SANDRA DOSDALL

HER too

SANDRA DOSDALL lives in Calgary Alberta and spends her free time focused on creating literature that she believes is relevant to our changing times. Her, Sandra's debut novel is the first in Her series, a storyline that has captivated readers and has brought 5-star reviews. She is excited to release Her too, a continuation of Her story, a journey through life while discovering one's purpose. A Corporate Director, Sandra spends her days involved in mergers and acquisitions. She is an established business figure, a wife and mother of three. Her newest literary accomplishment, "The Wanted" is a thriller that will bring you to tears.

May this book be dedicated
to all of those who choose
to believe that there could be a
higher power of some kind,
that there may be an afterlife,

and

that the possibility exists that
intervention occurs
in our activities,
altering the choices,
and consequences
of our daily lives.

ACKNOWLEDGMENTS

Having published work was always a dream for me. As a younger person I fantasized about being famous, about putting words together in a manner that brought life to the stories that have rumbled about in my head for so long. The people in my books have been in my life for many years, it is only now that you get to meet them, that I dare to share from the depths of my secret places, the songs of their hearts.

For those who have endeavored to read my work, I am grateful and indebted to you. I appreciate the time and attention that it takes to fully engulf oneself into the lives of the characters that I create. I can promise that I will never end the life of a character that I love, nor will I punish you by having them disappear or suffer inconsequently.

To my dearest husband, I am filled with more love for you today, than I was so many years ago. To have granted me the freedom, with your unconditional support, to do what I love has meant the world to me. I thank you, and offer a trip around the world, let us see the vastness the world has to offer, let us partake in the splendor and enjoy the fruits of our labors.

My children, all three of you inspire me, your compassion, wit and unbridled intelligence leaves me in awe.

I was trusted with three souls, three unique and delightfully bright souls that might change the world someday. I encourage your faith, I hope that your search is without consequence and that you reap richly the rewards of your works. I love you and thank you for choosing me to bring you into this world.

My comrades, my friends, those who know me better than I know myself. Sabrina, and Candice your support and acceptance is unprecedented. I offer my love and dedication to you both as we walk the path towards maturity together. I am grateful that you can tolerate my literary dabbling and appreciate your input and feedback. Our protagonists wouldn't be who they are without you.

To my Mother, I continue with gratitude to honor your contribution to my life every day. I would not be able to do the things I do if not for your love and support. Thank you for being my friend as well as a parent.

To the Lord, my God. I trust you have my back.

Prologue

The world was not expecting to encounter Her. By Her, I imply the one who was sent to save the people of the world. She came more than once, and to those who saw Her, encouragement was always given. A quiet knowing that the word was true, a validation of centuries of questions. Her manifestation was a gift to all that were in Her presence, a sentiment of the promise. She brought with Her truth, enlightenment and inspiration. Her mission clear, she set about the path endeavored for Her and brought change and encouragement to the world. He knew from Her existence that he too was sent to do more, to encourage positive change. He recognized Her gifts and her messages as what they were. He devoured Her promise of affinity, a kinship of hope missing for so long in the vastly desiccated and loveless world. She promised optimism, he held on to Her promise as he rose through the ashes to leadership; in a place where only the chosen can accomplish true greatness. For many are called, but only a select few are chosen.

From *HER*, CHAPTER 80

Released January 26, 2017

She watched out the back window of the cab, the
Black SUV chasing them through the streets. She wanted to
believe that her father was sad that they were leaving, but
her instinct told her otherwise. The hair on Her arms stood
up as She watched him manoeuvre the vehicle around others
and wanted to wave to him. Like She would have if She was
leaving on the school bus, or if he was just coming home from
a business trip. She felt gloomy on the inside, Her heart was
heavy, as though she was carrying around that knapsack that
her father refused to leave behind or let her see inside. She
still found his behaviour strange, his movements and
meetings. She kept reflecting on the vision with the man in
the suit, and the exchange of bags. She continued to wonder

what was in the navy school bag, and what Her father was doing with it.

The cab driver pulled into the airport entrance, slamming on the brakes of his beat-up Toyota Corolla as he reached the departures' doors. "Lady, here we are. The airport."

Madam smiled at him, she was reluctant, to speak, but needed to. She took the hundred from her purse and held it towards him. "This is all that I have."

He looked at her in the rear-view mirror, a smirk on his face. "You kidding me, Lady? That's all you got? I don't have change for a hundred."

Madam was on the verge of tears again. "It's all I have. I am so sorry, but I don't have any pesos. This is the best that I can do today."

The cabbie looked in the mirror again, he could see the SUV and the Federal vehicles approaching. "Lady just go. Forget about it. Go. I dunno who those guys coming are, but they been on our tail since we left your house. You need to go. Go. Be safe. Hurry."

Madam grabbed her purse and the hands of the two children. She had heard the term "Be Safe" twice today, she assumed it was a sign. She opened the door of the cab and escaped the tin box. She paused before she closed the door, looked at the driver and said, "Thank you." She noted the number of his cab, 3447; turned and ran into the building.

Madam could see the Continental Airlines check-in counter, in front of it was a cluster of people. She instantly worried about lining up and the probability of a clean exit. She hadn't told Agent Mendez of her planned departure, and she was now certain that her husband had not believed she would actually leave him.

The two children ran as quickly as they could, falling slightly behind her. Madam could hear commotion happening, she chose to ignore it and forged onward. She focused on the check-in counter. She was able to see the face of the Canadian Consular, Sarah Ryner, and the head of immigration Señor Felipe Calderone standing at the counter for the airline. She ran to them.

"Madam." Sarah Ryner spoke first. "Your Father called me regarding paperwork for the children. I have brought Señor Calderone with me to exercise the signatures." Madam looked behind her and saw her husband running towards them, he had his knapsack over his shoulder, and in his hand, he carried the navy-blue school bag. Behind him just coming through the doors to the airport were the Federal Agents, Mendez leading them in the chase.

"Thank you, Sarah, I cannot thank you enough."

Sarah Ryner looked at Madam empathetically. "I spoke with your father in length this morning, Madam, I am so sorry for all that you have gone through. On behalf of the Canadian Government, I would like to wish you safe travels, and please if there is anything that we can do, please do not hesitate to let us know. Your father is a very special man, he obviously loves you very much."

"Yes, he is, and yes he does." Madam was grateful for the acknowledgement.

Señor Calderone spoke. "Madam, for Mexico, we too wish you safe travels home to Canada, these papers are everything that you will need to clear Mexican customs with the children. Please pass through security with me now. I will accompany you. Come now please."

The head of immigration for the state of Jalisco, walked with Madam and the two children behind the glass partition, to where they would need to clear security before boarding their flight. The children could still see their father as he approached the area, screaming and crying. Behind him the Federal Agents were on top of him. A crowd of people had gathered, all of them watching the episode as it unfolded.

Her brother broke free of Madam's grip and ran towards the glass. He could see and hear his father without physically touching him. The agents were now attempting to manipulate him onto the ground. Three of them using force to bend his arms and legs at the joints. His knees buckled, and he went crashing down onto the tile floor. His face smashing into the glass his cheeks and lips distorting his appearance.

"DAD!" He screeched! "Mom, what are they doing to Dad?!"

Her father managed to get one hand free and reached into the knapsack that Juan had provided him the day before, he felt pressured and he knew that this was one time that he could use some help. He reached deep into the bag but without checking his own intentions, he pulled from the empty bag a Colt Pocket Hammerless Pistol, which filled his hand and startled his opponents. Time slowed to a crawl. Everyone's movements became magnified.

She screamed. "Daddy has a gun!"

Her father's eyes met hers. Sorrow filled her heart as She saw a broken man in front of her. On the floor, he was desperate and needy, wanting change but ignorant of how to accomplish it; she saw into his soul, the pain, the history, the anguish. She saw his transgressions and his path of destruction, his lies and deceit. She felt his desire for women and his hunger for money, his lust for power and his hatred for her own mother.

The Agents drew their own weapons. "Stop! Don't hurt him," She shouted. "Please don't hurt my Daddy!" He looked up at Her and saw the tears rolling down her cheeks, her hand still in Madam's. Her brother stood just inches in front of him. His blond hair falling on his forehead, his palm pressed against the transparent barrier between them. A single pane of bullet proof glass was all that physically separated them, their worlds however would never again meet.

The Agents handcuffed Her father, and stood him to his feet, the children watched as he was marched away from them. She could see only a red box in her mind, red for anger, red for sorrow.

Madam stood shaking, looking at the empty knapsack on the floor. Her plane tickets, passports and immigration papers in hand; a senior immigration official beside her.

Juan Maria de Salvatierra pushed a tooth pick into his teeth and turned away. He smiled at Mary Mack who stood beside Her. Mary nodded at Juan, and straightened the front of her black silk dress, silver buttons shining all down her back. She hoped the flight to Canada wasn't too long. She was never particularly comfortable on commercial flights. This one however would be her pleasure.

HER too…

SANDRA DOSDALL

CHAPTER 1

Her brother sat, his seat slightly reclined; next to the
window looking out at the clouds as they soared the skies
near 34 000 feet. His eyes were focused on the billowy cotton
candy puffs of white misty fluff as they jetted on towards
home. Home? He pondered the thought of home, where is
home? They had just left his home. Everything he had grown
to know was in a country he knew, as Mexico.

And he loved it. He loved the country, he loved the
culture, he loved the climate and the people. The natives that
had embraced him, accepted him and that made him feel
welcome. His mind locked onto the events that had
transpired in the airport earlier. He felt angry, he felt
betrayed. He felt like it was their mother's fault. She could
have done something; she *should* have done something.
Everything had unraveled so quickly, spiraling out of his
control, he felt helpless; like a fool.

The Feds, his father, the immigration people and his own mother, it was a myriad of confusion and lies. His mind was racing with uncertainty, with grey muted images of reality. How had his own mother left their father behind? To him it was unimaginable. To leave a team member behind was the greatest expression of treason. He lost himself in his own thoughts and placed his head on the icy cold windowpane. The plane continued to soar high above the clouds. He watched through the small window as frozen droplets of condensed water vapor created grand images of animals and abstract forms; clouds, ever changing and varying depending on personal perspective. His mind wandered from the clouds to the activity in the airport, to his sister; he would figure out what had happened. Someday, in his own way he would somehow get to the bottom of how all of it had unfolded. He would find the truth. He would unravel the mystery of what had happened to their father; what had been in that old stinky backpack, the blue school bag, and why their father had been arrested in the middle of the airport, as they stood and watched from behind the glass, with immigration officials and the Canadian Consoler as spectators.

CHAPTER 2

Germany- 1940

Frost was all that anyone could see. Ice was upon the surface of everything. It covered doorknobs, and coffee tins, it crusted the windshield of every vehicle that was still drivable, even those operated by the Third Reich. No one could outrun the cold, there wasn't one soul that was exempt from its reach and most certainly not from its biting freeze. Temperatures once again plummeted to numbers so incomprehensible they would be studied for decades to come; future generations would refer to the era as the Little Ice Age. It was not only a climatic anomaly on the European continent. Deviations in overall surface temperature and air pressure extended to the entire global stratosphere. Apart from affecting the Second World War, climatic irregularities resulted in droughts, flooding, wild fires, and crop failures around the world. Mother Earth was weeping because of the catastrophic indignity to her inhabitants.

The planet survived for over four and one half billion years; the essence of her survival not relative to the survival of mankind. Her evolution evident in the changing of the wind, the alteration of temperatures, the starvation and extinction of species, the burning of forests, the sudden cracking of her surface. Like an aging woman, the constant grinding and gliding of the tectonic plates caused profound faults in her ethereal skin. Her beauty becoming weathered and wrinkled, she was aging. Mother Nature had been here for eons, carving her light upon the oceans, harvesting her hand in the soil.

Mankind continued to refuse acknowledgement of a connection between the universe, it's gifts and their own existence. A continual misuse of power resulted in a surge of climatic abnormalities; earthquakes, hurricanes, tsunamis, and the Little Ice Age of the 1940's.

Beginning in the late 1930's, a network of Nazi concentration camps were built by the Third Reich with the intent of gathering political prisoners, Soviet prisoners of war, Jehovah's Witnesses, the Polish, Romani, Serbians, homosexuals, Catholic Clergy and all members of the Jewish Faith. From 1933 until the fall of Germany at the end of the war, the erection of approximately twelve hundred concentration and extermination camps in Nazi occupied Europe resulted in the demise of over twenty million souls.

The freeze wasn't enough to stop the Nazi's on their path of experimental genocide; their momentum continued despite the frozen winters and the prevailing war. They tortured and executed those which they believed to be radically undesirable.

Mary Mack considered the dark and dismal holding pen where a group of women were being corralled. She saw in some an intense fear in their eyes, a sense of panic. And in others a complete resolve; a resolve that comes from knowing that you have reached the end; an acceptance that you are at the end of your days. The women disembarked from the train that had delivered them to the camp. The boxcar filthy, the rotten stench of urine, sweat and fear saturating the air. All the women had been separated from their husbands and children, isolated from their families, now alone on a journey to which they knew not the destination, nor the agenda.

Mary Mack straightened her black silk dress, her hand on the silver button near the hem at the bottom. Her eyes focused on a young German man wearing an immaculate Nazi uniform. His black overcoat thick and generous, cinched at the waist by a thick leather belt. The notorious red band bearing the Nazi symbol snuggly tied around his left bicep. Black boots riding his calves to the knee, Mary though how warm he must be. His coat was buttoned tightly, she watched him as his breath eased into the air in circles of white dissipating vapor.

She glanced again at the group of females that he had been allocated to guard for the time being; some wearing nothing more than basic house dressings and stockings. He offered them nothing, not a smile, nor compassion of any kind.

The women huddled together, attempting to warm themselves. Necessity breeding friendship, a kinship not known to them before, from it came a resourcefulness that in another circumstance may not have been apparent. Women that had not earlier known each other now huddled together, their skins rubbing together in a weak attempt to find warmth. Vanity absent in the face of necessity.

Mary Mack watched the women as they shivered, their lips blue, their skin a muddled shade of grey. The

German officer was unmoved, stoic, his face remaining refined and still. His straight nose looking down upon them as they tried to warm each other with their cool breath.

Mary Mack stared at his tall athletic build, strong but lean, a runner perhaps. She made a mental note, and moved towards him, making herself only appear to him. "Hello, I am Mary Mack, with silver buttons all down my back, back, back, I've come to warn you of darkness, that follows your path, halt now and don't look back, I speak only truth to you, the light is right, cross the ocean for freedom and full flavor, reap stillness of night. Loss of souls forever mourned will haunt you both day and night. Children born will pay your price, for the rest of their life."

The soldier looked at Mary Mack, not certain from where she had come, her dress clean, her hair shiny and beautifully brushed, her curls neatly rolling forward, falling over her shoulders framing her tiny face. "Who are you! From where have you come? Get back with the group."

"I am Mary Mack."

"What are these riddles you speak to me?" The German soldier was stern, taken aback by Mary's forward approach. He looked from side to side as if to see if anyone else was near, if there was anyone else listening. He wondered from where this girl had come, with her beautiful dress, and brightly clean skin. During this terrible war, when women were dirty in the camp, their hair not washed, their nails and their teeth dirty, their privates unclean; she was bright, with a smell of fresh lavender. He fancied her no more than ten or perhaps eleven years old. Her shoes were shiny patent leather, with a strap across her arch.

"I speak only truth, of which you must eat, if your descendants are to thrive you must help the weak."

"I am a member of the Third Reich; I don't help anyone who is weak."

Mary was dismayed but not surprised by his response, "Hugo, yes you are a member of the Third Reich, I question why you would choose to go left instead of right? Do as I say, do not betray your noble house, protect those in need, and benefit long lasting indeed."

Hugo Fromm, the German soldier was becoming frustrated, but mesmerized at the same time. Her beauty and wit were like a wine that was enchanting him. He was becoming captivated by her rhymes; her voice was soft and silky smooth. He listened despite an awareness that he should not. He wanted to shun her but didn't have the will to follow through.

"Do you know that my family won't speak to me? My own mother hates me? She thinks I have betrayed the family by standing with the Reich. What am I to do? Not standing with them means that I would be against them, which would draw attention to the abnormalities in my own home. I cannot have that. I am protecting them. Don't you understand. I am protecting *my* family by standing with the Reich. I cannot save everyone. This war is a terrible thing. But I cannot change the entirety of it. The suffering, the freezing temperatures and the dying. I cannot make it stop because I chose not to wear this swastika on my arm. I get paid to be here, I have a warm coat, and with my pay I can buy food for my sisters, and my poor brother at home. My poor crippled brother."

Mary smiled, and reached for his hand without touching it. Tears were rolling down his cheeks. "I empathize with your plight, really I do, but the Lord is not pleased, not with the terrible things that ensue. You mustn't turn the other cheek. You mustn't let any child suffer. It is not His will. He is not pleased, not at all. We are all created equal, and the same, all perfect in His eyes. Our faults and errs are only the judgments and justifications of others. Not our own, and certainly not His. You see. Your own brother is not a cripple, he was created perfect, his inability to walk is not a hindrance to God or himself, but to his mother, and to his siblings. It is by their judgement that he is labelled as substandard. Through their eyes he is a cripple. It is they that have something to learn from the limitations that have been given him. Do you understand Hugo?"

Mary Mack continued. "There is nothing wrong with the individuals that the Third Reich has determined to be radically undesirable. Their beliefs are only different from your leader. These women," She lifted her hands towards the pen of freezing females, huddled together shaking and blue. "are not deserving of any medical experiments, or intense labor, they don't deserve the gas chamber, starvation or execution. You do not have the right to judge the last days of their lives for them. You were not granted that power. You are just a grown-up boy in a very nice uniform staying warm, who is very scared, doing a very terrible job, for money so that he can protect his family."

Hugo looked at the women, he looked at Mary Mack and then at his own hands. "What am I to do? What would you do? I don't even know who you are?"

"It matters not who I am. You need to escape. You need to flee. Once the war has ended, for now, you must help as many as will be."

"Where would I go? Where should I look? Do I take my whole family?" Hugo was feeling desperate, lost; he felt as though he was betraying his mother by doing this job.

Wearing the warm coat and boots was supposed to be an honor and yet it felt nothing of it. It felt dirty, it made him feel dishonorable, dastardly; like he was wearing the coat of a defector.

"I cannot provide all of the answers, only the riddles and rhymes, to make you think all of the time. Take note young Hugo, mark my words and see, this war will end badly, be on the right side of it, or so too your destiny will surely be." Mary Mack waved her hands at him and was gone.

CHAPTER 3

She sat next to her mother on the plane, her seat belt tightly fastened. She had been frightened during take-off and the ascent, but something had happened to her in the air, a sense of calm had come over Her. She had refused the offer of food and beverages from the flight attendants and had no interest in watching a movie or reading a magazine. She sat, her hands in her lap. Her voice quiet, her mood somber; she was still.

It felt to Her as if they would never arrive at their destination. She had heard grumblings about a change of planes in Houston, a layover and a delay before their next flight. She was exhausted, physically and emotionally. She was hungry and felt a slight throbbing behind her eyes. Poking gently at Her, insistent and pesky. She was excited to see her grandparents, and to settle into a quiet place with them. Their grandparents' home was comfortable; and safe. She longed for safe right now.

She had missed seeing Her grandparents terribly during the years that they had lived in Mexico. Quite a long time had passed since She had last seen them. She enjoyed a relaxed and easy relationship with Her mother's family. They were content to accept Her, and Her brother, they were not strict disciplinarians in the traditional sense of the word, not consistently barking orders or commanding change. They were full of love. Accepting and encouraging of her quirkiness, they embraced her limitations and gifts as an opportunity to learn about themselves. Her cup runneth over with love for them, she said a silent prayer of gratitude for them as she sat with Her eyes softly closed.

Her mind wandered to Lupita, Her Nanny, Her only friend; she wondered what was happening now that they were gone. What was happening in the house, were they still searching it? Were the Feds looking through all their things? Again, now that their mother wasn't in the house watching over them; were the group of federal agents rifling through her personal things? Were they questioning Lupita? Asking her about Mother and her movements? Her alliances? Her friends and business associates?

She silently prayed for her dear friend, her nanny that she knew she would miss for a very long, long time. She knew in her heart that they would not be returning to the land of Sombreros and Bull Fights. Their entry into the country had been illustrious, their departure traumatic. This escape was not a temporary retreat, it was a permanent solution to a long-time problem. Her mother had made some life changes, and this was part of it. She closed her eyes, prayed silently to herself, she placed the day's events carefully within her Purple Box in her mind, for she had faith that change would bring tranquility and a peaceful rendering to her own landscape as well as to Her mother's and Her brothers.

CHAPTER 4

With the fall of Germany came an open window of opportunity for Hugo Fromm. He had done his best to aid without being detected, prisoners within the camps to which he had been assigned during the war. He rationed food, and blankets, and when he could he would provide pencils and paper for them to write short letters and notes to loved ones and friends outside of the walls of the camps in which they were held. He would see to them being delivered when he could, and when it was possible, in the event of a death, he would take a personal message if there was loved one or family friend left to be contacted. Hugo knew that what he was doing was little in the way of saving lives. He did his best to lessen the suffering, knowing that he could not risk being detected.

After the ruin of the Third Reich, Hugo removed the red banded swastika once worn proudly, that now instilled feelings shame and remorse; and his uniform, replacing them with regular street clothing. He travelled south through Germany to Switzerland where he boarded a train for Genova. In Genova, he wagered his way onto a ship sailing for Barcelona. Once he arrived on the doorstep of Spain, he basked in the sun and enjoyed the glorious women until it was time to move to the north. Eventually Hugo managed to make his way through wine country on the northern shores of Spain all the way to A Coruna, a small coastal town on the northwest coast of the picturesque country where he waited and worked for his meals. He hoped that one day he would save enough money to board a ship that would take him across the ocean as he had been instructed to do by the beautiful young girl in the black silk dress with silver buttons all down her back.

While he waited, and saved every penny he could in A Coruna, a young Spanish woman caught his eye. With long dark hair and dark olive skin, a tiny waist and the smile of an angel, she was a true beauty that mesmerized him. Their romance was quick, passionate and intense resulting in a young pregnant Spanish bride. The two of them boarded a sailing ship to the North America, with a promise of a new life, a new beginning, and a new frontier for them.

Weeks later, when they landed in Vera Cruz, Mexico, the two were still very much in love. As a newlywed couple, they collectively decided to assume her family's surname Alvarez, making it easier to blend into their newly chosen community. Hugo never looked back to Germany and his life as a Nazi. He tried desperately not to think of the thousands of women in the camps where he had been stationed, those who had suffered so terribly. He rested on the notion that he had done his best, aided those in need, while protecting his family.

Before he went to sleep each night, the one person he was not able to escape the thought of, was Mary Mack; who just never came back.

CHAPTER 5

Mary Mack hated the feeling of flying in an aircraft; she much preferred the feel of a horse drawn carriage beneath her. She like the feeling of solid ground. The comfort of hooves on turf brought to her a sense of power and confidence that was absent in the air.

As she sat on the plane next to Her, Mary reflected on three major airline crashes that had taken place in 1951, and 1952 in Elizabeth, New Jersey. Mary had been an observer in all three; watching the unfolding of destruction, the breaking of hearts, the loss of life. She was rarely able to escape calamity; an observer of loss was her vocation. She maintained a positive outlook always, sadness and devastation trapped deep within her mind. On occasion, she attempted to will alternative results, in vain. She had been present for all three devastating accidents. Such a tragedy the crashes had been, a terrible loss of lives; with one innocent soul in each crash having had their life sacrificed. It was all for the greater good in the end, part of the master plan, the horrible catastrophes had been ultimately necessary.

President Truman had then implemented a full commission in May 1952, where after months of deliberation he recommended a clearing of space at the end of airport runways. The introduction of zoning laws in accordance with President Truman's commission then prohibited in the construction of future airports, the building of hospitals, schools, private residences and of buildings of worship in a fan-shaped area beyond the runway safety zone. Never the less, the three crashes in *one* city in a span of two years had been devastating to the people of Elizabeth; some individuals might have even suspected that the spirit realm had been involved in the three crashes.

Mary Mack had vowed to recognize the lost souls of these three tragedies by acknowledging them in some way. She would somehow use the name Elizabeth as a memorial. Mary Mack had spent a long time pondering the acknowledgment; then one day the perfect opportunity presented itself.

Mary Mack was assigned to Her upon Her return to the human world in 1991. Her journey had been long, the preparation had been intense and detailed. Mary had been provided divine instruction to protect Her at any cost. She had returned on a mission to save Mother Earth. She was to be gifted a human name, unto which that name must hold biblical **reasoning**.

Mary Mack reflected in the birthing room that day in 1991 and considered a similar appointment from long ago when the son came; *"When Elizabeth heard Mary's greeting, the baby leaped in her womb, and Elizabeth was filled with the Holy Spirit. In a loud voice, she exclaimed: "Blessed are thou among woman, and blessed is the child you will bear!"* Elizabeth, a messenger to Mary, the mother of the son of God.

Upon Her return, Mary Mack acted ensuring that the name Elizabeth be blessed upon Her, and now she was permanently on duty. Assigned to Her; as a warrior, a guardian, a guide of the Lord. The name Elizabeth gifted unto Her as a memorial to those who had been lost in the horrific air tragedies of the 1950's.

The safety implementations taken in Elizabeth New Jersey pleased Mary Mack, but the loss of life troubled her, even when it was necessary. It seemed senseless at times.

And she deeply feared being in the air in this tin can. She much preferred being on the ground, on her feet, worst-case scenario in a car. She could control the movements of such. Airplanes felt as though they were manoeuvring out of her control.

She wanted to check in with Juan but had been instructed to "Stay with Her" -message complete, end of her instructions entirely. So, Mary Mack, a young gifted warrior of the Lord, brutally slain during the war between the Scots and the English in 1060 was on assignment and currently invisible to everyone but Her. Resting quietly. Preparing for their descent into Houston.

CHAPTER 6

India -1966

"Please don't take my Mama!" he shouted with all the conviction and might that a young ten-year-old boy could manage. He wept, he watched as the ambulance pulled away from the curb, tires rolling on the dirt road, sirens howling as the medical bus pulled into the moving traffic and then disappeared with the trucks and rickshaws around the corner. He could hear the wail of the siren as it screamed and then faded into the distance and the sorry, broken cries of his brothers and younger sisters from the window of the house.

His father turned and walked toward the door; briefly looking back at all three of his boys, who stood watching where their mother had just vanished. Her frail body and wounded soul had been wheeled away to a quieter place he hoped, of respite. His aging body was tired, weathered from the sun and many years of hard laborious work in the fields. His mind ached from exhaustion; he pondered the events of years past. His skin was leathery; his hair was greying and lacked the luster and sheen of a young mans. His pants hung too low, his derriere disappearing as he aged. His shirt was permanently soiled, the color faded. He reached forward and opened the door, holding it for the children as they passed through into their humble abode.

"Come now boys, there are chores to be done today, let's keep our chins up and our chests out, be strong for the girls. We are proud men, no time for this remorse and anguish."

The boys all moved into the house and took to the chores that their father spoke of; they tended to work in teams as it made the work more palatable, and less tiresome. As they worked sorting the laundry, Rohan looked at his older brother, with tears in his eyes. "Do you think she will come home soon Bhavin?"

Bhavin, older than Rohan by just thirteen months was stone faced, when he answered. "Who knows, who cares, everything I need I will do for myself. Mommies are over rated, and I don't need one. I'm going to go do my chores, and you should get to yours too Roh, and stop that crying. You look like a little girl. Tears and all; wipe it off your face and move on. Father needs you to help and be strong. Let's get to it, don't be a baby!"

Rohan considered his brother's words and agreed with nearly all of them except for not needing a Mommy. He felt like he needed one, he was sure that he needed one; and he didn't understand why she had to leave. He wondered what his father was not willing to tell them and why, or for how long she would be gone. Maybe his father was glad she had been taken away. He couldn't imagine that to be the truth, but he also was not able to comprehend that complexity of the situation or the misrepresentation of truths.

He felt an urge to gather facts, to dig deep into the depths of the realities. He hungered for it, for he knew that the truth would set them all free; he knew this promise to be factual. Or at least he had heard it to be true.

He walked into the back of the small house to where he could hear his sisters crying. The twins were not even 2 years old and didn't understand where their mother had been taken. Jiya was just 4, and knew that mother was gone, but had no idea why. Rohan stayed in the kitchen with his father and the girls and helped in preparing rice for the afternoon meal.

"Rohan pass me those carrots please form the cold box, and would you please take the dog outside. I can't have it around when I am trying to cook; filthy beast!"

"Yes father, of course, I will." He did as he was asked, passed the carrots to his father and then took the dog out into the front yard. His dog plopped himself down and lifted his leg to scratch behind his ear. Rohan looked at him and stroked his head. The dog appeared to be oblivious to any changes what so ever. Life remained the same regardless of who provided the meal, or who took him outside to pee. The dog was superior in Rohan's eyes, and yet a filthy beast in the eyes of his father. He wondered about that, about perception and perspective and how it applied to this situation and to his mother's departure today. What was to be thought of it? Whose perspective was correct? Or were they all right and wrong, just for different reasons truthful to the beholder. Who would be the judge, and would they ever know the answers?

Rohan sat outside with his dog, for what may have been hours. He lost track of time and forgot about helping in the kitchen; the two of them listened to the sounds of the neighborhood, children laughing, other dogs barking, and chickens and roosters crowing and cocking at each other. He sat, and he sat, and he watched as the clouds rolled through, constantly changing formation and moving amongst each other. He saw a dinosaur, and a rabbit; he believed that he might have seen a lion and maybe a tiara. He wondered how the nebulous would look to his father, to his brothers. How their own perspectives would change the shapes that so clearly were obvious to him.

He waited, hoping that someone would call him inside; his father, or maybe Bhavin, his abdomen growled and gurgled, reminding him that he hadn't eaten for quite some time. His stomach cavity was calling him for food, for substance. He knew that his stomach left no cause for interpretation, hunger pains were the same for everyone, there was no room for perspective in the need for food. Or at least he believed this to be so.

He waited until the sun was setting, and his stomach was then aching from hunger. He prayed, that his mother would be okay where she was, that she was safe and that she might come home to them soon.

He finally gave in and went into the house, which was fragilely quiet; there was no one in the kitchen, no one in the living room. The bathroom was empty. Roh knew that no one had left the house, because they would have had to pass by him on the front step to get out. It had become dark. He snuck into the hallway and peeked into his parent's bedroom. His father was asleep, lying flat on his back, snoring loudly. His twin sisters, Amelia and Angelica were both asleep on the bed with his father; Jiya was on a mat on the floor next to his father's bed.

He crossed the hall to the room that he shared with his brothers Bhavin and Himmat. The light was dim, but they both seemed to be awake. Bhavin was reading what appeared to be a textbook from school, but Rohan wasn't sure what he could possibly be studying. The language on the front of the book was not something that he was familiar with, so he decided to ask.

"Bhavin, what's that book about that you are reading."

Bhavin looked up from his text book and answered Rohan, "English, I am studying English so that I can travel afar. I will not stay here any longer than I must. I'm not going to let what has happened to Mama, happen to me."

Rohan listened carefully to Bhavin's answer and pondered the complexity of information. A dummy he was not, Rohan was capable of many things, he was certain that his destiny would be greater than many of those before him. He wondered why his brother despised their mother so greatly, or did he? Was he resentful that she had been taken away, or remorseful that she was absent?

"What happened to Mama exactly Bhavin? Is she coming home soon?"

Bhavin threw a small pillow at his brother, "She's not even been gone a day silly, of course she will be back, she just needs some time away from us for a while. She will be fine, and we will be fine."

Rohan thought hard about his Mama, "But why did she have to go in the ambulance, is she sick?"

Bhavin sighed; his twelve years of life experience were hardly enough to allow him the luxury of explaining medical circumstance to his younger siblings, especially Rohan, with his ever-inquisitive mind.

"Look Roh, Mama is just having some trouble making sense of some things. Her mind isn't quite in the right place, right now, but the doctors will make it better for her, and then she will be able to come home to us. Okay? Look don't fret about it, there is nothing that any of us can do, except help Father to keep everything together. There are six of us kids. So, I should quit school and get a job somewhere. But that's all right; I can work and learn English. And then, as soon as Mama comes home, and I'm old enough; swoosh, I am taking off on a plane to New York City. The land of opportunity and I'm going to see Disneyland." Bhavin looked towards the window, "and you little brother must study your butt off. University is where you need to be; maybe study to be a doctor or a lawyer. Something big so that you can support all of the rest of us." He ruffled the hair of his younger brother, smiling. "You little Roh are the smartest one of all of us. There is something special planned for you, but I don't know what it is, so please don't ask me!"

Himmat rarely had anything to say, but today he spoke up. "She isn't coming back Roh, she has lost her mind and she is gone. Get used to it. Bhavin is just trying to make you feel better."

Bhavin retaliated, "That's not true, Himmat please why be so negative, she will be healed, the doctors will heal her, just like they did when you were sick."

Himmat stood, "I was not the same kind of sick as she is, I was sick with illness, and not of my own doing. She is just sick in the head."

"Listen to me, Mama did not make herself sick, geez is that what you think Himmat?" Bhavin became frustrated. "Ok I will agree with you that getting that disease that you had, was no fault of your own, but neither is this Mama's fault."

Himmat flushed, "Oh yeah, well I talked to people and they say that she is crazy, that Mama is has lost her mind, and that it is her fault; that she did this to herself, she might not have started it, maybe it happened because those men attacked her, or because father was gone working, or maybe it's my fault for being in the hospital for so long, but she isn't in her mind right anymore; she isn't the mother that we knew once, she won' be the same again, they just can't fix crazy, so there you have it."

Rohan watched the two of them as they fought. He remembered his brother Himmat being sick, and the entire family fearing that he would die at the hand of the disease. Himmat spent many, many months in the hospital, recovering from Diphtheria. The outbreak in early 1964 had rattled the entire country; over 15,000 people lost the battle to the disease, Himmat, however had not been one of them. He had managed to fight through and remain strong. Resisting the temptation of eternal rest. Everyone believed that because he had recovered that there was a special calling on his life, that the Lord had a purpose for him. Rohan wondered if that too was subject to perception or was it just idle talk. Did people believe the things that they said, or were they just making noise to be heard?

Rohan spoke, "You Himmat were very sick indeed, and we all prayed for you; for you to be healed of the Diphtheria and to be healthy again. It worked then, the Lord heard us, and I think we should do the same again. We should pray earnestly with our hearts; this time focused on Mama, she needs our strength; she needs our prayers. Mother can be healed in the same way that you were healed. That's the promise, that all shall be healed, that all shall be provided for, on earth, as it is in heaven, right? Doesn't that mean that it's the same for everyone?"

Himmat frowned at his younger brother, "Oh boy Rohan, aren't you something hey? That's your answer for every issue, isn't it? Well you know what I think? I think that you pray because you don't know what else to do. You are so narrow minded and dumb, that you just assume that praying will fix everything. Guess what bro? It's not happening. I got better because I am strong as an ox, like father said, and Mama got sick because she's not right in the head. Go ahead and pray for her if you want. If you think you can make a difference. But I will be looking forward, to what I must do to help Father, and finish school. I will not be wasting my time chanting to some God that is in no way going to answer any of us. It's just gobbledy gook Rohan, it's just all words, just dumb wasted words."

Days turned into weeks, and the weeks quickly passed into months. Rohan waited for the return of his mother and prayed to his God every day for her safe passage home. He held onto his belief in a greater good, in a higher power that was aligned with his spirit, able to promote goodness, and apt to adhere to the promises given. His brothers had resorted to quitting school. Both had been given jobs by family friends who were willing to help their father. There were just too many mouths to feed, and too much laundry to complete. There were just too many chores and not enough daylight. One man could not complete all the work; their father needed the help of the older boys. The clock idled on, the calendar flipped. A year had passed, and then soon another.

Rohan and the girls were still too young to work, even in India. And so, they had gotten used to doing all the household chores. They collected eggs in the morning from the chickens that fluttered around the yard, and each child made their own bed. They fed and walked the dog, helped with meals. Rohan made sure all of them arrived at school for their daily teachings and ensured that everyone made it home again before the sun set. He made lunches for himself and his father, and of course for Jiya and the twins. It was an exhausting endeavor, one that at times Rohan wished would end.

He often hoped for change and fantasized about his mother's return to them. That she would come home to them, allowing everyone to return to what they had once accepted as normal. Where she, as their mother did the chores, and the children had time to play, to learn and to grow.

Sleep had become something of a luxury, even he as a now 11-year-old boy was learning that he wouldn't always get what he needed in the way of rest and that many mornings he would wake, wishing that he could sleep for longer. His bed wasn't as comfortable as it had been when his mother was home. Her presence made everything smell like rich vanilla. He wasn't sure if it was her perfume or something special about her, a type of magic that she performed. Or perhaps it was only that she created her laundry charm more often. She had always left the sheets and towels fresh and crisp; always inviting the children to crawl into a clean bed, after a hot shower and while wearing clean pajamas. Fresh naan bread, and warm chutney, always warmed his heart and the very thought of her made his heart skip a beat.

His spirit yearned for her presence. Rohan craved for his mother's touch, her caress and her embraces. He often cried himself to sleep, remembering a time when there was laughter in the house, and when he had felt loved, instead of only being needed. He knew that his father loved him, but the love of his mother had been lost that day, when the ambulance had left with her in it, screaming as it rolled down the street.

Time began to pass more quickly, and the days grew one into another at a more rapid rate. Bhavin worked hard to help, sending money to their father every week from where he was working, but it was becoming apparent that the ability to feed all the children was becoming impossible. His father succumbed to the strain of it all, the financial pressure, the emotional absence of his wife and the support she provided to him. Rohan would be sent to the Catholic Boys School. He would live with the Priests and in exchange for payment of his tuition and room and board, Roh would work on weekends and for the summer. He had already become accustom to hard work and living at the Monastery would allow him a superior educational advantage. His moving was a promise of a brighter future. Hope for a life that would be different.

His mother had never returned to the house, her medical bills were crushing his father. He had become trapped beneath the legalities of hospital politics and billing systems. He barely had time to work himself and was no longer able to manage with all the children. Bhavin was helping by working and supporting the girls, Rohan though was the smartest of the children, there was something unique about him and extraordinary, he had the chance to become something bigger and better than a laborer. Roh's intuition and strong inquisitive character ensured that.

He had no idea what Rohan would become, but he would forever have regrets if his son's life ended up wasted, scrubbing toilets, or pulling Rickshaw. He now resented his wife, and her inability to manage her emotions. He saw her sickness only as a weakness, an excuse to run from them; all of them, himself and the children. He questioned her loyalty and wondered if she had ever loved him. He resented that his life was in ruins, that he had more children than he could afford to feed and clothe. His heart ached with loneliness for her, in her absence, he lay in the darkness at night and wondered if she too thought of him; or of their children.

Roh too cried for her in the darkness after his chores were complete and he had crawled into his bed. He sobbed silently at times forgetting what the touch of her hand felt like, or how her face looked when she laughed. He tried to focus on the positive things that she did. The small notes that she placed in his lunch box every day, "Roh my most special boy, I love you, have a great day!" These sincere notes were sweet little surprises for him. They lifted his spirits, it was something that he would welcome today, if she were here to provide them. He missed her preparing his bath, washing his cloths and fixing the meals. Her culinary creations always tantalized his taste buds, with hints of curry and coconut, sweet chili peppers and cardamom, cinnamon and cloves. The memories of them were vivid in his mind, he could smell the goods cooking on the stove, and hear her laughter as she stirred the pot. The quiet times at night were a refuge from reality and a salvation of her memory. He trusted his memories not to fail him, to support his desire of goodness and clarity in his mind. To preserve all that she had always been to him, to allow him to remember her love.

He prayed that one day he would be able to return the favor and make her see how much each note, each meal, each smile had meant to him. He knew in his heart that she loved each one of her children, and to him that was all that mattered.

At the age of 11 years and 10 months Rohan packed one small suitcase, containing all his personal belongings and boarded a train to Bangalore where he would live and learn within the walls of the monastery for the rest of his childhood days. He wistfully thought of his mother as he waved good-bye to his family. He wondered again for how long she would be away, and if she knew how desperately he missed her. His father stood tall, a half smile crossing his face as he waved good-bye to his youngest son. He held the twin's hands, one child at each hip as he watched Rohan leave for what could be a very long, but potentially very productive and advantageous adventure.

CHAPTER 8

The planes descent into Houston was smooth and without incident. The airline pilot made the usual announcements about gate changes and weather, baggage claims and immigration. She looked up at Her mother and asked.

"Mother... is this going to be difficult for us?" She wondered because their departure had been abrupt and had not gone without confrontation. She did not like any type of unpleasantness.

Madam shook her head, 'No baby, it won't be difficult, this is the easy part, we have already finished the hard part." She closed her eyes and saw the face of her husband pressed against the glass in the airport, his hands awkwardly twisted behind his back, federal agents pinning him against the floor. His old and dirty back pack strewn awkwardly over his shoulder. She grimaced. She was uncertain of what would be waiting for them on the ground in Houston, she wasn't sure that the transition was going to be painless, but she presented the case as such, regardless of her lack of confidence.

"Mom" Her brother was pointing at something outside of the window of the plane.

"Yes sweetie" She turned to him, gently touching his soft blond hair, caressing his head.

"Look how the heat is glowing off the asphalt, see? You can see waves and waves of it. The heat I mean. Can you see it? It appears in waves Mom. Did you know that it looks that way because of the bending of light waves? It happens when light passes between substances with different refractive indices, in this case, cool air and hot air. Because hot air is less dense than the cool air, the light speeds up when it reaches a hot surface and then curves back upwards, allowing us to see an image of the sky and the surface to appear wavy in the heat. The asphalt is the hot surface, of course, I think it looks so cool."

"It really does, it really, really does honey." Madam didn't understand light refraction or how air density was affected by light speed. But her boy was interested, and so

she tried to at least be interested in him. He was important.
His thoughts were important, and his ideas were interesting.

CHAPTER 9

Madam approached the United States Customs official with her head held as high as normal, her children one on either side of her. She felt oddly warm and was starting to feel tired, and a bit anxious to see her parents. The children were travelling well but were also exhausted from the trauma that had transpired that day right before their eyes.

In her hands were the three passports that had been stamped and sealed by the Mexican Government and the Canadian Consular as they had left Puerto Vallarta. He waved her forward.

She made eye contact but didn't smile.

"How are you today mam?" He had sandy brown hair, a mustache and was a-typical border patrol clean, pressed and broad shouldered. He had been doing this job for a long time. He didn't love it. It had started as a passion, as most jobs do, with excitement, and reverence. A slightly misguided desire to right the world; a hunger for justice, an appetite for service, he came to work every day expecting the same.

Through his station of entry, passed many people, from of all walks of life. He saw many foreign dignitaries, a plethora of celebrities and famous athletes. Faces known and unknown, there were those who were happy to be under the spot light, and those who preferred to hide in the dark shadows. Some individuals were physically undeniably beautiful, others not as much. He believed that he enjoyed the diversity of his work, and he thought he had seen almost everything that there was to see.

"Fine Thank you."

"Just the three of you today?" He held her three documents in his hand, hers was open, he looked at her picture, and then up at her face.

"Yes."

"No husband travelling with you?" Her photo was black and white, which he thought was odd, as most passport photos were taken in color.

"No."

"Where is your husband Madam?"

"My husband? Why do you ask?" She was suddenly feeling a bit nervous, agitated. She didn't understand the necessity of the question. She was a woman, travelling with her children. Her documents were in order. Why did he need to know where her husband was?

"Madam, new legislation prohibits the crossing of borders without court documents. You are required to have a court order, at minimum written consent of the father, signed in the presence of a court approved notary to enter the United States. Are you saying that you have nothing? No paperwork of such for the children?"

"Correct. I have nothing of the sort, only the passports."

He looked at Madam, and at the two children. Who to him appeared to be very well cared for. The Girl was pretty, she had wise eyes and a kind smile, she seemed gentle; beautiful auburn hair, red almost. The boy was cute, in a movie star kind of way; he had huge blue eyes and blonde hair. The woman had an appeal that he couldn't explain. She wasn't stunning, not in a classic beauty kind of way like Audrey Hepburn or Natalie Wood but she was alluring. He was drawn to her. Her dark hair falling in ringlets long past her shoulders. Her skin a dark golden brown. He wondered where they had been, and for how long? The passports were

Canadian, but it was clear to him that they had been abroad somewhere. They were all very darkly tanned.

"Madam, can I see your boarding passes please? From your arriving flight? Where are you arriving from?"

Madam reached into her purse and retrieved them. She carefully placed them on the counter top in front of the Customs Official. "Mexico." She said. The corners of the boarding passes were slightly bent. His eyes scanned them, and then he looked up at her. "Madam, I am going to have to ask you to come with me please." He picked up the passports and the boarding passes and moved towards a room to the left of the receiving area.

Madam and the children followed. The children holding each other's hands. The room was plain, painted white, with navy blue plastic chairs, the seats of which were supported by chrome legs, placed carefully against the wall for them to sit in. The Customs Official indicated for them to take a seat, and he left them alone in the room for a few moments. It was quiet. When he returned, he took a seat on the front of the black and metal desk on the other side of the room. Another taller man in a suit joined them, Madam made eye contact as she always did. Discerning previous interaction. There was none.

She had taken a seat next to Her brother and held his hand. For his sake, more than for Hers. She could sense a feeling of panic rising from within him. She knew that her physical contact would calm him. Their mother remained standing.

"Is there a problem, other than that I do not have the required paperwork from the children's father?" Madam nodded towards the children as she finished her sentence.

"Madam, your paperwork raises concern. These boarding passes are hand written, yet you seem to have arrived on a commercial flight. And your passports are stamped and sealed by very high-ranking Mexican Officials and the Canadian Consular. You are not travelling with your husband, nor do you have the required paperwork from him." He took a breath before continuing, "Yes, Madam, yes I would say there is a problem."

The second gentleman in the suit spoke, "Madam, can you explain to us please, the situation? It is our responsibility to ensure the safety of the United States, we must look into the past of every individual entering our country, especially those with paperwork that is lacking or strange. We need to ask you-Why your boarding passes are irregular? Why you required these high-ranking individuals to see your exit from Mexico?"

Madam stared at him. Not in a demeaning way, but only a firm one. She was staking her ground. Her eyes were piercing, they penetrated too deep within him, his soul was exposed to her, his secrets became apparent, like a quick flash she saw them in front of her eyes. A wave of energy passed through the room as she did so.

She took a deep breath and exhaled. "Do you know who I am?"

A gust of air burst through the room, the two men looked at each other, both men smiled. The taller man in the suit took the paperwork from his co-worker, grabbed a pen and placed his signature on all three after stamping the passports.

"Thank you, Madam, for clarifying everything. We appreciate it. Have a safe flight home."

Madam and the children moved through the corridor and into the terminal. She was pleased with herself, she had managed to dodge yet another bullet. Yet she had no idea what had happened or how she had altered the situation without needing to defend herself.

CHAPTER 10

The train pulled into the station at Bangalore, and fear welled in Rohan. The British had ruled Bangalore since the early 1800's and so English was widely spoken. The climate was pleasant in the city, warm, and humid; but not excruciatingly hot. Rohan looked out the window of the passenger car to the platform below. Searching for a familiar face and found nothing. He reached beneath his seat and pulled out his simple leather suitcase, the entirety of his belongings contained within. He stood and followed the other passengers towards the exit at the rear of the passenger car.

The platform was filled with people, travelers and peddlers, women, men, young boys and a few girls. Some were moving with suitcases quickly hopping around, moving and bustling towards their destinations. Others were standing still, singing and attempting to sell their wares. Some wore earthen pots on their heads, filled with herbs and oils. He looked at their colorful clothing, the stacked boxes and animals scurrying around. He saw dogs, and monkeys. There were birds of various species and colors, and a few pack mules; loaded with the wares of the day. It seemed chaotic, and very exciting all the same. His fear melted away, replaced by an eagerness to explore, to see a new world, one that none of his brothers nor sisters would have the opportunity to experience.

After lowering himself to the platform he looked up to see a Priest wearing black slacks, a black short sleeved shirt, and his collar. The Priest held a sign with Rohan's name on it, written in black ink on brown corrugated board, and so he approached him.

"Good afternoon son, you must be Rohan. I'm Father Raul." The Priest extended his hand for Rohan to shake, Roh grabbed the Priests hand, but didn't shake it, he held it, and didn't let go. He was afraid, and this man seemed as though he would save him, if not today, then someday soon. As Rohan held the hand of the Priest he saw a clear path through a meadow filled with sheep. There were colorful flowers and green grass on either side of the pathway. The

Priest was at the gateway to the path, smiling, holding open a gate.

Roh took a breath and let go of the man's hand. He was kind. He knew that he could trust him.

The two of them walked along the platform, holding hands again, the Priest having taken the suitcase from Rohan, carrying with ease the bag that had weighed down the younger man. Father Raul asked Rohan about the train journey and questioned his interest in the Monastery. He did not ask about Roh's mother, or the situation in the home before he had left.

When they had arrived at the Monastery where he would live out his teenage years, Rohan met more of the Priests and was soon introduced to the other boys who were all studying in their rooms. These boys had all come from wealthy Indian families and had lovely cloths and suitcases. His own clothing consisted of hand me downs from Bhavin and Himmat that were tattered, mended and the colors faded. He was embarrassed by his personal belongings but was assured by Father Raul that he too would be totally outfitted with uniforms the same as the other boys were wearing. Rohan wondered how his father had managed to afford such a luxury as private education for him; as tuition and boarding wasn't economical at all. He was quite able-even with his limited exposure to the world, to understand the simple expense of this schooling.

He took his one suitcase up the stairs to the room where they had instructed him to sleep. The stairwell was wooden and dark, and void of pictures or decorative touches. A large Crucifix was hung at the end of the hallway at top of the stairs. He opened the door to his quarters, which was wooden and large, and heavily polished. It smelled of lemon and was gleaming enough to see a reflection. The doorknob was shiny brass and as he turned it, the door creaked. The room was small and sparse. The walls were painted white and were bare of any extras. The room contained a small twin bed and a dresser with three drawers for his cloths. There was a nightstand with a lamp and a Bible on it, a single Cross neatly hung directly above the head of the bed. This was for protection; he was very aware of that. He knew in his heart that he might one day rely on the cross.

The small window with gauze draperies, was functional, allowing a soft breeze to flow into the room.

The concept of not being required to share his personal space was very foreign to Rohan, and he wasn't entirely certain that he would be able to sleep at night surrounded by silence. He was accustomed to having to share with his brothers, and often one or two of his sisters.

The solitude seemed very luxurious to him and he felt as though he was being overindulged.

Upon arrival at the Monastery he had been given a manila envelope full of papers. He opened the envelope and poured its contents onto the bed. He was searching for his dining and class schedules for the following day. He was hoping that dinner would happen soon as he hadn't eaten since breakfast and was feeling famished. He was curious about his classes and whom he would have for teachers. Not that it made much difference to him, as he didn't know anyone besides Father Raul. Curiosity got the better of him and he dug through the paperwork like a mad man.

Within the pile of papers, he found a tuition contract signed by his father. He read through the lengthy document and was surprised to find many things. He was first astonished at the amount of his tuition and boarding fees. With all the medical bills that his father had had in the past 4 years with his brother's illness and then his mother's he was quite certain that they were not able to afford the outrageous price for his education. His tuition for each year alone was more than his father made in nine months. He shook his head and kept reading through the pile that had come so neatly packaged.

He was equally as surprised when he came across an agreement for services in lieu of his annual tuition. Clearly outlined on the pages that followed were the requirements of the Priests for Rohan, the services he would provide to the school and his father's acknowledgment and acceptance of their terms.

Rohan would be expected to clean all the dormitories and restrooms including showers twice per week, he would assist in the kitchen with meal service to the other students and clean up after the final meal was complete. He would sweep and mop the dormitory floors and run errands as the Priests saw fit. And in addition, Rohan would not return home. He would remain on campus, and would paint the dorm rooms, refinish any of the hard-surfaced items as needed; such as desks, bookshelves, tables, doors, and stairwells. He would be expected to maintain his keep and provide a neat and tidy surrounding for the other students. Roh had been hired in trade for his school fees as a janitor.

His father had negotiated his tuition and had exchanged his son's time and efforts without his consent or even having asked him about it. Rohan sat on the bed and thought about his situation. He felt lonely and he felt dejected from his family. How could he be traded away?

He wondered what they would be doing now? Here he was sitting alone in a room, in a very large school full of boys, with no warmth, no comforts of home. The space was to be his, his own room, with no sharing required.

Rohan had essentially been traded by his father, to the Priests as a servant in exchange for a pre-University entrance education. He was disappointed; hurt by his father, and he wondered if his brothers knew of the conditions of his education. He was far too angry to cry, so instead he began to run scenarios through his head. He decided at that moment that he would learn to take care of himself; and that he was his only friend. He resolved to study hard, complete the chores as the Priests required him to do, and move ahead into a life that would be far from here.

He thought about what Bhavin had said to him months ago, that he was learning English to escape this horrible place, this country that kept them chained to poverty and uncertainty. He would do the very same for himself, except that he would have a formal education. He would complete an education that would be recognized, one that would make his father and his mother, regardless of her illness very proud.

CHAPTER 11

Jorge Alvarez was ecstatic to have his lover's husband in custody. Even if Madam had fled the country; and he didn't know where she was, at this moment in time, he couldn't be a happier man. Of course, the opportunity for happier could present itself later, but Jorge was willing to be patient. Patient with Madam, patient with the soon to be ex-husband, and patient with the legal system that would send him deep into the prison system for many years to come.

The personal belongings of Madam's husband; which included two bags that had been confiscated, had been placed into the evidence holding. Jorge was anxious to see what exactly was in the old smelly backpack that had been the forefront of everyone's attention on the day that he had been arrested. The blue school bag was also of great interest to the Chief of Police. The man had held on to both the bags as though his life was dependent on them. Most people when being taken into custody would easily release their possessions. Not this jackass. He fought to keep them.

Jorge took the stairs down to the holding area and nodded at his Sergeant on duty.

"Chief, top of the evening to you, what brings you down to my neck of the woods so to speak…?" He was a portly and round fellow who had been on the force for over twenty years. His olive skin was shiny and his smile always bright. His black belt sat beneath his rotund belly, essentially disappearing when he stood.

"Buena's Nochas, listen, I would like to have a look at the personal belongings that came in a few days ago, the ones from the gringo that was arrested at the airport."

"Oh Ja! I know juss the one, interesting stuff. You were on that bust Chief, no?"

The chief wondered what was so interesting about it. "I was yes, can you bring the box forward for me, please sergeant."

"Of course, Chief, I'll be right back."

Jorge put his hand in the pocket of his chinos and took a breath. There were times when doing the job were difficult. To him this time, this year, this month, this week, this day, was particularly trying. He cursed himself for falling for the woman, and yet he couldn't help himself. He couldn't stop himself from going head over heels. She possessed some kind of magic, or at the very least she had cast some kind of a spell on him. He wondered where she was and if she had gotten to her destination safely. He understood her need for secrecy, for her own safety, but he hoped that she would contact him soon. He would feel better if he knew where she had disappeared to, Jorge felt if he knew at least the location of her whereabouts, he could rest at night.

He could hear the sergeant coming back down the hallway, shuffling his feet as he walked. It was apparent that he was carrying something. It sounded as though it was something of substance, as though it had a heaviness to it.

"Here you go Chief. It's all in here, I placed it all in this box myself. I have the list here, on the lid. Juss the way you like it. See?" The sergeant, pointed to the lid on the box, and to his neatly detailed and organized listing of items contained therein.

"Yes, thank you. Good Work Sergeant, if there were more men like you my job would be an easy one." He nodded at him as scanned the items on the list and then lifted the lid. There was one thing in particular that grabbed his attention. One thing that stood out the most, the fifth item on the list, *one blue canvas school bag*, and the sixth item on the list, *one hundred and fifty thousand American dollars in one hundred-dollar bills, found in the blue school bag.*

Jorge scanned the rest of the items on the list and opened the box. He noticed first the old backpack and opened it immediately. It had a smell, like old papers that had been wet. It was empty. There was a wrist watch, some peso coins, a few bills, a laundry ticket, a set of keys, a wedding ring, a wallet that contained only a picture of Madam and the children, nothing else. He saw the blue school bag; and at the bottom of the box, a shitload of cash.

"Sergeant, there was nothing in the old backpack? No revolver? The man had a revolver when he was arrested, what happened to that?"

The Sergeant rubbed his chin. "No, no chief, no gun of any kind. Just that stinky old back pack. Empty. The blue bag though, had all that cash in it."

Jorge was perplexed, he had been absolutely certain that there had been a gun, he had seen it himself. "Thank you, Sergeant, that's all for tonight, you can return the box and its contents to its resting place."

"Yes Chief," Jorge left the room and walked back up the stairwell to his office. He wondered how many people knew about the money. What had been the husband's intention for it, and where had it come from. What happened to the gun? He looked up the stairs to the top. The climb seemed overwhelming to him tonight.

CHAPTER 12

Juan Maria de Salvaterria watched Jorge climb the stairs. He used every ounce of power he could find within himself to make the climb seem farther to Jorge. He wanted this man to exhaust himself. He smiled contently as he watched his steps slowing. The chief's hand holding the handrail as he never had before. He had always run up the steps, usually two at a time. Tonight though, his feet sounded heavy as they hit each stair. The soles of his shoes sliding onto the next foot plate, and the next and the next.

If the thought of Madam made him physically exhausted, there was a chance that the man would eventually move on. Physical exhaustion made for emotional drain, Jorge would tire of the chase, his wanting of her would fade, his desire would become a distant memory, like a black and white movie that would play on at night as her memory would drift though his consciousness, becoming more and more faded, the reel playing less and less often. Making Juan's job a little easier.

Juan liked the idea of that. He enjoyed a challenge, but at his age, he loved a smooth ride.

CHAPTER 13

Rohan studied diligently, attended all his scheduled classes, and took extra classes when he could fit them in. He washed and pressed his clothing at night, so as not to waste valuable study time in the early morning. He worked in the kitchen of the cafeteria during supper hours, helping to prepare and serve meals for the other boys, teachers and Priests. Father Raul assured him that to serve others was an honor and that he should be proud that the Lord had chosen him to be the servant of all. He was skeptical, but he continued to do his very best at everything every day.

Some of the boys, who were from Mumbai, and Delhi, from wealthier families; felt obligated to bully and tease Rohan. They clearly didn't see the prospect of service as a blessing in the same way that Father Raul did. They threw their plates on the floor for Rohan to pick up, they slopped their soup on the tables and tripped him when he was carrying large plates and trays of food and dishes. They urinated on the floors in the restrooms. They laughed when there were no Priests within earshot to hear. They did their best to make him a miserable as possible.

Roh chose to not allow them to triumph.

Roh was determined despite the tirades of his peers, to succeed. He relished in the fact that the boys were teasing him. He came to understand through prayer and meditation classes that in some mysterious way they felt threatened by him. He considered himself to be favored because of this knowledge. He kept his newly acquired information to himself, and he smiled on the inside where only he could see.

Many nights were spent alone in his room writing letters to his Mother, which he wasn't able to mail or have delivered to her. He knew nothing much of her whereabouts. Only that she was still in hospital, and that there was no certainty of her return to the family. His heart ached for her. His loneliness was his greatest obstacle. He spent many hours dreaming of her, remembering and willing her return to the family.

He became forlorn as the days turned into weeks, and the weeks into months. He made no progress in the fortifying of relationships with the other boys, he was a loner, one that was completely ostracized, by his classmates but was very often preferred by the Priests and teachers. He was smarter than most of the boys at the school. It had taken only a short time for him to figure that out. Some of them understood him to be academically superior. He just believed that he was academically alert, when they were not inferior to him, but merely lazy.

He studied harder and more often, he passed on football practice, and tennis lessons, spending more time than the other boys on the required and optional academics. He didn't honestly see the point in frivolous games of athletic prowess. He realized that his competitive nature was only nurtured by an intense love for knowledge. He thrived in the areas of World History and Economics; Psychology and Sociology were also favorites of his. Chemistry seemed to pose a bit of a challenge, however it wasn't a challenge that he was not be able to overcome. The more difficulty that he had with a subject, the more he studied it. The more he dove into the textbooks, the more time he would spend on the learning of every detail of information provided and available to him.

Languages also tended to be very easily absorbed by Rohan, he excelled in studies of new tongues. He thought back to his discussions with Bhavin and had to laugh to himself. He was now fluently speaking English and French and was working on Latin and German.

As his confidence grew so did his ego, he became stronger and more confident; he wondered if his dear older brother had gotten through the first book of English yet. He thought often of his family and missed them all terribly. He did however realize that his chances for a life outside of India were far greater if he continued with his education at the Monastery. He had come to enjoy it, despite his being homesick.

Christmas Vacation time was approaching and Roh knew that all the boys would be returning to their homes to visit with their families. They would receive gifts from their parents, eat an abundance of rich and delightful foods, and sing carols. It would be a merry time in which they would rejoice. He would not. He would remain on campus and would paint all the restrooms, and the classrooms on the 3rd and 4th floors of the main hall. Apart from Father Raul and himself the only other who would stay behind would be the janitor. He would help Rohan with the painting of the classrooms and the restrooms and showers. He was a large man, heavy as though he had always eaten too much, and his face was always red. His pants always hung a little too low, sweat always stained his shirts in great circles under his arms and on his back.

Thinking of the sweat made Rohan shudder, he wasn't even aware of what the man's name was, but he knew that he must not do anything to annoy him. Roh had heard him bellow at two of the other boys one afternoon, he wasn't sure what they had done, but he knew that he would never deliberately do anything to upset the apple cart of the terrifying janitor.

When the final bell rang on December 22nd, Christmas vacation presented itself. All the boys hooted, hollered and prepared themselves to catch the bus to the train station. There they would all board different trains; which would take them to their respective homes. Rohan sat in his room as the boys filled the hallways. He could hear them boasting about what gifts they expected to get, and what their favorite foods were. He thought of how he enjoyed having food, and how grateful he was that there was a meal for breakfast, lunch and a hot dinner every day. He could not imagine having a favorite of anything. He did enjoy a nice curry, but he didn't have the mind to be picky.

He waited out the departure of the masses, and then reflected on his own family. He took time to pray for his mother, and his father. Hoping that they were both well, and that his mother would soon find happiness. He prayed for the success and health of his siblings and wondered if they would think of him in his absence this holiday season. After his prayers, he spent some extra time reading his Bible, and wrote a letter to each his mother and to his father.

As the room began to darken, with the setting of the sun, he suspected that there might be a nice meal made for him. he put shoes and a sweater on, tidied the bed, placed the Bible in the drawer of his night stand and left his room. The hallway was dark and seemed frightening to him, which it never had before. He looked up and down the hallway and towards the stairs. He thought he heard someone walking behind him and turned to look towards where the crucifix hung at the end of the hall. He saw nothing; shrugged his shoulders and began down the stairs to the lower level.

As he placed his foot onto the first step he felt a warm rush of air blow past him, and he again turned and looked to where it had come from. He felt warm all over his body, like he was sitting in the sun on a hot day. The air became still, completely void of sound, except for a whisper that came to him from above.

"You have been chosen child."

Rohan scanned the area, afraid to inhale, reluctant to move. His eyes moved to the left and to the right without a turn of his head. His knees felt weak, slightly wobbly and unable to hold him upright. He placed one hand on the wall to his left, acknowledging the need to stabilize himself. A fall would upset the janitor for sure. He waited, holding his breath, hoping to hear something else. Waiting to ask to question. "Chosen for what?"

The whisper sent warm air again to surround and comfort him. All fear and trepidation left his being and he felt at peace. There were no glowing lights, no band, and no fireworks, just a whisper.

"I have chosen you child."

CHAPTER 14
1980

Tears continued to fall, relentless and un-subsiding. She looked at her grandmother moving robotically, nodding and agreeing to arrangements. She hesitated to speak, wanting to share what had happened with her. Knowing that she would appreciate the exchange, the offer of kindness and would likely feel relieved of the pain that was ailing her.

The small round kitchen table now had six chairs nuzzled around it instead of only the normal four; and many others were standing in the landing above the stairs. Her father seemed to be directing the meeting. With a notepad and pen he jotted in point form important facts and information as others interrupted him. His glasses seemed to be fitting him tighter than normal. She noticed that his temples seemed to be pulsing; his forehead tense.

She listened as they discussed flowers and cars; the need for limousines to and from the church. Who would bring food by and at what time the minister should be expected to arrive at the house, how long he would stay. She wondered if anyone would make her favorite walnut squares, if she should ask or if asking would be rude. She decided to wait and see. No one liked a rude girl. She should be seen and not heard, with her hair neatly done, and her dress nicely pressed. Her father would see to having all the children's shoes shined. And her mother would insist on all of them behaving well. She didn't comprehend the idea of misbehaving under these circumstances, but she wasn't like other children.

She moved across the room to where her grandmother now sat alone. Her grandmother's hair had been done at the salon early in the morning, her nails were neat and polished. Although it was still early, she wore a pretty dress, it was not black, it was a floral; in rose tones, simple but elegant, a regal picture of a lady of importance. She noted how her grandmother looked. She was sad, broken hearted in fact, but she was poised, composed and still majestic.

"Nana, can I sit with you?"

She wiped her nose with a handkerchief made of fine linen. "Of course, my Dear, come over here." She gently touched the velvet chair beside where she sat.

She sat closely beside her grandmother, who was now mourning her husband of over forty years. "Are you okay?"

"Oh, Sweet thing. No, not yet, but I will be, one day. I just can't believe he's gone. I don't know yet what I will do without him. You don't know this, but he was everything to me. I have loved my boys, so much, but my John, he was my whole world. He took care of me when I needed him most, he was a real man, he was different than the rest. He could do things, and handle things that other men just could not. One day Sweet-heart, you will understand what I mean."

"He loved you too Nana, more than anything. He told me." She smiled up at her grandmother through teary eyes.

Her grandmother returned the smile to her. "He did? When did he tell you that Sweetie?"

"Last night."

Her grandmother took her granddaughters shoulder in her hands and held her gently, she looked at her from the side, "But that's not possible Sweet-heart, and you know that."

She nodded. "Yes, I know, I understand what you are referring to; but he came to me last night. After I went to bed. Remember you put me to bed in his room. I had some trouble falling asleep, I wasn't feeling well; my stomach, and a terrible headache; there was that storm that was scary with the wind and the thunder; and then he came to me. He was wearing his nice dark pants, and that light shirt that he liked so much; the buttery colored one, with his wing tipped shoes, they were all shined up nice. He said that I shouldn't be scared, it was okay, that his soul was at peace. He told me that I was going to do great things for mankind, and that he loved me. And that he loved you more than anything in this world. He said that he had always loved you, and only you. He said for me to pray, every day until the end of time. Then he kissed me on the forehead and said too much chocolate isn't good for a girl. Then he was gone."

Her grandmother held her breath a moment, visions of her John passing through her mind. Tears spilled from her bottom lids and rolled down her cheeks as she realized that her husband, partner, and best friend had crossed over to the other side but was still able to communicate. "Good Heavens child."

CHAPTER 15

Houston is the home to four major airports, Ellington, William P. Hobby, West Houston airport and George Bush International Airport. With thirty daily flight destinations to Mexico, Bush International offers service to more than Mexican cities than any other U.S. airport. Houston is the headquarters of United Airlines, and George Bush International Airport is United's largest hub, with more than eight hundred daily departures. Over thirty-nine million passengers a year travel through the Houston Hub, making it an easy place to disappear. A place to use if one wanted to become just another face in the crowd. It wasn't an accident that Madam and the children had been booked to transfer through Houston, and it wasn't by chance that they would be doing so at the busiest time of day.

She moved behind Her mother, watching the crowd as the people hustled and bustled from gate to gate. There was a flurry of colourful coats and purses, suitcases on wheels being pulled behind while people chatted on cell phones. The pace was irrational. She made a mental note of this. It was indeed very unlike what She had grown accustom to. She loved the comfort of the slower pace of life in Mexico, the tranquility and joy. The pleasures taken from the sun and the sand, the peace found in siesta and the gratefulness for life. These people moved quickly, they all had purpose, or seemed to. They all appeared to be important, they carried themselves as though they were individuals of great significance. They had an air to themselves. Noses slightly elevated, shoulders back. Phones engaged. Chests forward. This was a nation of driven souls, she had been on their soil for only moment and She could identify a difference already. These people were prepared for war. She could sense it. Not a war of the traditional sense, with conventional weaponry but a different kind of war. One that might be fought using the very things that seemed to keep them connected to their loved ones, bosses and friends, their business contacts and other important individuals. She saw those phones as a threat.

She looked around for Mary Mack and couldn't see her, but She knew that she was near as She could sense her presence. She had spent a great deal of time on the plane in prayer and meditation. Her quiet solitude was enabling her visions of others. She however wasn't certain if it was her imagination or actual spirit contact.

She reached forward for Her mother's hand, "Mother, I'm feeling hunger."

Madam turned, relaxing slightly now that they had successfully navigated the US Customs office. "Okay, I'm hungry too. I think though that we should find our way to where we need to be. We need to change hangers completely. And it's quite far. It might take us a half hour just to make out way through the people and hallways to where we need to catch the bus to another hanger. And we will need to stop at a restroom along the way, can you hang on for a minute?"

She frowned. 'Why do you do that? Why do you always ask for a compromise? I haven't eaten since breakfast today. It is now five o'clock in the afternoon. I don't ask for much. I am patient, I understand that my dietary restrictions make it difficult for everyone, but could a girl get a simple carrot? That's all! Or some guacamole. I know that you too have had a tough day, but please, I cannot go on. I simply cannot."

Madam looked at her daughter and then at her son. "Are you hungry too?"

Her brother nodded. "Well yeah, I mean, I ate on the plane though, they gave me a tray of food, but She couldn't eat it.

Madam swallowed. "Well then we shall find some food. I apologize. I do not get hungry. I don't have the same need for nutrition as the two of you. I am no longer growing. And sometimes I forget. So, I will try to do better. I have relied on Lupita for that. So, I am sorry. Let's see what we can find that is yummy and that will satisfy our needs shall we?"

She pulled Her long auburn hair back into a ponytail and put an elastic on it. "It's hot here Mother." Beads of sweat were forming on Her nose. She was beginning to feel weak, and wasn't certain if it was from the heat, or from the lack of nutrition.

Madam was silently and aggressively searching for a safe place that they could rest and eat when she noticed a dark-skinned man watching them. Her heart began to beat faster.

She maneuvered the children into a small restaurant with red vinyl seats and arborite tabletops. She deliberately chose a table in the front, which was visible on all sides. She ordered water for all three of them hamburgers no cheese, no buns, extra lettuce, they would use the lettuce to hold the hamburger patty, and although She didn't typically eat meat, today everyone would need to make exceptions. Extra French Fries would settle a lot of upset. Her brother was happy with anything as long as it came with ketchup and a smile.

Madam kept her eyes on the dark-skinned man who continued to watch them. He was not travelling alone. She made note of him signalling someone. She hadn't yet figured out who it was however. Her mind wandered, she was not able to eat the food that had been placed in front of her. The children chattered on about meat and cows, and respiratory systems in living beings and why it's wrong to consume them. She half listened as she watched the man and attempted to discern who he was signalling.

The children ate, oblivious of the men who were watching their every move; every lift of every French fry. Madam kissed the tops of each of their heads and lifted her lettuce burger to her lips.

CHAPTER 16

Abraham sat in the cold, damp cell with nothing more than his bible and rosary beads to calm his wandering mind. He spent most of his days in meditation, attempting to climb his way out of hell and into the realms of what he believed to be an elevated position, with a seat next to God himself. He prayed endlessly, he sought understanding and wisdom from a creator he couldn't understand. He prayed for Her, giving thanks for the opportunity to have known Her, for the time he had been in Her presence. He knew without hesitation that she was the one, she had touched a place in him that no one else ever had. In his err She had provided comfort, compassion and forgiveness.

His mistakes had allowed him to ask himself the questions that he had been afraid to ask. Who am I? And for what is my purpose? Time spent alone in the darkness opened his mind to the question, what his role was in Her life. He knew now that his greatest expression of himself could be manifested through the art of experiencing time with Her. She encouraged truth in those She encountered, she embraced and accepted individuals as they were, raw, real and flawed. He was grateful that through his selfish acts She had shown him kindness, She had tested the boundaries of his patience, his understanding, his love, and fears, She had kept not a record of his misgivings but instead had prayed for his release from the clenches of evil; and from that he knew the existence of his God was more than just a probability, it was surely reality.

He would sit, for the days that were necessary, for the nights that were required, he would wait in the dark and dingy cell to which he had been sentenced. The act of kidnapping Her and Her brother he understood was punishable, he accepted his punishment. He would do as was required of him by his creator as penance for his sin, and then he would find Her. And in Her he knew that he would find resolve. He knew She was the way to freedom.

CHAPTER 17

Rohan waited again holding his breath. There was no movement in the hallway, no more sounds, no breeze, no more whispers. But he waited. He waited because he wanted to be chosen. He deeply desired to be the *one* that everyone wanted to be. He wanted to be the teacher's pet, the Priests darling, the most favored of children. He wanted it. And so, he waited. He stood on the stairs without moving. He refused to move. Not to the left, nor to the right; not up the stairs and not down. He stood still, and he waited for a message, for another whisper. For direction, and for acceptance, not to be discarded, but to be chosen. He waited.

The next morning Roh woke to a banging on the door of his quarters. "Boy get your little ass out of that bed, it's time you were painting walls."

Rohan opened his eyes and scanned the room. He didn't remember coming to bed, and he was most certain that he had not had any supper last night. He looked for his glasses and for his pants. He stood quickly and pulled his pants on, slipped his feet into his shoes, grabbed a sweater and pulled it over his head, and then in one swift movement he grabbed his cap, put his glasses on and opened the door, to find the janitor standing right in front of him.

His breath stank, and he reeked of dirty sweat and unwashed cloths. Rohan held his breath and fought the need to gag. They moved down the hallway together and as they approached the stairs, the janitor turned to him.

"Missed you at dinner last night. Which is okay because I ate yours. Father Raul wanted to come looking for you, but I said, nah, he's probably just in his room reading. That's really all you do, right? Read? You just read?"

Rohan looked back at the crucifix and silently prayed for temperance.

"I do enjoy reading yes and thank you for eating my portion so that it didn't go to waste. I am terribly sorry that I missed the meal, I will have to apologize to Father Raul when I see him today."

The Janitor grunted at him, and then continued down the stairs. He mumbled as he walked,

"Weird, the kid is weird, and I get stuck with him over the holidays, weird, weird, weird."

Rohan spent the day painting, and by noon he was becoming quite proficient at it. He was quick and made only a few mistakes. The walls were being redone in a soft grey instead of the basic white that had been there before, and he thought it an improvement. He splattered only a small amount on his pants and noted that his sweater remained remarkably clean.

At the end of the day, Father Raul stopped to see how the day had gone for both Rohan and his new friend, the janitor. Both acknowledged that it had been productive and then Father suggested that everyone take a one-hour break and meet for dinner in the main mess hall. He would prepare a hot soup and some bread for a meal. Just one hour, he said. And both of Rohan and the janitor nodded.

Rohan was anxious to sit with Father Raul so that he could ask about his experience from the night before. He returned to his room, closed the door and lay down on the bed, thinking that a short nap would just refresh him enough that he would feel well for dinner. He removed his glasses and closed his eyes. Feeling the magic of sleep overcoming him.

His body melted into the bed, he felt heavy and lethargic, but as though he was floating, soft like cotton candy, fluffy and light.

His eyes refused to stay open, like the slamming of a great door, they closed, and he tumbled head over heels into a deep sleep. Colors of red, purple and blue flashed before his eyes as he saw himself walking through a field of sunflowers. The sun shone brightly and burned his skin from high in the sky. The flowers gently swayed in a soft cool breeze that seemed to come at him from all sides. He felt relaxed and calm. He looked down at his pants and saw the paint splashes on them. He giggled to himself, thinking of how odd it was that such an easy job could end up so messy. As he walked through the field of sunflowers he saw people that he knew but was not able to speak to them. They were too far from where he was to hear him clearly. He attempted to wave but no one seemed to notice him there.

Off in the distance he saw a young girl that he did not know. She was beautiful, with an angelic quality that he found mesmerizing. He watched her skipping rope from a distance, she was singing and laughing; and appeared to be alone. He moved towards her and she turned towards him, she waved her hand, beckoning him to come nearer. Rohan began to run towards the young girl. Her dark curls falling down her back and bouncing as she jumped rope. He could hear her voice more clearly now. She sounded sweet and innocent while singing.

"Miss Mary Mack, Mack, Mack All dressed in black, black, black With silver buttons, buttons, buttons All down her back, back, back. She asked her mother, mother, mother, For fifteen cents, cents, cents, To see the elephant, elephant, elephant, Jump the fence, fence, fence. He jumped so high, high, high. He reached the sky, sky, sky, And he never came back, back, back Till the Fourth of July, lie, lie."

Rohan looked at her with an interest greater than he had ever felt in anything. He was so incredibly awestruck that he was unable to speak. It was as though he had been hypnotized by her; he stood now right beside her and watched intently. She jumped rope without ceasing, bouncing and laughing as she repeated the rhyming song over and over. She would look at him and smile, but continued to skip, and never spoke a word; until finally she said, "Are you an elephant?"

Rohan thought her question odd as he was clearly a boy, a twelve-year-old boy now. Growing up quickly but certainly not an elephant. "No, no I'm not an elephant." He said. "I'm a boy"

"Hmmm," she muttered, "Then why would He bring you here now?"

Rohan was becoming lost in her dialogue. He thought it odd that a girl so beautiful would speak in these riddles. "I'm not sure what you mean." He said.

"Well, if you are not an elephant, then why have you come to me? I am waiting for the elephant who jumped over the fence...isn't it clear?" She placed her hand on her hip, her fingers smoothing over the black silk of her dress. It was quite a lovely dress, a shirtwaist dress with a pleated skirt and silver buttons down the back.

Rohan shook his head. "No, it's not clear to me at all Miss, I am a boy, I go to school and I do my best. I look nothing like an elephant. Why would you think me to be such an animal? Why do you speak in such riddles?"

She began to look frustrated with him. "I don't know what you are talking about, you look exactly like what I thought an elephant would look like. I do not know what is a riddle, my name is Mary, Mary Mack and I am waiting for the elephant to come back. Do you happen to know what the date is? It must be coming close to July now. I've just been here skipping and waiting for July to come and bring my elephant back."

Rohan was not able to take his eyes off of her. Her beauty resonated into every leaf on every tree, and into every pebble on the ground. He had never seen anything anywhere that was so captivating. A glow escaped her and filtered into the air around her. He stared at her, "it's December, not July. I could be your elephant if you like. We could be friends, you and I. I don't have many friends, but I might like one that is as pretty as you are. I could stay and play with you, I have nowhere to be." He found her to be most confusing, but he was willing to make every effort possible to win her over; and was not certain why. He would do anything to be her friend, to become her elephant.

Mary Mack began to skip again. "Don't be silly boy. I need an elephant. You are clearly just a young man. You will never do. You can stay if you want, and I will play with you, but I will still be waiting for the elephant. At least until the 4th of July. Do you understand? My elephant will come… but you will do for now." She turned her rope around and around and skipped without missing a beat. Her curls began to bounce again fascinating him further.

He didn't understand her conundrums and he wasn't clear on why he would have to be an elephant. He was willing after all to be whatever she wanted. Even if it was just pretend, even if it was only for a short time, until the Fourth of July, or until her elephant came along. In the distance, he could hear a voice calling to him that sounded much like that of Father Raul. He chose to ignore the call and stay with the girl. She gave him pleasure. He realized how interested he was and how appealing she was to all of his five senses. Her smell filled his nose suddenly, clean, and floral, with a hint of sweet vanilla, he breathed in deeply, inhaling the scent to the depth of his toes. Taking all of it in and holding on to it; the color of her dark mahogany hair and her dark brown eyes he was sure he would never forget.

She bounced, and she bounced her rope clicking on the ground with each rotation. She looked at Rohan. "You like me, don't you? Well we should be friends, special friends. Miss Mary Mack and the Elephant sitting in a tree, K-I-S-S-I-N-G, first comes love, then comes marriage, then comes Elphie with the baby carriage." She laughed uncontrollably, giggling until her eyes watered. "Did you get that? Elphie? Like Elephant? Or did you say your name was Rohan?"

He jumped back from her. "How do you know my name? I never told you my name! Who are you? Mary Mack? Why do you speak in such riddles?"

She looked at him, tilting her head to one side and smiling she answered. "You are not the elephant, of this I am sure. He has been here before and he will come back. I am everything that you will ever want. I am love, I am feminine energy, I am the power and electricity you desire. I am youth, and vibrancy, I am peace, comfort and serenity. I am all that you will ever need." She turned her face away from him then. And continued to skip. He could only see her hair bouncing. Her face had become obscured. He tried to catch her gaze once again. But she seemed focused on something in the distance. Her skirt bounced up showing him the length of her leg from where her sock began above the ankle to just above her knee. He felt something in him stir, something that was completely new to him.

Rohan had never spent any time with girls other than his sisters, this was an experience that was completely original, and one to which he had no point of reference, he began to feel nervous, and his mouth began to feel dry. He was not accustomed to situations that were outside of his control. Mary Mack had most certainly taken control of this situation and he didn't like it one bit. He was not able however to stop himself from watching her, and he most definitely was not about to leave her side.

He heard the voice again of Father Raul, calling to him,

" Rohan, Rohan, Rohan." He ignored the call, he shut his ears to the beckoning. He wasn't able to help himself. He wanted to do nothing but to be in her presence, to be in the same space that she occupied, he stayed, and he watched her skip.

"Rohan, will you skip with me? I will take care of all of the rhyming, you will just need to jump when I tell you to. Can you do that?" Mary smiled coyly at him.

He was certain that he didn't know how to skip, but he would be able to figure it out quickly. Her olive skin looked so smooth he wanted to touch her, but he didn't dare. He was afraid, but excited at the same time, bursting of a new source of energy that resonated directly from her. He jumped in when she signaled him to do so, and he skipped with her. She began her rhyming song and he hummed along as the rope turned over and over. Clicking as it broke the ground between them. She giggled as she reached the end of her song and she stopped turning the rope. "Oh, Rohan you are so good at skipping. It almost seems like you were born to skip with me."

Rohan could still hear someone calling him but continued to ignore the pleas which were beginning to sound more and more urgent.

"I like skipping with you, I feel free and happy to be with you."

Mary Mack reached out and touched Rohan's cheek. She said nothing but ran her hand over his cheek and into his hair. Her touch sent an electrical shock through his body. He felt it from his cheek to his toes, and it ignited a magnetic pull to her. He was compelled to reach out to her. He placed his hand in her hair and moved closer to her. Her fragrance was now over powering him, he was becoming unleashed. He no longer felt like a boy. He felt older and more confident. He touched her hair and drew it towards his face so that he could smell it. It smelled of sweet vanilla, the fragrance stirred memories from within him. He inhaled deeply, deciding without consciousness to give himself to her, all of everything that he had; every ounce of his being would become hers. He wanted nothing more than to be with this girl forever.

The loneliness that tormented him disappeared, his fear of failure was gone. He felt strong and powerful and invigorated. He moved his hand from her hair and touched her face. Her skin was just as soft as he had imagined it to be, his own skin began to tingle, his breath began to become faster, more rhythmic, his heart was beating quickly.

He looked over her shoulder towards the trees in the distance only to see them disappear. He blinked, startled by their vanishing. The sky began to darken, and the temperature began to drop suddenly. What had been warm and comfortable was now feeling too cool to be outside and very breezy. He shuddered. "It's turning cold and I don't have a sweater on, I might catch a chill, we should find somewhere to warm up. It feels like there might be a storm coming."

Mary Mack said nothing.

Rohan reached for her hand and scanned the horizon for a place that they could escape the chill. Leaves began to blow around them. The sky continued to darken, and the temperature continued to drop. "Come, Mary, we should find shelter, there is a storm coming."

Mary stood still and said nothing.

He pulled at her arm, and pleaded with her, "Please Mary; come with me now. I will take care of you, come Mary, let's find a safe place together."

Mary Mack's face distorted, what had been angelic was now of demonic proportions. Her teeth were long and fanglike, her soft luxurious curls became a matted and tangled mess of dreadlocks. Her olive skin was grey and leathery looking. Her fragrance turned sour and was putrid smelling. Saliva hung from the corners of her mouth, mucus ran from where her button nose had once been; which was now pointed, warted and gnarly. Her dress was tattered and torn now, a black mess of ratty fabric that looked hundreds of years old.

He jumped back and fell to his backside. He held the ground on either side of him, it was cold and mossy feeling. He tried to scoot back away from the beast in front of him. It moved towards him, coming close, spit dripped from her and fell onto his cheek, his skin now felt clammy. He shuddered as it began to hiss at him. He scurried backwards, the breath of the beast hot on his chest. He couldn't bring himself to look at it. It was so horrible looking, and the smell churned his stomach.

"See what Little Girls are *really* like: stay away from them boy; they could be the death for you, *you have been chosen to do the Lord's work.*"

With that Rohan woke and sat up with a start. It was dark in his room, the moon was high in the sky, and shone through the windows. The clock ticked midnight. He had missed dinner again.

CHAPTER 18

Chief Alvarez sat in his office in the center of town, with Madam's husband in a cell in the basement of the building. The federal authorities had temporarily remanded the bastard into municipal custody. And so, he sat behind the bars of a cell in Jorge's own lockup.

The irony of it all provoked a grin, and it took all of the strength he had not to stroll down to the dark and gloomy depths the cellar himself. Jorge was tired. Today had been a long day, all he really wanted to do was go home and have a hot shower and get some sleep.

He had his own questions, he had his own secrets, and his own investigation was about to begin, he needed to know why and how Madam's husband had been operating. He planned to investigate the near drowning incident from years before, he felt guilty that during the original investigation, he had potentially overlooked something that may have made a difference, a potential payout would have changed things. His own curiosity provoked in him a need to investigate the life insurance angle further, as the feds had suggested; and he would. For his own sanity he needed to clear up the loose ends on the case, and Jorge felt he owed it to Madam. He was fairly certain that he had lost any chance if there had ever been one, of any kind of a future with her. But he still wanted to make it right. To set the record straight, make things okay for her, she deserved that. He needed to figure out what had happened to the revolver, it was crucial. He knew without any question that there had been one, he had seen it himself. He needed to know which one of his officers had taken it or hidden it. Revolvers didn't often disappear. He wondered about the backpack and the fact that it was empty. He didn't understand the desire to carry an empty bag. And one that was so old and smelly should certainly not be carried if it had no apparent purpose. He owed it to himself to find out where all the cash that the husband had been carrying had come from, and what it was for.

CHAPTER 19

Juan Maria de Salvatierra walked the streets of Puerto Vallarta in the dark of night. He looked for nothing in particular, he observed the movements of the community randomly. For once in a very long time, he believed his assignment had been completed. His khakis hung loose, his t-shirt was tattered and torn. He loved his new look. After a period of adjustment, he had decided that his robes were truly a thing of the past. He liked the new fashion. It was liberating and allowed him more freedoms. The formality of his robes was comfortable, but liberty was eternal.

He watched the people pass as he walked, pleased with how well he seemed to be fitting in to this environment. He made a mental note that the majority of individuals passed him as though he was a ghost; many without making eye contact; as if they hadn't even seen him. A warm sense of pleasure filled his belly as he sipped on an iced limonada. He enjoyed not being seen, his job relied upon it.

Juan enjoyed his work. He had always been gratified while serving the Lord in the literal sense. As a servant of the cloth, a man of the Church during a time of great movement. He had been faithful and had lived his life doing exactly what his heart directed him to do. He believed fully in a world where a higher power ultimately controlled his movements, he lived by faith and he felt that he had been justly rewarded. This part of his work, *this* was the reward. This was part he loved. There were aspects of the job that weren't desirable for sure, as there were in any type of occupation. To suggest otherwise would be less than forthcoming. He never enjoyed death, and suffering was less than optimal. But on occasion, it was necessary to achieve success.

For as Juan saw it Life is all but a test, a journey of learning our boundaries for love, our willingness to forgive, our abundance of courage our ability to inspire. An assessment of our capacities, are we able, can we apply the rules, are we certain to follow instruction as laid out for us? Can we be present? Fully aware and abundant for ourselves? Also, for others? Are we too proud to limit ourselves to the guidelines given? Or do we believe ourselves to be deserving of more? Are we lustful? Egotistical? Boastful? Can we live as His Son did? Would we?

For Juan service was always a question of heart, and he always knew. He knew when he was a boy that he had been chosen. He fought his parents from the very beginning, and he disobeyed them to answer the great calling that was upon his life.

Juan sipped on his limonada and thought about the human condition, the greed and the wanting. The pushing of reality farther and farther from reach, leaving the average individual unlikely able to achieve their goals, but left with despair, dread, disappointment, and disgust in themselves.

"Forgive them Father, they know not what they do." Juan looked up to the stars, knowing that although a part of this assignment might have been completed, Her mission was far from over. He would take rest now and prepare for his next orders. For he knew they would be coming, if not tomorrow, soon enough. He was aware of Her importance and he was honored to have been awarded occupation on an assignment of such caliber.

He moved on with the crowd, throwing his cup from his limonada into the trash receptacle. He noticed Chief Alvarez across the street on the other side of the Malecon walking into the Police Station, Juan thought he might just check in with him, and moved towards the corner.

Whistles of traffic cops were blowing; the ocean was crashing against the shore. The sound of laughter from tourists and locals filled the night air. Juan shoved his hand into his pocket and pulled out a bundle of papers. He glanced at them quickly. He smiled quietly to himself as he approached the police station. This was going to be fun. He did enjoy a good game of chess. And he believed Chief Alvarez was going to be a worthy opponent. 'Giddy up Jorge', he chuckled to himself as he slipped into the building un-noticed.

CHAPTER 20

She watched Her mother watching the dark-skinned men watching the three of them and hoped that her mother didn't notice Her watching. She giggled on the inside at the silliness of it all. Everyone was watching, but no one ever listening.

She could see into a partial thought of one of the men, she wasn't sure which one, but she was certain that the three of them were in danger. Permitting they chose remained in clear site however, they should be fine. Her mother had done a fine job of selecting a table, in the center of a high-volume traffic area. She thought her mother to be a fine care giver. It was almost as though she had insight, or as though she had done this before. She was quite proud of Her mother. Pleased that she had gotten them this far safely.

She sipped on Her water and nibbled on the vegetables on Her plate. The meat tasted vile to her. Visions of brown calves and cows with long eye lashes and tan colored tails came to mind. Chewing on grass in fields, roaming free, grazing in the sun where they should be; not mashed into a patty on her plate for Her to consume. She did understand the need for protein and she was grateful for her mother's concern. She found it difficult to swallow however. Her throat tightened, and her gag reflex enabled, balls of meat clogging in the back of her throat. She spit the meat into her napkin and took sips of water to eradicate the taste from her mouth. Lettuce and tomatoes were a better option for her, when Mother wasn't looking she would slide the hamburger patty onto her brothers' plate and no one would be any the wiser. He would be appreciative and would potentially be indebted to Her further. She enjoyed the feeling of leverage. She smiled to herself.

"Mother, at what time should we begin our journey to the next gate?" She looked up at her Mother who was scanning the terminal area and seemed to have eaten nothing.

"I think soon, I am just attempting to discern the best way for us to get there. With the least amount of difficulty." Madam was intently watching the dark-skinned gentlemen who were doing their best not to be noticed. She pushed her dark curls back from her face and applied pressure to her temples. A tension headache was settling in nicely. Throbbing in her central lobe. The pain was certain to make her nauseous for the remainder of the day and a little edgy.

She assumed that despite her mother's apparent concern, these men would not have weapons of any kind. She believed this to be a secure area, and to the best of her knowledge, the three of them wouldn't be leaving the area that they were in. So, the worst that could happen is that one of them could be taken. As that had already happened to Her and to Her brother once before she thought the likelihood of it happening again was negligible. The odds of it were just not in favor of a kidnapping. She felt comfortable walking safely.

Her mother seemed to have harvested a plan, she could tell by the way that her brow was furrowed. The two of them waited while her brother finished his food. He wiped his face and hands carefully with several napkins and then placed them on his plate on top of the remaining food. Her mother paid the check and then they pushed in their chairs back from the table and stood.

The three of them walked together through the crowd towards the bus transport station. Having come into the United States through the international terminal, they now had to make their way south through the crowds to Terminal A, and to the Air Canada gates. As they moved, she could see that she had been incorrect and that they indeed were leaving the secure area, this meant that there was indeed a possibility that the dark-skinned men were carrying weapons or might have them hidden somewhere near. The three of them would need to clear security once again eventually. She stayed close to her mother, her brother was mesmerized by the television screens and hand-held devises. Captivated by technology he had stopped moving and their mother hadn't noticed.

She tugged at Her mother's skirt, "Mummy, He's back there, by those men."

Madam swiveled on her heel in the crowd, her heart leaping from her chest to her throat. Her eyes scanning the clusters of people, seeking him out frantically her eyes darted from left to right.

Madam saw him, and the dark-skinned men closing in on him from the left. She lifted her left hand to the air and yelled his name, her voice deep and echoing loudly off of the concrete walls that surrounded them.

She looked over and saw Mary Mack quietly watching, her hands held tightly together in prayer position, her face barely visible. The dark curls that so eloquently covered her head falling forward past her shoulders. The dark-skinned men alarmed at Madam's interference, slithered back into the crowd. Disappearing much more quickly than they had appeared, like seals retreating into a cold ocean water.

Her brother looked up from what he was doing, oblivious to the activity that surrounded him. "Sorry Mom, I'm coming, did you see that television? Mom? Mom? Did you see it? It was so thin? They make them now so that you can hang them on the wall. Can you imagine? Hanging the television on the wall instead of having it on a stand, or a table? Incredible right? And the color is spectacular. Well way too expensive for now, but in a few years the prices will come down I think."

Madam looked over at the men who were now certain that they had been made. She made eye contact with the tallest of the three men, he refused to look away, and stared at her hard, his eyes piercing hers. His teeth rolling a tooth pick back and forth from left to right.

"I didn't notice the televisions sweetheart because we were supposed to be walking towards the gate. Remember?"

"Yes, I didn't forget. I just saw those cool televisions and I wanted to look at them. I'm sorry Mom. I should have said something to you. Did I make us late now?"

Madam hugged him tightly and then took his hand in hers. "No, we are not late. I just don't want to lose you. This is such a big airport, and we need to pay attention, okay?"

He smiled at his mother, still unaware of the dark-skinned men, or Mary Mack who was now smiling and making silly faces at Her.

She was frustrated by her brother's inability to be aware, oblivious, frightfully childlike and so easily distracted. She caught a thought wave from Mary Mack... *'patience, he too is a child of God and loved abundantly, forget not that we are all accepted as we are.'*

She wanted to send a message back to Mary Mack, and tried, but wasn't successful. She was thrilled to have received one so clearly however. She would practice this new form of communication in Her quiet time. When She was supposed to be sleeping...she would instead be intent on mastering the skill of telepathy.

CHAPTER 21

Christmas vacation seemed long to Rohan. He painted everyday with the Janitor who although they never said much to each other, came to a certain understanding. There was a mutual respect between them. The two of them found solace in working together in silence, neither one needing to speak just for noise.

Rohan knew nothing of the man's personal life, or if he had one. He didn't know if he was single or married, or if he had any children of his own. The janitor came to work each and every day, he did his job in the very best way that he knew how. Rohan knew in his gut that he like him, but more so that he trusted him.

The other boys returned from vacation to a newly painted school. Between the two of them, they had managed all that was on Father Raul's list and a few additional rooms and dormitories. The place smelled clean. Of fresh paint and cleaning supplies with a lemon fresh scent.

On the first day back at school, the popular boys sat together around the lunch table. They boasted and hollered about their family gifts and Christmas expeditions. Rohan listened to them, without making any comments. He kept to himself that day just as he normally did.

There was one boy in particular that seemed to really enjoy teasing and tormenting Rohan. Nigel Sharhim, He held up his arm, to show the crowd the Cartier watch that had been given him over the holidays. It was gold, and it was shiny. Rohan couldn't help himself but to stare at it. it was the most beautiful piece of jewelry that he had ever seen. It glistened with diamonds, set into a perfect pearl face.

Nigel caught him staring. "Hey poor boy, what the hell do you think you are looking at? Are you staring at me? Is it me you are looking at? Or is there someone standing right behind me?"

Rohan despised confrontation. He shook his head, and answered, "No I am not looking at you. I was admiring your beautiful time piece. Congratulations, it really is stunning. You must have behaved so well. And made your father really proud to get such a marvelous gift."

The boy laughed, he looked at his friends - all of them laughed too.

"What are you talking about Rohan? Proud and behaving well? Roh I think you have officially lost your marbles you know? Why do you think a guy like me gets a gift like this? Oh, are you not sure? Ok well I'll tell you. A guy like me, gets a Cartier watch because my Daddy is the president of the bank. That's it man. When you come from money, you breed more money. It's just a natural progression. When you don't have money, well as you very well know Roh, you get to paint on Christmas vacation. Paint the walls, paint the halls, paint it all. Oh, and what did you get for Christmas ole chap? Nothing this year? That's too bad." The boy made a pouty face and smirked at Rohan.

Rohan was hurt, and he was very upset by the actions of this young man. He picked up his lunch tray and left the room without saying a word to anyone. He sat alone in his room and read his text books. He thought about his mother and he wondered how she would be doing now. He hadn't seen her in so long, and sometimes forgot what it was that she looked like. He could hear her laugh as he fell asleep, and he imagined her touch, her caress as she stroked his cheek, or as she cut his hair. He missed her.

He studied late into the night. Escaping from the torment and torture of the boys who ran the school.

In the morning he rose and prepared himself to go to class as usual. He got up, he washed his face and hands, brushed his teeth and dressed himself. He packed his book bag for the day and went to class. He had forgotten about the events of yesterday. They were not of importance, nor mattered to him what so ever.

When the first bell of the morning rang, all of the boys were in their classroom, in their seats. The professor entered the room and took roll call just as he always did. It was chemistry that they were in, and chemistry that they would study. Roh continued to struggle but had learned some study techniques that made it more tolerable, and manageable.

Within a few minutes the Dean of Studies knocked on the door and entered. He was a tall man, and wore nothing but three-piece suits, he looked stiff, professional like a banker or a lawyer. He was tall, and his hair was clipped short, he was shaven close, he had no facial hair. In a large room of individuals who wore similar clothing, he would be indiscrete. He was someone who would blend in, and perhaps never really be noticed, a Ghost. In the school of the Monastery however he stood out like an orange ball in a basket of green ones. He was the shiniest, the most noticeable.

"Rohan Gupta, may I see you please, not here, but in my office., not after class but right now."

Rohan stood, not sure what he should do, he picked up his books, and placed them neatly in his book bag, not because he was a neat freak, but because he was not certain how he should handle the situation. He had never before been to the Dean's office; he was historically a good boy. Always followed the rules, always obeyed the guidelines and understood the expectations of him as a man.

He walked the hallway, a feeling of dread overcoming him. His palms became sweaty, his mouth and tongue were dry. He was nervous, and yet he had done nothing wrong, what so ever.

The Deans office was large and was at the front of the school. As he approached the office he passed by the janitor's quarters, his door was open, and Rohan looked in. They made eye contact as Roh walked past, his head hanging low, his gait unhurried. He was scared, he had never felt so alone as he did at the very moment when he entered the Deans office, it was large, and it was to him very intimidating.

There was a man there that he had never seen before, he wore traditional Indian clothing, not a suit like the

Dean. He was very smartly dressed though and seemed of great importance. He had an air to him; an aura that plead respect.

As he entered further into the room he saw the likes of *Mr. Cartier watch*, Nigel Sharhim. He was baffled by the presence of these two individuals. Had the boy come forward and explained how he had hurt Rohan's feelings yesterday at lunch? Was this an effort to clear his conscience, and apologize, make it right?

The Dean spoke first, "Rohan, I have known your father since we were boys at school ourselves. It was because of that, that I agreed to have you come to our school. I have heard nothing but good things from your teachers and the Priests regarding your behavior and study habits. Which is why the events of today have come to me as such a shock."

Rohan stood still, the door was still ajar behind him, he thought quickly about running, but wasn't sure how far he would actually get before someone grabbed him.

The Dean continued, "Mr. Sharhim is here with us today because his son here, who is one of your classmates, has had a very expensive Christmas gift stolen. His Cartier watch has gone missing. And you were seen last night entering his room while he was attending volleyball practice."

Rohan stared in disbelief, "Sir, please it's not true."

The Dean cut him off, "Rohan please, we have more than one witness, you were seen at lunch time admiring the watch, is that not true?"

Rohan nodded, "Yes sir, it is true, I did admire his beautiful time piece."

"What do you have to say for yourself then Rohan? Hmm? Would you like to return the watch now?"

Rohan fought an uncontrollable need to cry, his words came stuttered, "No sir, I would not be able to return it, as I do not have the watch in my possession."

The Dean was becoming frustrated, his desire was to wrap this up quickly and get this gentleman out of his office so that he could return to doing what he liked best, which was leading these young men into successful and prominent lives. This episode was uncomfortable for him, and a nuisance.

"Rohan, please, let's just be honest, and stop this ridiculous behavior now, everyone has other things to do today, it would be in your very best interest to accept defeat at this point, own up to your transgressions and take your punishment, if you do not you will leave me no choice but to expel you from the school."

The Janitor was emptying the trash cans from the main office and was able to over hear the conversation from inside of the Dean's office. He was appalled. He had seen what had happened, and he knew that Rohan was telling the truth. He had been in his room the entire evening. He wondered how it was that these people could do this, how these boys could lie, and put the poor innocent boy directly and purposely in harm's way, with the full intention of having Rohan expelled, shamed and sent home.

He knocked on the door to the Dean's office which was still slightly ajar.

"Yes, what is it?" the Dean shouted.

He pushed the door open and stood tall in the opening of the man's office. "Sir, I have some information about the incident that might help you to resolve the problem."

The Dean looked at Mr. Sharhim, and then back at the janitor, "Please if you have something that will help, I would greatly appreciate anything that you have to offer."

Rohan was wide eyed, fear ran through his body making him feel hot. He felt sweat beading on his brow but was scared to brush it away. He had worked all through the holidays with this man and had enjoyed his company. How could he come forward now and what had he seen?

The janitor cleared his throat and began his tale." Well Sir, if I may, I would like to do everything that I can to not only enlighten you on this situation, but on many incidents that have occurred since the onset of this school year. As you have always asked me to Sir, I have kept an eye on certain boys here, never interacting with them, but watching their conduct and behavior. I am grateful for the job that you provide me, and I have many friends within the walls of the school. Some are old friends, and some are new." He looked at Rohan, and then continued. "There is an unbalance and abuse of power here sir, where certain boys believe themselves to be greater and more powerful than others. A superior class one might suggest. Some of those boys at times feel threatened by the presence of boys such as Rohan who show immense promise. Father Raul has shared with me that so many boys are called Sir, and yet so few are chosen. All of these boys believe that they have been chosen for something great. A service or a splendor or such, they are here at our school because of that very thing. Because they believe, or better yet their parents believe, that there is a purpose to them being here. Anyway Sir, as you are aware, I had the opportunity to work over the holiday season with Rohan, spending a great amount of time with him, and with Father Raul. It is my opinion that he is of very strong character and would never take an item, of any value that belonged to someone else. Since he has come to the school Sir, I have witnessed this boy," he nodded at the other boy in the room, "Mr. Nigel Sharhim harass and torment Rohan incessantly. This boy is not worthy of our school, this boy should be the one expelled Sir."

The Dean was watching the face of the boy's father. His anger apparent in the color of his cheeks, a red flush rising. "Do you have anything more to share with us? Anything other than opinion that could actually substantiate your position?"

The Janitor continued his story. "Well yes sir of course, Yesterday the two boys shared a table during lunch. Rohan commented on the beauty of the watch that Mr. Sharhim had returned to school with. Nigel took that opportunity to once again belittle Rohan. Rohan returned to his room at that point and didn't emerge until the morning Sir. What happened was something much different than what you have been told, and I will do my best to help shed some light sir,"

"Please, help us here." Said a frustrated and somewhat impatient Dean.

"Well after lunch Nigel and his boys had a good laugh at Rohan's expense; once again. Then Nigel followed Rohan down the hallway towards the dormitories, which are all freshly painted sir. Thanks to Rohan and myself. Nigel then removed his watch and placed it behind the crucifix at the end of the hallway, outside of Rohan's room. That is where you will find the time piece, sir. Of this I am certain."

The Dean looked at Mr. Shamhir and at Nigel. He was now uncertain of himself and of these boys, he knew not who to believe, but was confident that he should question each and every individual's motivation. The truth was inevitable but was most usually reliable and defined by its deliverer. He was positive that he would get to the very bottom of this matter. His sincere hope was that Rohan was innocent as he claimed to be. He dreaded the idea of having to call Rohan's father with the news of his being expelled. He would much rather be calling to share the news of an appointment to the honor roll, or rather a scholarship allocated by the Diocese for outstanding performance. To the depths of his very soul he knew the boy was innocent, what he questioned was the validity of the janitor's pleas. He silently prayed as they walked the hallways towards the boy's dormitories. He implored the great universe for the evidence he needed to be present. His future was dependent on it.

The bell tower hummed and clanged as the group approached the entrance to hallway of the dormitories.

Rohan was sweating profusely, his nerves eating at any confidence that he may have had before this meeting. He repeatedly padded his brow as he removed the sweat that was beading and tolling from his hairline. He was completely aware of the seriousness of the situation. He pictured the face of his mother as they walked towards the staircase to the upper floors. The entire group seemed to be moving in slow motion, an eternity passing in the moments that it took the group to walk the short distance to the dorms. The outcome of their investigation would not only determine Rohan's educational future but may have an impact on his life categorically.

The Dean was the first to reach the stairs, he turned to Rohan and offered a look of sympathy as the ensemble of boys and men moved down the hallway towards the crucifix at the end of the hall, outside of the entrance to Rohan's dormitory.

CHAPTER 22

Chief Alvarez waited until it appeared that there was no one within the station but himself and a few guards. It was late. He descended the stairs again to the holding station when he knew that his Sergeant would be on dinner break and the evidence holding chamber would be empty. He slipped in and moved back to where the itemized boxes were held. The evidence boxes were neatly labeled and placed on shelving units, stacking critical clues for important cases from the floor to the ceiling. Jorge found the one he was looking for easily and removed it from the shelf.

Jorge was quite certain of what his intentions were for the cash, and at this very moment he was positive that it was his time, he was due a pay day. He had saved Madam's children when they had been kidnapped, he had helped Madam escape this country and it was time for him to reap the rewards. No one knew of the money but himself and his Sergeant, he was certain that no one would ever suspect him of stealing from the evidence lock up.

He was not able to see Juan Marie de Salvatierra, it was Juan's intent to remain invisible for this game. It was for Juan the likes of a game of chess, and he was making the rules up as he played along.

Jorge lowered the box to the floor and removed the lid. He moved the blue canvas bag to the side and was surprised to see that the old back pack was gone from the box. Also missing from the box was all but one, single one-hundred-dollar bill of the original cash. The money was gone, one hundred and forty-nine thousand nine hundred dollars-missing. All of it was missing. He shoved the blue school bag to the side, and then back again to where it had originally lay.

A single one-hundred-dollar bill, laying neatly inside of the blue school bag, and the remainder of the husband's personal belongings was all that remained.

Jorge spun on his heal and looked on the shelf for an additional box. There was nothing. He focused again on the items list on the lid...it clearly stated that there was an old backpack, and item number 5 was a *blue canvas school bag,* item six, *one hundred and fifty thousand American dollars in one hundred-dollar bills, found in the blue canvas school bag.*

Jorge shoved the remaining items to the left and then to the right again, subtly hoping that the cash would reappear as though he was caught in the midst of a Vegas Magic show. There were a few papers on the bottom of the box that he hadn't noticed earlier that evening. He lifted them out hastily and looked at them.

Copies of a Life Insurance Policy with Her name listed as the insured. Alvarez couldn't believe that he had missed this. He might have potentially spent weeks looking for this and it was right under his nose. Right in front of him, he had been so focused on the cash he had missed this important clue in the case. He read through the paper work quickly, scanning until he found what he had been looking for. Clearly identified, the name of the beneficiary of the policy. He slammed the lid onto the box and ran back upstairs, intent now on finding his Sergeant, and the whereabouts of the missing money.

CHAPTER 23

Mary Mack sat on the plane as they waited to taxi and depart from Houston, she was restless, but rather pleased with herself for managing to maneuver Her through George Bush International Airport in Houston, all by herself without the need of additional assistance. Of course, it helped that Madam was always on her best behavior; alert, always readily prepared for the worst.

Mary looked at Her brother now nearly sleeping and at Her mother, sitting quietly. Madam appeared to be resting, sitting quietly with her eyes closed, her hands in her lap; but Mary Mack knew better, she was never resting. Madam was preparing her mind for the next leg of her journey.

She sat with Her hands carefully folded in Her lap, she was so tiny, a wee bit of a child, one might think her to be only 5, when she was actually now nearly 7. Her eyes were closed, but Mary knew that She too was awake. Mary slipped her a quiet message, unsure of Her ability to receive it.

"When Christ shall come, with shouts of acclamation, and take me home, what joy will fill my heart. Then I shall bow, in humble adoration, and then proclaim, 'My God, how great thou art.'"

She opened Her eyes and looked up at Mary Mack. She smiled and sang for everyone to hear, "Then sings my soul, my savior God to thee, how great thou art, how great thou art, then sings my soul, my savior God to thee, how great thou art."

Madam leaned over and kissed the top of Her head. "Perhaps you should try to get some rest baby." She stroked her daughter's auburn hair gently. "I do love the sound of your voice, but you must be exhausted."

She took her mother's hand and squeezed it. 'Yes Mother." she said as She winked at Mary Mack.

"You can hear me then?" Shared Mary Mack.

"Oh yes, loud and clear, I wondered however, how difficult it would be for you to hear Me." Sending the message made Her head ache a little.

"Depends on interference. This tin can we call an airplane is good for telepathic endeavors. Let's not bother with the why, they just are. Bravo to you though. You catch on

quickly. Just like the day we started with languages back at school." Mary Mack smiled at Her, an endearing loving smile.

She kept Her eyes closed. But She desperately wanted to look at Mary Mack. *"Why is this happening to me? How can I do this? Can everyone?"*

"Absolutely not. Everyone has the ability but lacks the desire and the discipline to tap into it. You; through your meditation and prayer have opened channels in your brain that others never utilize."

"And why can I see you? And no one else can?"

"I'm not really at liberty to discuss that with you. Not at this time anyway. Perhaps later... You will one day understand completely."

"Fine, F. I. N. E., to be satisfactory. She accepted the reasoning and declared it to be fine. *"I like being able to talk to you this way. It enables us to share top secret things without the knowledge of others."*

Mary Mack's heart warmed for this young girl. *"Yes, exactly. One day I will show you things that will help you to understand why you can see me, and why we can talk in this way without speaking. But not today."*

"Okay. I'm a little sleepy Mary Mack." She closed Her eyes tightly, and thought that, this fragment of Her adventure; learning yet a new language; telepathy ought to

be placed safely into Her Purple Box, with other items accomplished by faith. She drifted off to sleep, while Her mother and Mary Mack watched over Her.

CHAPTER 24

Jorge looked for the Sergeant after the dinner break, and found him rather quickly, right where he should have been, in the evidence holding locker, behind the counter, completing paperwork. Alvarez took a deep breath before entering the room and approaching the man, a man that had given his entire adult life to the force, was loyal, honest and until today had been totally trustworthy.

Juan Maria de Salvatierra was watching, unseen by the two men. "Chief Alvarez, what brings you back tonight?" The Sergeant was taken aback by the presence of his superior three times in one day.

"Evening Sergeant, I came back specifically to see you, I'm glad that it's quiet tonight so that we can talk."

"Oh, that's nice of you sir, thank you, but you really should be out with the ladies by this time of night, or at the very least, you should be, like they say in the papers, catching bad guys." He chuckled at he said it. His happy body reacting to the laughter as it erupted from him causing a subtle shake of his midriff.

"Sergeant how was your dinner break?" Jorge rested his hand on his hip. His mind racing with scenarios and possibilities. His thoughts produced short films of the sergeant shoving the cash into his pants pockets and sneaking out the back to a waiting Toyota. Racing through the streets, a high-speed chase ending in a shoot-out in the middle of the downtown. Chief Alvarez once again the hero overcoming his rotund officer. He would manage to sneak the cash into his own pockets before anyone noticed.

"Fine sir, nothing out of the ordinary, you know I went home and had a bowl of Pozole, the wife makes a lovely bowl of soup you know. One-day sir if you may, I would love for you to come to the house. Join me for a dinner. It would be quite an honor for us to have you in our home."

Jorge looked at him. Not sure what to think. He knew if the man had taken the money he would not likely be inviting him home for soup. Into his home, to meet his family. However, he was at a loss for other options. He couldn't imagine what had happened to the cash. "What did you want to talk to me about Chief?"

Jorge looked at the Sergeant and smiled subtly. "Nothing." He shook his head. "It can wait until tomorrow Sergeant, you're right, I think I need to go catch a bad guy. Have a good evening." He turned on his heel and moved towards the stairs. His heart heavy, his mind racing, but with different movies than just a few minutes earlier, he now saw the sergeant in a happy home, in a small kitchen with an ample table, covered with a cloth hand sewn, dotted with small flowers. He saw soup bowls with small chips in the porcelain but filled with love. Robust with flavor and laughter. He felt sad for himself. He realized at that moment, that although the sergeant made less money and had less accolades in the papers, or none, he was a much happier man. The sergeant had an abundance that he was missing; the sergeant was happier than he was himself.

Jorge quickly thought about every decision that he had made and realized that all of the fighting to get ahead, the fitness, the running, the chasing of steps on his career path, were just in vain if there wasn't a bowl of Pozole for him to go home to.

His feet felt heavy as he climbed the stairs back to his office. He felt tired again, over tired. He noted that this was the second time today that he had physically felt exhausted. This puzzled him as his fitness level was always of extreme importance to him. He rested his hand on the handrail, just long enough to catch his breath. He closed his eyes for a moment and could see her face. Her dark hair falling down her back, her mouth open ever so slightly as she laughed. He winced and plodded up the rest of the stairs to his office.

Juan watched Jorge's face as the vision of Madam rolled through is mind. Juan was good at creating images, an expert at projecting emotion onto people and was pleased when he was succeeding. He knew that Jorge was in pain, and he was delighted. Juan didn't believe Jorge was well suited to Madam. There were times when Juan couldn't help but feel the raw emotions of man. His own spirit was still whole, his soul still remained in-tact, the memories he possessed were all real. Juan Maria de Salvatierra dug deep into his own resources and was about to act on the remnants of his own human flesh.

He knocked on the door of Chief Alvarez' office. "Adelante' come in please." Jorge sounded drained as he called out from behind his desk.

Juan passed through the doorway, the shear height of his body filling the entrance. Jorge looked up from what he was doing, "Yes, can I help you sir?"

Juan was feeling playful, he was missing Mary Mack, but felt that on his own he was capable of many things that would only further advance their cause. "Good evening Chief Alvarez. I think I might have something that you believe belongs to you."

He had Jorge's attention, "Yes sir what might that be?"

Juan reached into the pockets of his khaki shorts and pulled out one hundred and forty-nine thousand nine hundred dollars in one hundred-dollar bills. It had been bulky, and heavy, filling his pockets entirely. He had snuck into the evidence holding and replaced the cash with the insurance papers. He had been unnoticed, and he believed that the impact he would create presenting to Jorge would be well worth the risk of having been caught.

Juan felt better having the money out of his pants and placed it onto the desk between the two of them. He stroked his beard and shook his head to the left and back to the right. After setting the money down on the desktop he said. "My gosh that is a lot of cash isn't it?"

The Chief's eyes grew wide. He placed both hands onto his desk and began to stand.

"Oh please, don't get up." Juan spoke again. "There really is no need at this point. You have done quite enough today. This is the money that you were looking for."

"How did you get that?" Jorge wasn't certain who this man was, nor did he know how he had gotten into the station, up the stairs, and into his office without being stopped. He wondered more importantly how he had gotten into the lock up and managed to get his hands on the cash.

As though he had read the chief's mind, Juan snickered, his left hand raised to the sky "I really am a master of things and can't say more than that. Sorry Chief."

Alvarez reached forward and touched the money, the feel of it exciting him, his mind racing. "Who are you, how did you get in here?"

"Names Juan, Juan Maria de Salvatierra, and I came through the front door actually."

Jorge's mouth opened slightly in surprise. "Juan de Salvatierra? Like *the* Juan Maria de Salvatierra, the Apostle of California?"

"Like that yes... except that would be impossible, now wouldn't it? If you told anyone that, they would assume you to be a lunatic, Juan Maria de Salvatierra has been dead a very long time I believe...so you probably should not, um...say *that*. I'm afraid Jorge we have a bit of an issue with this cash here. Would you like to explain to me just what it was that you were thinking about doing with it?"

Jorge swallowed hard, his pulse beginning to elevate. "I don't know what you mean. Why don't you sir, explain to me how *you* got it? How is it that you are in possession of this money sir?"

Juan laughed, a deep and throaty laugh that instilled fear in the Chief, not amusement. "You don't know what I mean? Tread carefully Jorge, please and thank you, you never know who might be watching. And let's be clear, I need not explain anything. Not to anyone, most especially not to you."

Jorge pushed his hair back off his forehead, he made a quick decision in the heat of the moment, to tell the stranger the truth. He would never be certain why he made the choice, never clear as to why he felt obligated to answer the man. He would wonder for a long time after, if he had been justified in doing so, and if the decision had been in his best interest. "Look, I don't know who you really are Juan, but I had reason to believe that the money was at risk in the evidence lock up."

Juan was receiving instructions from afar as he listened to the Chief. "Yes, and so you thought that it would be best to take it yourself then? Is that what you were thinking? And leave the blame to fall on the Sergeant? He's such a great man, the sergeant. Loyal, honest, a good husband. Such a crime would ruin him, and his family. He would suffer, his wife and children would be destroyed."

"No, no of course not. I would have returned it. I was just planning to move it to a secure location."

"A location more secure than the safe inside of the evidence lock up? Which by the way, is fully surrounded by armed officers twenty-four hours a day? Where would that better location be exactly, Jorge?"

Jorge had been trapped. He had been pushed into the corner with nowhere to go. He knew it. "Okay, look. I was going to take it; plain and simple. Who would have known? Nobody. The only people who even know that it's there are the Sergeant and myself. I figured I could cut him in for ten percent and that would be the end of it. It's drug money anyway. It's his drug money, her husbands. Madam's husbands. It's dirty and no one would ever miss it. You don't know the half of it, and I still don't even know who you are."

Juan sat in the chair in front of the Chief's desk and placed his hands neatly in his lap. He slowly stroked his beard and paused before saying. "I actually know all of it. The truth is Jorge, that *you* don't know the half of it. But I am going to tell you. I would like you to sit down again please, and I would like your full attention. The few words that I will share with you are going to impact the remainder of your life. Are you prepared for the unfolding of truth?"

Jorge nodded as he prepared to listen. The wheels of his rustic secretary version office chair creaking with his weight as he settled in for what he thought would benefit him greatly. "I would love to hear it actually, lay it on me."

"The cash in the blue school bag was not drug money. You are wrong. It was not achieved under criminal nor malice circumstance. Madam's husband had stashed away a portion of the cash that he had taken from Madam's bank accounts with a friend of his-for safe keeping. He picked up the money in the morning and had been planning to return it to Madam on the day that she left. He was aware that Madam was leaving and that he was finally unable to stop her. He knew that he could no longer hold on to her. He also was very aware that choices he had made had negatively affected her and the children. It was his way of making a peace offering. Unfortunately, his plan to return the money to her never came into fruition, he lost his temper and didn't give her the money. Then when he was arrested at the airport, the funds with the blue bag were confiscated. You Jorge, were about to steal Madam's money, not drug money, and not anything of Madam's husband. You see Jorge sometimes when we don't have all the necessary information; we can just make a bad choice. We act out of haste, we jump to conclusions, we can make mistakes. Things are rarely as they seem. Best thing to do here would have been to have left it in the evidence lock up, with your sergeant, where it belongs for now."

Jorge's face was full of immense sorrow, Juan could physically see it, and he could feel it radiating from the man. He continued. "Tell you what we are going to do here Chief, I know you feel bad, I can see that. But it's just too late for that. You can't be part of the plan moving forward. I need you to do me a favor, would you do that?"

Jorge could do nothing but nod. His heart was aching. His mind drifted to thoughts of Madam. "You will return this money to the lock up, and then you will forget that you ever knew Madam. Don't attempt to find her, I know that you have been thinking about that all day; but it's time to forget about it. Forget about her Chief, you will move on."

Jorge couldn't help himself and blurted without thinking, "But she is the only one that I have ever loved. How can I just let her go? When people ask me what I see in her, I just smile and look away, because I'm afraid if they knew they might fall in love with her too. And now what do I do? What? Live alone forever? Lonely cop, solo crusader? The local papers will love it, they will relish in my demise, headlines will read...'*Cop crusader-lost cause; forever lonely, eternally saving lives; stopping one bad guy at a time'.*"

Juan liked that this guy had a sense of humor. "Look take it from me, Jorge, I speak from experience, it's not as bad as you think. A man can live many, many years waiting for a woman to return. Waiting for the fragrance of their skin to surround you, for dark curls of hair to fall gently on your face, to hear gentle laughter and silly rhymes and rhythmic songs. We are very capable of being alone for long periods of time. We are strong. You are lucky that you found love, even if it was only for a moment. Some people never do."

"What if I don't agree?" Jorge looked directly in the eyes of the large stranger that sat in front of him. The eyes were dark, like onyx, but clear as water. The depth of them created a sense of clarity in Jorge's heart, he decided that without knowing why that he must not pursue her. It was as though he was looking through thousands of years of history in one moment. He knew that he mustn't seek Madam out.

"Not an option. This is not a negotiation. I regret to inform you sir that you will not be seeking interest in Madam furthermore."

The light in the room was beginning to dull. It seemed to Jorge as though he had been in his office for a century. It smelled suddenly very old. It felt damp and musty.

"So, for the sake of one night of romance I shall pay the price for a lifetime?"

Juan stood. "I'll tell you what, I'll check back with you. Behave and perhaps there will be an exception made for you. But for now; yes, Jorge it appears that you are exactly correct. Your attempt at a relationship with her was a fatal blunder."

Juan stood and prepared himself to leave the room. "We understand each other then? You've got it Chief Alvarez?"

Jorge nodded. The door to the room closed behind the visitor as he left, leaving only behind a room filled with regret, torment and intense sadness. The Chief sat alone with one hundred and forty-nine thousand nine hundred dollars on his desk and wept.

CHAPTER 25

Clearing customs and immigration when returning to their own country was a breeze. She watched Her mother as she handled the officers with a smile, a nod, simple answers and grace. She was proud of Her mother. She felt glad to be solid on Canadian soil.

The three of them exited the secure area and entered the main airport terminal where Her grandparents were waiting. She saw Her grandma from a distance, her blonde hair shining under the fluorescent lighting. She ran to her throwing herself into her arms. "Oh my gosh how you have grown! And grandma has missed you so my Dear." Kisses were exchanged between the two, and the woman held the child tightly to her chest. "Oh goodness, Grandpa is going to want a hug too. And why is your brother taking so long to get over here?"

She giggled, "I do not know Grandma, but I am so happy to be here with you, I can't even tell you how much." She nuzzled her head into Her grandmother's neck and settled in to where she was comfortable. A gentle ease fell upon Her and she relaxed as she smiled at Mary Mack over the shoulder of her beloved Grandmother. She allowed her eyes to gently close as she placed this memory safely into Her Pink Box.

Pink for favorites, pink for pretty, pink for things she loved. They were home, and at last, they were safe.

CHAPTER 26

Rohan narrowly escaped demise. Mary Mack watched the events as they unfolded from the doorway of his room. Her black dress glimmering in the sunlight that penetrated through the open draperies of the window across the hall. She listened to the dialogue between the men. A disgust rising in her belly, a burning anger forming in clenched fists pounding on either one of her thighs.

The boy's innocence had been proven, the janitor had shown clearly that the watch had been placed behind the crucifix in the hallway, and not by Rohan; but by the owner of the watch himself, Nigel. It was clear that there was a profound resentment of Roh and jealousy in Nigel. An envy of Rohan's special gifts. Rohan possessed many talents, which had become apparent to not only his teachers and the Dean of the school, but also to the other boys. Mary Mack would ensure that Roh completed his schooling and that his passage to maturity was completed in the manner which was directed under His plan. If need be, she would eliminate obstacles that were in his way. She had been directed to do exactly so.

CHAPTER 27

Their father was held for weeks in a dark prison cell in the heart of the city in which he had originally been detained. Puerto Vallarta continued to hum and sing, the people of the Puebla enjoying their lives as though he didn't exist. Eventually, when the federal government failed to provide any evidence of wrong doing, and Madam had not pressed charges herself, Jorge had no choice but to release him.

Much to the Chief's dismay he had let him loose himself, unleashing the beast into the street with nothing more than what had been left in the evidence box after the feds were through with it.

The feds had lost interest in the case after Madam had left the country, after they had confiscated the one hundred and fifty thousand dollars in cash; and her remaining assets had been returned to the bank as directed. There was no reason for them to pursue him. The trail of evidence in the case opened on Her near drowning incident had run cold. Although Madam's husband was indeed the beneficiary of the life policy; the child had not died, and therefore there had not been a payout by the insurance company and no crime had been committed.

The trail ran also cold to his offshore holdings, there was no way to legitimately tie Madam's husband in any way to the mafia or anyone of their key players. Of course, Chief Alvarez was not surprised by this fact; the group of individuals in question didn't often leave a trail of evidence behind; nor any connections that could lead to their own prosecution.

Madam's husbands Mexican visa was consequently then cancelled; immigration placed him on a greyhound bus to Matamoros and the vast country of Mexico was for a time, finished with the likes of him.

He found his way by bus to Louisiana, he disembarked just outside New Orleans, where he could hide until his ego had time to heal. Like a snake deep in the bayou, he could slither into the darkness, disappear into the marshy swamp unknown; unable to be found. Waiting for the appropriate time to strike next.

CHAPTER 28

"Mary Mack why does my head hurt so much?" She looked at Mary Mack, her hands holding her head, her fingertips pressing her temples, massaging in circles, an effort to release the pressure.

"I'm Miss Mary Mack, all dressed in Black, Black, Black, with silver buttons, buttons, all down my back, back, back, I am afraid, fraid, fraid, that I do not know, know, know, but if we go, go, go, to see, see, see, the old grey man, man, man, before July, July, July, we might see an elephant, elephant, elephant, so tell your mother, mother, mother, but don't say why, why, why."

"Mary, why are you rhyming? Why don't you just say what you want to say?" Her head was pounding, she was frustrated and wanted nothing more than to lie down. She didn't want to play games with Mary Mack right now.

"You must tell your mother that your head is hurting, but you cannot tell her why."

"But I don't know why Mary. That's the point. It hurts all the time. I wouldn't know what to tell her anyway."

"Yes, I can feel it. I am so sorry for you. I wish I could make it stop. I would you know, if I could."

She looked at Her friend Mary Mack, their friendship had grown stronger and stronger with time, a sense of trust between them had flourished, Her skills becoming heightened, more profound. Mary Mack was mentoring Her and loving Her at the same time. They had become like sisters, without the ability to ever physically touch or feel anything other than spiritual presence of the other.

"I know you would Mary, Mary can we talk about your childhood? About what happened to you? Now that I'm almost ten I think that I can handle it."

Mary smiled at Her. Almost ten. Time was passing, and She was growing up, maturing and becoming the person that She was always intended to be. There were many things that she could handle, but Mary's childhood was not one of them. "It was difficult, I was a princess, my father was a King and a great warrior. My mother, the Queen was gloriously beautiful."

"What happened to you Mary?" She needed to know. She wanted to know the truth. She wanted to extend a hand to Mary, just as Mary had to Her. She wanted to be a friend, to Mary Mack, as Mary had always been to Her.

"I am afraid that I have been sworn to secrecy. I cannot ever speak of it. It was a tragic death; however, I have been released of my pain. My heart and my soul are free of the incident, for me; it is as though it never happened. The memory will always be there, imbedded deeply in my carnal thoughts; but the anguish is gone. I now have good memories of my childhood. The bad parts were expunged, there are only grey areas where bad the memories once were. Small fragments of time that I still remember, but that I am not able to associate emotion with."

She took a moment to process, inhaled, and said, "I think I understand. So, it's as though it happened, but like you read it in a book, or as if someone told you about it. But not that it happened to you."

Mary nodded, "Sort of like that yes."

"So, it doesn't hurt you anymore then? If the pain is gone? Whatever it was that happened?"

Mary Mack took a moment and then answered. "Yes, that is correct. The hurting is gone."

"Mary Mack, if you could have anything, anything in this world, anything at all...what would it be?" She waited on the edge of Her seat for the answer. She knew for Herself, if she could have anything today, if would be to have a head that didn't hurt.

"If I could have anything? Anything at all? I would be a child again. I would like the chance to live again. Sometimes I watch you experiencing life and I feel as though I was cheated. Tasting mango, or avocado, riding your bike or trying snowboarding for the first time. Losing a tooth, scraping your knee, hugging your family. Tasting your own tears as they roll down your cheeks when you feel sadness, the smell of fresh grass when it's been cut. All those things that you are doing that you love. I never got to experience, or I would like to try again. I would really like to. And all of the things that you don't like to do; the swimming lessons, making your bed, brushing your teeth, and brushing your hair out every day, doing your homework; gosh I would love to have a chance to do all of that. I would like to grow up and fall in love with a boy, I would like to have the chance to get married one day, feel the love of a man and have a baby. I never got those things because they were taken from me. I missed out. I don't know what ice cream tastes like, I don't know what it feels like to want something so bad that your stomach aches. I lost out on everything, not because I did anything to cut myself short, but because someone else decided for me. In a moment of rage and hatred my life was taken. In a split second my life changed. I have enjoyed what I have been given as a chance at life very much, and I love watching over you. I have gotten to see many parts of the world and do many things that I would not have seen or done. I am one of the lucky ones. I am fortunate. I am blessed beyond words and have gifts in abundance. But if I could do anything, anything at all, I would like to be a little girl again."

She took a deep choking breath as she wiped tears from Her own eyes. "I will pray for you Mary Mack." She reached for the hand that she could never really hold, for although it was near, it was never reachable. There was merely a hairs distance between the heavens and the earth, but she was not able to cross it. Her skin would never touch that of Her best friends, Her heart understood her, and Her mind wanted for her all of the things that Mary wanted. "I will pray."

And from that moment forth, she made it her daily goal to pray earnestly each morning for the one and only friend that had been by Her side through tragedy and triumph. Her friend that she could not speak of, for no one could see Mary Mack, and no one could hear her.

She carefully placed the exchange into Her purple box, for faith events, safe within Her mind, sacred in Her heart. Each day she gave thanks for the little girl in black with silver buttons all down her back and prayed that she might have one more chance to live as a little girl.

CHAPTER 29

Chief Jorge Alvarez had allowed Madam's husband to leave Puerto Vallarta without incident because there was no evidence linking him to any crime. Instinct told him though that there had been many crimes, many wrongdoings, and that he himself had allowed a felonious individual back onto the streets by his own hand. Jorge had personally watched him board a greyhound bus headed for the United States, but regardless of that he felt obligated to connect the dots to Madam's husband's criminality in some way.

For months, he dug, he researched, and he investigated quietly. He felt lucky that the feds had moved on and he could now poke and prod around without being noticed. His own local officers paid no attention to his comings and goings and the state police didn't seem to care.

An additional blessing was that Juan de Salvatierra had not returned. There passed many weekends where Jorge considered a stop at Sunday Mass, a visit to the clergy. He had turned his own back on the church, telling himself that he didn't have time, that his Sunday mornings were important, that he needed his sleep more than he needed to hear the word of God. His heart was aching for answers, his mind required the peace that came from of knowing that he was sane. He needed confession, he required a connection to a higher power.

The likelihood that the man who had crossed his threshold was Juan Maria de Salvatierra, was actually zero. But the memory of the exchange burned in his mind, his instructions heavy on his heart. It had however seemed very real to him; a trip to confession he felt might ease the weight on his heart and his consciousness if nothing else. The priest would not tell anyone. He couldn't think of a better place to dump his woes.

His heart still ached for Madam and despite the command to forget about her, he had not been able to. Nights seemed long as he lay in bed thinking of her, tossing and turning, waiting for the dawn to come. He was certain that eventually she would dissipate, like fog in the morning and he would forget. With time Madam would fade from his memory and become just a shadow. A glimmer of what once was.

He followed the direction of his visitor, and never spoke of her. He never mentioned her name, nor did he ever ask about her. Public opinion would suggest that he was over her finally. Her memory erased. Then one day a letter came, to his residence, address to him, in her handwriting. He thought of discarding it but could not. He opened it with shaking hands, his heart beating fast, a lump in his throat, tears streaming down his face.

> *My Dearest Jorge,*
>
> *So much time has passed, that I feel afraid to reach out to you, but frightened if I do not, the consequences may be worse. I wanted to believe that I could walk away from you and never look back. My life is a continuum of momentum, decision making and strategizing. And now I realize that at the end of the game, the king and the pawn go into the same box. We are all but one. Of one, to be one, unified, not against each other, but we should always play for the same team, and when we can't we should know that we will return to the same place of origin. Returning to the same box, with the same lining, fighting the same fight,*

with the very same sword. From one Universe, of one universe, serving one for the good of all.

I think fondly of you every day, my heart breaks each moment that I think of our eyes meeting, our hands touching, our hearts beating in unison, our souls a match next to each other's. I regret that I had to leave you, and I hope that one day you will understand the reason why I had to. One day I hope that you will forgive me, for I will never stop loving you, until the ends of time,

Madam

Jorge read the short letter, and then ripped it to shreds. He threw the pieces in the trash can under the kitchen sink. He grabbed an apple from the fruit bowl, picked up his cell phone off the coffee table in the living room, and slammed the door as he left his condo.

CHAPTER 30

The leaves changed color once again and the snow fell to the ground. Her mother had become very thin and she worried for her. She watched her as she dressed for work, her hipbones protruding.

"Mother are you feeling well?" She asked as she watched her mother pull a sweater over her head. It had turned cold, snow had begun to fall, the weather was cooler now. Madam was wearing layers of sweaters to ward off the cold, and in a feeble attempt to keep her frail body warm. She glanced out the window at the falling snow. The silence of it appealing to Her, the fresh snow absorbing sound, lowering ambient noise over a landscape because the air trapped between snowflakes attenuated vibration, the quiet was peaceful, comforting to Her.

"Fine darling, why do you ask?"

"You look tired, and very skinny." She looked at Her mother who was standing across the room, in front of the mirror, and She could see her collarbones, her hipbones and her breastplate. Her cheeks were sunken, and her eyes were larger than they had in the past. A silent alarm went off in Her head. She was frightened. Her mother's hair didn't seem shiny to Her, and it didn't appear as curly as it had once before. It seemed dull, lackluster, almost mousy looking. Her skin which had now been out of the hot sun for much too long was pale, the sun kissed glow a thing of the past; a story page turned.

"Skinny, is a compliment. You can never be too thin or too rich, that's what my Nana used to tell me." Madam looked at herself in the mirror as she said it. She thought back to a time when she had heard her grandfather tell her that too much chocolate was never good for a girl. She thought of him often. His death had been hard for Madam, at the time she had been strong for those that required it, standing tall, behaving as she should. But inside she was broken, shattered; splintered fragments of his soul remained with Madam always, as she remembered him affectionately. She smiled at her daughter in the mirror and caught sight of a shadow as it passed behind Her. Madam turned quickly to face Her. "You are also pretty tiny yourself..." She reached for her petite child and hugged her tightly. Giggles erupted from Her.

"Oh Mommy, do you think I will ever get big?" She asked Her mother.

"Probably not. There are plenty of big women in the world. And that leaves just enough room for tiny You. You were made in the size that is perfect for you to be. Don't try to change that. We should never wish to be something other than what He intended. It is His will, our task is to accept, not to change." Madam looked her daughter in the eye. "Do you understand? You are special, in every way. You were sent here to do special things. No one knows what those things are. But one day your plan will become clear, to all. The best gifts come in small packages after all. Am I right?" She poked her daughter and kissed the top of Her head.

She did understand, and She acknowledged the truth in what Her mother was saying. She watched her as she dressed, instinctively She knew that something wasn't quite right. She made a mental note to talk to Mary Mack later about it, but for now she brought up Her own issue. "Mom, I have been having headaches, bad ones, they don't ever go away."

Madam nodded before replying, "I have noticed that you have been short tempered with your brother and that you have been holding your temples a lot. What type of pain is it? All over or is it area specific?"

She was pleased that Her mother had noticed and wasn't surprised by the turn in conversation. It made things easier for Her. "All over. Sometimes I feel faint from it, and it makes me feel sick to my stomach. When we go for swimming lessons, like when you are at work and Grandma and Grandpa take us, sometimes the cold water makes me awfully ill Mom." Secretly she hated swimming lessons. She was aware of the necessity and she participated in the lessons out of respect. However, Her encounter with the bottom of the ocean, and her near death experience had left a faint lack of interest for Her in the area of water sports. She certainly would not ever call Herself a water enthusiast. She endured, like with many things that she did not enjoy, she managed a smile as she facilitated the pleasure of Her mother while she participated.

A day would surely come, when she would be in control enough, that she would make Her own decisions and she would decide for herself just exactly what she would do and who she would do it with.

The pounding in Her head was relentless. Not a dull ache or throb, but a piercing probing global pain that taxed

Her vision and disabled Her extra sensory perception. She had limited contact with Mary Mack. She felt isolated, secluded and alone.

Her mother was reluctant to respond, selected her words as though from a carefully written script. "We will call the doctor on Monday and I will get you in as soon as we can. There must be a reason that you are in so much pain. We will figure it out. Why don't you lie down for a bit? See if you can rest? Maybe that will help?"

She looked at Her mother with disbelief, "Lie down? You think I need a nap? My headache has been aggravating me for as long as I can remember; more than a year. It makes me vomit some days. My eyeballs ache so bad that I can't stand reading anymore; one of my greatest pleasures. Grandma makes me lie down all the time, in the dark. She says when she gets a headache it helps. It doesn't; I hate the dark. Things happen in the dark that no one can explain nor understand. And my head just continues to pound relentlessly. I need you to make this go away. I need you to do something. Please."

Madam thought back to when she had been a child, and she too had suffered from extreme headaches; however not for prolonged periods of time. She reached for her child and held Her. "What happens in the dark? Would you like to talk about that?"

She was disappointed with Herself for letting it slip. A small sliver of information that she had vowed to keep to Herself, she knew that if she divulged Her secrets they would start asking more questions than she was willing to answer. "It's nothing mother, really. You don't need to worry about it."

Madam wasn't buying it, but she was already late for work. "Tell you what Sweet-heart, how about if when I get home from work today, the three of us go out to dinner? How would you like that?"

She sighed, "I think that I would rather just stay home, if that's okay with you. I really do not feel well."

Madam hugged Her tight, "Okay Sweetie, okay." She was concerned. She knew that there was something strange happening, she just had no idea what it was, and she had been so busy herself with work and learning a new job, the divorce proceedings, the juggling the children's schedules that she had not had as much time to manage their affairs. Adjusting to having to do everything as a single person; was taking a toll. Not only had she lost a husband, whether he was truly help or a hindrance, but she had also lost her sidekick, her beloved nanny.

CHAPTER 31

Rohan had grown into the Monastery, memories of his childhood and of his mother were distant in his mind. Fading into the past, freeing him of the chains that once bound him. Replaced by spiritual doctrine and prayer. His focus primarily on the Lord and His directives in Roh's life.

His friendship with the janitor had manifested into a relationship, one that Rohan cherished. A trust had formed, stemming from the incident with the missing timepiece that Christmas in his first study year. He often considered how the outcome might have been, had the Janitor not intervened on his behalf. Thoughts of his plan, his direction and enlightenment filtered through his mind. The mysterious ways in which his fate had been altered were not a mystery to him. Had he been expelled from the school, he would have had to return home, shamed and with no chance of further education. Instead, he calculated the immeasurable and profound ways that his life had been managed by a power unseen, one that projected positive and boundless substance for him. His faith in Him, ensured that it had to be so.

In gratitude Rohan prayed each day, giving thanks for all the grace and abundance that had been provided and the protection that had been awarded.

He continued to study, maintaining top placement in his grade. An honor to which great privileges were awarded. On Saturday's he was permitted to leave the grounds of the Monastery, in search of his heart's desire. Freedom meant that he could wander the streets of Bangalore in search of small treasures and simple pleasures.

Rohan enjoyed the theatrical manner to which the Indian people moved. The colorful sari's the rickshaws and the banter. As a smaller child he had feared the commotion, as a teen, he embraced it. In each flutter of a heart in love; he saw hope, in every echo of laughter; he heard joy. From the daylight he knew that there would come night, and tomorrow a new day, another opportunity for learning and enrichment of his mind.

He relished in the flavors of the foods, his palette becoming more mature, enjoying a vast array of tastes. His time was spent in awe, touching, breathing, watching, listening and savoring the ways of the Lord.

Mary Mack watched him, from the shadows of the marketplace, pleased with his advancement, proud of his accomplishments. She smiled to herself knowing that he was on a path set forth by divine design. He would one day lead the world. He would preach to the masses, heal the sick and provide comfort to weary hearts. She looked to the heavens, praying...

"Lord, thank you for walking with us through the seasons of our lives.

For the winter, when we are held safe in your arms through the darkness.

For the hope of spring, as we are filled with new promise and life. For summer with the warmth of love, and autumn as we prepare for the falling leaves ...we are grateful for the promise that comes with this life, and the hope that lies in his presence for humanity."

She considered allowing herself to be seen to him and decided against it. Having only ever appeared to him in his dreams. Mary Mack decided that her presence was better left a secret to Rohan, for by faith he walked, knowing that the Lord was leading him. Interfering in that may undermine his ability to believe and would be of grave detriment to his success. She remained invisible.

CHAPTER 32

She busied herself with things. She did her best to find activities and events that would fill the time each day. For from each day came twenty-four hours, filled with one thousand four hundred and forty minutes, broken easily into eighty-six thousand four hundred seconds. If she could only find something to busy her mind, occupy her thoughts, and free herself one second at a time, she could manage her day.

She thought of Lupita, she fondly reflected on the sandcastles the two of them constructed and the sunshine on Her back. Eighty-six thousand three hundred and ninety-eight. She prayed for Abraham, her abductor who to the best of her knowledge was still in prison. Rotting like a piece of bad fruit. She thought of ways that he might escape, that she herself might break him out of the cell that held him captive.

She remembered how Her father looked as the feds held him to the floor, handcuffing him, taking from his hand the gun that he had pulled from the old dusty back pack. How his face looked, the shame that eroded his soul.

She contemplated ways in which She could beat the headache that plagued Her. Eighty-six thousand, three hundred and forty-nine. She looked into her colored boxes, filled with neatly filed memories, things that she was keeping for later. Her Red Box was nearly half full. Next to the Purple box, sat a second purple box. The faith events that she had stored here spilled from the perimeters of the box; these filings were plentiful. Filled with things that to Her were acts of God. Things that made Her believe in a higher power. Ideas and events in time that to Her helped to make a difference in Her own life, and in the lives of others.

Her Pink box was pretty, on the sides of the box She had hung adornments. Flowers and glitter, pretty gems and butterflies. Her happy box. Things that to Her were fond; that made Her a better person, things that She cherished, that made Her feel nice.

She glanced into the darkest of Blue box, sadness lingered deep in the cavity of this crafty box, a colored box that stole joy from the spirits of people. She had filed the story of Mary Mack, her confident here. To be saved and looked at later; the memory of Mary Mack was of a time in history that to Her brought profound sadness. She knew that Mary Mack no longer felt the pain of her days as a child, but She wanted to alleviate her of the anguish. Crush the memories that still lingered, the images in Mary's mind that tormented her, the grey and hazy thoughts that kept her stuck.

She opted to acknowledge Her Green box, which was piled with events and memories that were not only good, but that were also provoking maturity in her; growth spilled from the interior of this box. Eighty-five thousand, nine hundred and eighty-nine.

She thought of Her brother, he too was growing. His maturity showing in his ability to grasp multi-faceted concepts, his willingness to accept others at face value. As they are, without expecting change or alteration. She thought this enviable. He maintained a love for things that exhilarated him. Notions and philosophies that engaged his mind and captivated his desires. He was to Her; perfect, without blemish, easy to provoke, and quick to forgive. A suitable sibling without question.

She wondered what it was that She would do with Her life. Would She be a nurse, or a neuro-surgeon? Could She perhaps sustain a life as a professional ballerina? Would a life as a wife and mother be enough? She thought about how she might best be used in service to the world. Her viewpoints and beliefs, how could they be best displayed and what would bring her pleasure? Eighty-four thousand, eight hundred and three.

Again, her headaches reached her frontal lobe. Like a spoiled child screaming for attention from the back of the room. Jumping and kicking, in an effort only to be noticed, to be acknowledged and confronted.

She saw the man with the black pants, the shiny wing tipped shoes and butter colored shirt. He waved at Her, a smile covered his face. She was quite certain that She had never met him. She had of course interacted with him. He had been in the water when she nearly drowned. But she was not clear on how he fit, how his piece fit into her puzzle. She paused here, watching him for a moment as he moved through Her mind effortlessly, creating in Her a feeling of security, of serenity that drew Her to him. She projected a query in his direction, confident that he would receive it. *"How do I know you? Where do you belong? How do you fit into my plan?"*

He only smiled again, his eyes beaming with love. No answer was provided. She did not smile back, frustration and anxiety rumbled, she felt the need to pee, and squashed it.

She would not could not give in to the needs of her bladder. Her irritation with the handsome man was gone. Distraction proved to oblige Her once again. Eighty thousand, two hundred and sixteen.

She continued to meditate, quietly watching him. His image remained, peaceful once again. Peaceful once again. *Peaceful*...once again. She recognized that he had not changed, he remained the same, serene; bringing a sense of calm. It was from within Herself that images of others changed. She herself, cast the emotions that made those around Her appear different. It was Her own frustration and anxiety that caused a small but noticeable rift in her observation of others. Her own perception of her own thoughts that rumbled in Her mind, that created doubt and anguish. The man with the dark pants and the butter colored shirt remained firm, genuine; unaltered. She made a quick but resolved decision to accept that it was through Her weakness that others fell short of perfection. She thought this complex. She decided to own her newly found awareness of Herself and filed it in Her Green box.

She continued to count the seconds, to grant each thought a moment where she would allow them to manifest in her mind. Permitting herself to see, inviting herself to feel, and accepting Her growth as it came. One second, one minute at a time.

CHAPTER 33

Mary Mack stayed with Her, holding her hand through the procedure; the droning noise of the machine aggravating the pain in her head. It seemed abnormal for her body to feel slightly warm, she had become accustom to being cold all the time, nurses had placed blankets on Her for her comfort.

She had been told that it was important that she remain perfectly still while the images were being obtained, which is typically only a few seconds to a few minutes at a time. She was also told that she would know when images are being recorded because she would hear and feel loud tapping or thumping sounds when the coils that generate the radio frequency pulses were activated. Some scanning centers provide earplugs, while others use headphones to reduce the intensity of the sounds made by the MRI machine.

The headphones that she had been given covered a great majority of Her head, obliterating any literal sound, hiding her rich auburn hair.

The technologist was able to see, hear and speak with Her at all times using a two-way intercom. He could hear her conversing with Mary Mack, but he saw her sitting alone. He wondered to whom she was talking and listened intently.

"Mary Mack, how long do you think this will take?"

The technician heard nothing but Her.

"Do you think they will find anything? I wonder what they will see in my head?" She giggled and remained perfectly still. "Maybe they won't find a brain at all. Maybe it will just be an empty cavity."

Her voice was the only human sound, echoing within the room.

"Oh my gosh yeah that would be hilarious. Right? Can you imagine?"

He heard no response from anyone, but she continued.

"I'm kind of scared actually."

Turning up the volume on his earpiece, he strained to listen.

"No, not of the noise, not of the test, MRI, whatever they call this, I'm scared of what they might find, a little bit." A tear rolled from the corner of her eye and fell into her hair piling on the deck of the scanner bed.

The technician turned up the volume on his headset again. He lifted himself from his chair slightly so that he could see into the room to where she lay. The thumping and bumping of the machine beginning again. He was certain that She was alone, completely.

"I am only ten Mary Mack, it's still okay to be scared right?"

He worried for her while he listened to the one-sided conversation.

"Well how old are you now? Actually, if you were to count every year? I mean seriously?"

There was no sound, but that of Her voice and the hum of the machine.

"No, I guess it doesn't count no. I *am* being still. Perfectly still just like I am supposed to be." She sighed. "Fine."

Children are given appropriately sized earplugs or headphones during the exam. MRI scanners are air-conditioned and well-lit to ease a natural claustrophobic reaction. Music is played through the headphones to help pass the time. She began to sing not to the beat of the music streaming, but Her own song, freeing and beautiful, sung to someone unseen by the technician…

"Once I stood in the night with my head bowed low
In darkness as black as the sea
In my heart felt alone and I cried oh Lord
Don't hide your face from me.

Hold my hand all the way every hour every day
From here to the great unknown
Take my hand let me stand
Where no one stands alone.

Like a king I may live in a palace so fine
With great riches to call my own
But I don't know a thing in this whole wide world
That's worse than being alone.

Hold my hand all the way every hour every day
From here to the great unknown
Take my hand let me stand
Where no one stands alone…"

She closed her eyes tightly and filed this experience away in her Yellow Box; yellow was a box that contained not many items, for it was one that was uncertain, anxious and unknown. There was rarely a time when she was not clear on the transformation of events, and not comfortable with the manner to which she was to conduct herself; today however she felt uneasy about her circumstances.

Mary Mack sat with Her and held her hand. In silence together they prayed, while the machine banged and thumped, the imaging of her inner brain near complete.

In some cases, intravenous injection of contrast material may be performed. The intravenous needle may cause some discomfort when it is inserted, and the patient may experience some bruising. Some patients sense a temporary metallic taste in their mouth after the contrast injection. She tasted copper on Her own tongue and thought it to be strange, but not totally unpleasant.

Magnetic Resonance Imaging or MRI is a non-invasive medical test that physicians use to diagnose and treat medical conditions not otherwise easily detected.

An MRI uses a powerful magnetic field, radio frequency pulses, and a computer to produce detailed pictures of organs, soft tissues, bone and virtually all other internal body structures. Unlike conventional x-ray examinations and CT scans, a Magnetic Resonance Image does not utilize ionizing radiation. Instead, radio waves redirect the alignment of hydrogen atoms that naturally exist within the body while in the scanner, without causing any chemical changes in your tissues captures images. As the hydrogen atoms return to their usual alignment, they emit an energy that varies according to the type of body tissue from which they come. The Magnetic Resonance scanner acquires this energy and creates a picture of the tissues scanned based on this information.

The magnetic field is produced by passing an electric current through wire coils in most scanning units. Other coils, located in the machine and in some cases, placed around the part of the body being imaged, send and receive radio waves, producing signals that are detected by the coils. The electric current is considered to be safe and does not come in contact with the patient.

A computer then processes the signals and generates a series of images, each of which shows a thin slice of the body. The images can then be studied from different angles by the interpreting radiologist.

Frequently, the differentiation of abnormal or diseased tissue from normal tissues is better with Magnetic Resonance Imagery results than with other more mainstream imaging modalities such as x-ray, CT and ultrasound.

Detailed Magnetic Resonance images allow physicians to evaluate various parts of the body and determine the presence of certain diseases. The images can then be examined on a computer monitor and transmitted electronically. The ease of such allows medical teams to share this information freely and quickly. Brain tumours in children if present, can be readily diagnosed.

CHAPTER 34

Mary Mack was doing her very best to adjust to Her daily routine, continuing on a forward path with Her training and instruction as she was assigned to do. Mary missed her typical contact with Juan, but genuinely enjoyed spending her days watching over Her. Her medical hiccup had caused some concern and had stirred some interest in higher ups. The Magnetic Resonance Imagining had gone well, and she had remained still as instructed, but Mary wasn't certain that the results would carry a message of clean health.

Mary Mack requested that assistance be sent in, as she felt overwhelmed with fatigue and stress herself. For her, the worry she felt was not a usual reaction to a human assignment. Mary Mack was not one herself to become emotionally attached to those she worked with.

Rhyming and games were something that Mary Mack had always relied upon to distance herself from her contacts. Her rhythmic games kept her assignments pondering her message at least for a moment; sometimes longer. Her theatrics had proven over many, many years to encourage not only engagement through listening, but had protected Mary herself from getting hurt. The games created a playful distance between herself and her assignment.

Many of her assignments were for much shorter periods of time than this one had been with Her. This mission was proving to become difficult. A kinship had formed, a bond between the two girls. Whether it be because of a similarity in age, or a general interest in each other, Mary Mack genuinely had fallen in love with Her. She watched over her during night, never leaving her side while she was awake. Mary Mack prayed for Her safety, prayed for her peace and for her health.

"God that is almighty, Lord that has made the heavens and the earth, Father that has created all, I worship you. I thank you for this day, and for your patience and understanding. For providing, and for granting us the will to live, the will to die, and permitting us the wisdom to know the difference, I am eternally grateful. I come to you now

Father, and ask in Jesus name that you protect Her, give her strength to face her enemies, temperance to teach her followers, faith that she may never lose sight of the truth, allow Her to love all that cross her path Lord, and allow us to continue to edify and impart on Her your ways Lord, that she may complete Your work. Of these things and those in Her heart, I ask of you in Jesus name. Amen"

Mary sat on the chair in the corner of the room, her black dress neatly pressed, black silver buttons all down her back. She watched over Her once more as she slept allowing thoughts to come into her mind of her friend Juan Maria de Salvatierra. Mary Mack had visited him just once appearing as a grown woman. It was the only time that she had ever had the opportunity to experience adulthood. The only time she had felt as a woman would feel. The event had frightened and exhilarated her at the same time.

Thinking about it now made her feel uncomfortable. For her relationship with Juan was not that of a man and a woman, their relationship was not romantic. Mary Mack was anything but naïve. She enjoyed the comfortable ease of their rapport now; their relationship was based on trust; it was a mysterious multifaceted friendship. Where there was conviction, and honor. She could count on Juan for anything.

She liked that about him. He was trustworthy, and genuine. She also believed that Juan had faith in her abilities and could equally expect that she was doing her job, just as she knew he was doing his.

Mary Mack focused on Juan's face in meditation knowing that by doing so she would be able to contact him telepathically. And in turn she would be able to gain the support that she felt she needed. She would be able to share her feelings and fears with her friend through transference of thought. She engaged and focused through meditation.

CHAPTER 35

Rohan continued with dutiful service to the school in which he was enrolled. Summer vacations were spent as was his Christmas holiday, on site working with the school janitor on issues that arose from regular use of the students. Desks were in desperate need of repair, dining hall tables and chairs needed small adjustments to their legs and a coat of stain to make them shine. Draperies and curtains throughout the entire building were removed, hand washed, hung to dry and then pressed by Roh before he rehung them all in their proper place.

For Rohan the feeling of cleanliness brought not only a sense of pride and accomplishment, but a true impression of value, and worthiness within the walls of the school. He felt empowered, respected and rewarded for his good works. Rohan studied diligently, his grades and placement clearly indicating his passion, a love for the Word as it is written and presence of the Lord in his life.

Nigel continued to be a thorn in his side, despite the finding of his watch that had never really been missing. Time rolled on, days turned into weeks which turned into months. Rohan adjusted fully to his school environment and began to reflect less and less on his home life. He was becoming more independent, stronger, academically astute, he was more and more a true servant of the Lord.

CHAPTER 36

Madam prepared herself for the doctor visit at the Children's Hospital, with the intent on reviewing the data collected during the MRI scan from weeks past. The length of time that had passed while they were waiting for results was not only difficult for Madam but was also immensely challenging for Her. She struggled while attempting to focus at school, she fought with her brother and didn't sleep well.

Her headaches worsened, elevating the problem even further, her imagination getting the best of Her, worry destroying her ability to deal with what should be normal everyday tasks. Her mother was concerned for Her, worried about the amount of time She spent in meditation, unclear the full benefits of solitude, uneasy about the results of the examinations.

A boundless amount of traffic, made for a long drive; apprehension building within her bloodstream, her mind growing more distressed. She was pleased to have her grandfather with them for the hospital visit, his presence soothing, and calming to Her.

"Mommy, can we play the big word game?" She questioned Madam who was focused on the roads.

"We can of course, we haven't played for so long, my goodness I have to think about where to start." Madam glanced at Her in the rearview mirror, her eyes dark with wisdom, full of energy and abundant in life. Her small frame easing back into the seat, her long auburn hair falling forward past her shoulders, she looked every bit her age, now older. "Okay I have a good one. Serendipitous, to be lucky in making unexpected and fortunate discoveries. S.E.R.E.N.D.I.P.I.T.O.U.S. She was serendipitous in finding Thomas for together they would share a lifetime of happiness; Serendipitous."

She looked at her mother and her grandfather from the back seat of the car and wondered to herself if in fact she would ever be tall enough to ride in the front seat of the car, to take Her place upfront. She longed to be a shotgun passenger, with a view out the windshield, of oncoming traffic and endless sights. She imagined herself with her feet on the dashboard, the window down and her hair blowing softly across her face. A road trip across the country, and endless adventure of pavement and laughter. The thought warmed her mind and engaged a part of her imagination that had for weeks been dormant. She felt elated.

"Serendipitous, S.E.R.E.N.D.I.P.I.T.O.U.S.- Wonder and awe struck them all as they realized Her arrival was serendipitous; and for the greater good of them all." She gazed out the window to the side of where she sat. Trees clicking by one by one, as they motored along, their branches full of leaves; robust, a dark lush green.

"Mother, do you think that we each have a purpose?"

Madam bit the side of the lip. Taking just a moment to think. Before answering Her, she knew that she must find the correct words, and the most diplomatic way in which to address the question. "I do. I do think we have a purpose, I think each individual has one, all bearing different significance, but yes, I most certainly do. Dad what do you think?"

Madam's father had become a solid source of reasoning and support for Madam and the children since their return to their home country. He was wise, and straightforward. He nodded and looked over his shoulder at Her sitting in the backseat. "I personally believe that everyone has a time, and a purpose. That we are here with a sense of reason, a direction and for a time that is unknown, I feel that we enter this world with an explicit objective; and with an expiry date. To suggest that we only have so much time to accomplish our tasks, our clocks are ticking; each one of us most definitely has a reason to be here, a purpose; yes."

She pushed her auburn hair back from her face, her dark brown eyes glowing brightly. "What is mine?"

CHAPTER 37

The doctors were prepared and waiting for Madam and her precious cargo. The hospital air was cool, not cold but left the skin feeling chilled. It smelled of medicine, and cleansers. She was uncomfortable. She held onto her mother's hand as they walked from the elevator into the waiting room. Her mother approached the receptionist and announced their arrival. While she and her grandfather sat quietly; her mother confirmed details of her medical information, pertinent phone numbers and emergency contacts.

Her mother wondered to what extent these were actually necessary? Not pertaining to every child who was in the hospital that day, but specifically for Her. Requiring emergency contact information suggested that there might be a need to contact someone urgently. She had been of the understanding that they had come for a simple review of the results of her recent MRI. Madam couldn't imagine what could go so array in a meeting that one would need to call an emergency contact.

Her mother took a seat beside Her on a simple chair, with her purse in her lap. The three of them refrained from speaking. She had nothing to say, and she suspected that Her mother's nerves would not allow her the gift of conversation. Her grandfather sat still and quiet, his very presence comforting to Her.

After what had seemed like a near eternity, her name was called by a nurse in a colorful scrub suit. She donned bright pink pants and a turquoise top that was swathed in pink flamingos. Her blonde ponytail pulled her hair back from her face allowing all of her features to be easily seen. Although she didn't wear a smile, she seemed gentle, and approachable. Her face was near expressionless.

She and her mother stood, motioned to her grandfather to do the same and followed the nurse down the hallway to a room where two doctors were waiting. On a computer screen were images of a brain; She thought it must be her own.

The doctors asked them to please sit, and so they did as they were expected to do. Madam and her grandfather sat in chairs. She on an examining table to the left of where Madam had been directed to be seated, the paper on it crunching under her bum as she sat down. She felt an odd flutter in her chest, her heart beating faster than normal. She quickly determined that nervous tension was causing it. She took deep breaths in through her nose, out through her mouth in a feeble attempt to slow her heartbeat.

The doctors greeted them formally and began to review tidbits of information that had previously been provided; the location of the headaches, the duration of them, the regularity of them. She was bored.

She listened to the sound of the doctor's voices as they interacted with her mother and wondered why it all came back to doctor's offices. Why She always seemed to be in them. The absurdity of it made Her question the medical profession in its entirety. She believed, that overall, medical professionals might know less about disease and illness with advancements in technology; or at the very least, the knowledge that medical professionals possessed opened many more doors of uncertainty. Perhaps in many years past, before technological advancements; the ignorance of one's fate could actually be a blessing.

Madam was speaking now, she listened… "and so what do we do next?"

The taller of the two doctors spoke. "Well Madam, frankly as I said, the tumor is inoperable, in the central lobe of her brain, as you can see here in this image." He motioned towards an image of a brain that showed a tiny mass within it. "If we were to attempt to operate, we would risk first losing Her, and second if she were to survive the operation she would likely not maintain basic life functions. The tumor, we believe is a Medulloblastoma, which would normally be found in the cerebellum, or the back and bottom of the skull. Typically, as in Her case, these types of tumors are malignant. It will continue to grow and interfere with Her daily activities. She will continue to experience the headaches, which will become more severe. Dizziness will eventually impede her fine motor skills and her ability to walk. Decision making will be affected as will her intellectual processing speeds."

Her mother stared at the doctor, unsure of what to say, uncertain of how to manage with the information that was being provided to her. Her mouth was dry, her hands shook with fright, she was not able to speak.

"We can control intracranial pressure with corticosteroids, but she will still be at a risk of vision and hearing loss, she may experience seizures and eventually become incapacitated."

Her grandfather spoke. "How can this be? She is only ten years old?"

The doctors both nodded in agreement, their faces solemn, and sad. "Yes, indeed sir, we agree, it is a common type of brain tumor, but it's positioning has us rather perplexed. We can treat Her with chemotherapy and there is radiotherapy of course but there are side effects to both. Both treatments may hinder the growth of the tumor, but without surgery we cannot destroy the essence of it."

Madam was frozen, she looked over at her daughter, she sat on the examining table and remained mute, as though she were not in the room with them. Her grandfather spoke again. "What is the prognosis for cases such as Hers? What can we expect?"

"I'm afraid for all of you, that it the horizon is rather grim. I should expect that as her health deteriorates, she will weaken overall. My best guess would be, as we cannot in good conscience remove the tumor surgically, that she is looking at twelve to eighteen months. The tumor will continue to grow exponentially and eventually brain function will cease.

The room was quiet except for the tick tock of the clock on the wall. She glanced at the taller of the two doctors, his height somewhat ominous. She had been listening and pondering all that was said and transpired, she thought of Mary Mack, and how short her life had been cut, and wondered if perhaps Her purpose was like that of Mary's. To guard and protect from the other side. She swallowed hard, the back of her throat dry, her tongue feeling too large for her mouth. After taking a quiet moment she found courage from within and quietly posed a question to the group in front of Her.

"When a child dies, for a moment all the angels in heaven stop, and say a prayer. Would it be alright if you think that I am going to die, that you can let them know ahead of time, so that my special angel can be with me?" Both doctors looked at their feet, unsure of what to say. "Because you see everything that I have done in my life that has been scary, I have done with her, and without her I don't think I could manage death."

Madam sat still, watching her daughter, watching the doctors and waiting for their answer. Finally, after the second hand on the clock had moved a significant distance around the face; the younger doctor responded to Her. "Darling, dying is a special gift, and even though I am certain that it is scary, I am sure that for special people like you, it is a great honor. For in dying we are able to meet our maker, and one thing that I am most sure of... is that He is pleased with you." He took a brief moment to piece together his next thoughts, a spiritual man himself he understood and empathized with Her position, with Her fears and with Her need for assurance. "If there is someone, an angel, that you need, and if the universe has not sent her to you when your time arrives, then yes; I will most definitely call her for you."

"Her name is Mary Mack, and she will always; always come back. She promised that I would never lack."

CHAPTER 38

Rohan lay in bed casually watching the moon through the open new draperies on the window to his left. On his chest lay the Holy Bible, his glasses on top of the scriptures. The moon appeared fuzzy, blurred and out of focus. As though it was present, but not reachable to him. He imagined himself bringing it closer, adjusting the picture to suit his own needs. Clarity; it seemed to him a sensible and achievable desire.

He set onto praying, his challenge only to find peace in the ambiguity of his mother's continued health concerns. Her condition had remained virtually unchanged, for years now.

Rohan remembered not much of what had happened to his mother before she was taken from them. He did recall positive things, her scent, the sound of her laughter, the feel of her warm embrace, the taste of hot curries and naan bread. He remembered the things that she had done that made him feel; loved, connected, encouraged and safe. His memories of her were warm and inviting to him.

He tried hard to forget the day that they had taken her away in the ambulance, the sirens screaming, his sisters crying. Rohan believed himself to be weak, a soft, but intellectually advanced child; capable of enduring many hardships. Mary Mack watched him from the corner of the bedroom. The simplicity of his environment was pleasing to her. She felt serenity exude from him as he prayed. A humble and heartfelt supplication, she was grateful for his temperance, and for the strength that was growing within him.

She chose not to be seen, for she didn't want to interrupt his quiet meditation and prayer time. Her black silk dress hung beautifully, her silver buttons down her back straight like a carefully crafted arrow. Mary Mack herself had suffered deeply, not due to her actions as a human herself, but because she felt that she had fallen short of her promises to her assignments. Her buttons representing souls that had fallen. She wore them with pride, knowing that the promise forthcoming ensured the surrender of each of them to the heavens. Good souls, making poor choices, most often in times of turmoil fell into the hands of the black angel.

She continued to watch Rohan as he prepared for class, refreshed by his steadfast and undying love for the Lord. He would one day make them all proud, representing greatness in the most exalted way possible for a human.

CHAPTER 39

Evening came, and then the morning light, many times. Warm turned to cold, and the leaves fell. Snow came, and then melted, as the evenings came and went. Time was passing and without change. One day was similar to the last, the monotony of life stealing time from Her last days.

He watched over Her as she slept, after the sun had set and the stars shone brightly in the night sky. Her chest rising and falling ever so softly as Her breath entered and left Her small body. Providing life that to which had so often been taken for granted by so many. Her auburn hair cascaded loosely over the pillow, a blanket of softness and innocence created without effort. He smiled upon her. He wept for Her as he knew Her days would soon be drawing to a close. He wanted so desperately to stop time, to be able to salvage for Her any fragment of existence that he could manage. Like so many in this situation, his desires were painfully in vain, the clock continued to tick tock, each second stealing precious moments.

Knowing nowhere else to turn, he knelt beside the bed, and with his hands in prayer, began a soulful journey to the Lord.

"Lord, I understand not your ways, I have tried, and cannot stop the days from slipping away, I have no choice but to beg for mercy. For Her. Take mercy on Her sweet life Lord and let Her live. I believe you have a great plan for Her, please help me to understand why you would take Her now? Please help me to understand the need for death, and for this terrible thing that has been growing inside of Her. If you are full of mercy as they say Lord, then let Her live. If you must have one, then take me instead. Take my life Lord and spare Hers that she may grow to experience and enjoy all the magnificence that You have to offer Her. I give you my life Lord, spare this child. For even though I walk through the valley of the shadow of death, I fear no evil, for You are with me, your rod and Your staff they comfort me, I have had a good life Lord, and although it has not been long, it has been fruitful, and You have blessed me. I am so grateful. I am ready Lord, make it my time, not Hers. In Jesus name, I ask of this. Amen."

He reached forward and gently touched Her forehead, her velvety skin flush and pink on Her cheeks. He swallowed the lump that had grown in his throat, attempting to stop the tears that were threatening to expose themselves on his own face.

He sat on the side of the bed, taking Her tiny hand into his own. He could feel the warmth from the down duvet on Her fingers. He traced each of Her tiny nails with his index finger while tiny drops of saline escaped each of his own eyes and rolled carelessly down his cheeks.

He thought back to Her birth, to Her beginning and how unfortunate and short Her life had been. To him it seemed that there was an apparent absence of grace in Her life, frustration brewed within him, opening the door of possibility, allowing the concept of non-existence of a Lord that he had always trusted in. He thought about Moses, Job, David and Jesus. He wondered how they maintained faith. How would it have been possible to do so with no manifestation of prayer appeals? How could a merciful being allow prayers to fall on deaf ears, to allow the innocent to fall sick, to permit the young to suffer and die?

Juan Maria de Salvatierra watch Her grandfather from the corner of the room. He heard his prayers and understood his thoughts, Juan knew from his own experience that faith grew by believing in something that could not be seen. He thought back to a time when he had waited for a young woman to return, someone that he had not even been certain was real. He had for years questioned the authenticity of his visitor, genuinely questioned his own sanity, and in the end his instinct had prevailed. He had been sane, Mary Mack had appeared to him in the garden, just as he had remembered.

His own heart ached for Her, in the midst of Her illness, he was prepared to intervene but was frightened that the consequences of Her grandfather's supplication might be grave. Juan said his own silent prayer for all that was great and good, and set off on his own duties.

CHAPTER 40

Her father settled himself in the greater New Orleans area, knowing that it's dense population would aide him in slipping away for an extended period, without running the risk of being easily found.

There has never been an official language in Louisiana, and the state constitution enumerates "the right of the people to preserve, foster, and promote their respective historic, linguistic, and cultural origins," whether English, French, Spanish, or otherwise. He enjoyed the civil liberties awarded by this. The area was rich with culture, pretty women and opportunities. He rented himself a small flat, bought a few groceries and some rum.

In the evenings, he would wander into Lafayette Square with the intention of entertaining himself. He appreciated the vast architecture and alluring nightlife. He found plenty of both on his trips to the American Quarter.

Many styles of housing were of existence in the New Orleans, including the shotgun house and the bungalow style. Creole townhouses, notable for their large courtyards and intricate iron balconies, lined the streets of the French Quarter. Grand trees and lush gardens surrounded them, making a visit to the area most pleasurable for anyone with no particular agenda in mind. St. Charles Avenue was famed for its large luxurious antebellum homes. Its mansions were placed on larger plots of land in various styles, such as Greek Revival, American Colonial and the Victorian styles of Queen Anne. New Orleans was also well known for its large, European-style Catholic cemeteries, which can be found sporadically placed throughout the city.

After stopping to eat dinner at a street vendor, he came upon one of such cemeteries and decided it fit within his plan for the evening. As the gates were not locked, he pushed through and began to wander amongst the tombstones, and plot markers, seeking nothing in particular. Up and down the carefully groomed rows he walked, reading but not seeing what was written on each stone. In front of some of the tombstones, sat small floral arrangements left by loved ones who had recently visited.

He felt an eerie stillness surround him, a sudden gust of wind blew past, alarming him, heightening his senses. He looked from left to right, and over his shoulder; and continued meandering.

Juan watched him from afar. His gate matching that of Her fathers. It was written in his orders to keep an eye on the man, and he continued to check in every so often. He contemplated the idea of interaction and decided against it. For today.

Today Juan would leave him to his own accord, eating, walking aimlessly and chasing women of the night. There would come a day, however, that Juan would take it upon himself to discuss his actions of the past, and his choice to hide. For today though, Juan thought it best to leave him alone. A little spooking was always fun for Juan however, and so he continued to follow him creating a feeling of nervousness and alarm.

Juan enjoyed the feeling that he achieved from human terror. Fright created by the presence of a spirit was invigorating to Juan. He enjoyed that he could put a rational person on edge. The cool air that surrounded them, the feeling of being watched, when the hairs on the back of their necks stood, and when the hairs on their arms stood at attention, he felt he was at his best. Doing the work of a warrior was problematic but entertaining at times. He followed Her father with the sole intention of making him feel uneasy.

CHAPTER 41

The summer finally came, fragrant blossoms flanked the sidewalks, the scent of fresh cut grass filled the air. She sat in a chair covered in a blanket, watching the clouds roll across the sky. She considered the idea that Her headaches could have been connected to Her mother. The experience of cranial tenderness intensified if She was drawn away from Her most comforting person. When Abraham had abducted them on one of the most frightening and eventful days of Her life, so many years ago now; she had suffered with a headache. She deliberated as to whether or not Her mother might have something to do with Her illness, with the pain, and with the suffering. Her hands held neatly in Her lap, she said a silent prayer; knowing that Mary Mack would hear Her, and with hopes of connecting with a much higher power.

"Dearest Lord, I have accepted your illness, and I thank you for the strength that it has taken to bear my fate. I am grateful for Your ever presence, and I hold steadfast in your court. Please Lord, if you can hear me now, I pray for a rendering of my situation. I am not one to beg, nor do I enjoy asking for help. Please be with me now as I surrender to you. I do not believe that I have the fortitude to continue, I am weak, I am not worthy of this life that You have given me. Release me of this pain, show compassion, and allow me to completely trust in You. I ask for freedom from this ailment, from the pain that shakes my faith. Free my mother who is trapped by her need to mend and restore everything, and my brother who will rise above and become everything that you need a servant to be. I thank you, for the presence of Mary Mack in my life, for granting me the kinship that I have with her. I ask that one-day Lord, you will see fit to allow her to return to this world as a human, to experience a full and bountiful life in the body of a woman. Enable her to feel love, and to be loved in return. That she may experience all the things that her heart so desires; if it be Your will. For these things, for the love and restoration of your planet Earth, for the wind and the sunlight on my face today, for the gift of Your son, a great leader and example of humility and strength I am grateful Lord. In Jesus name, I pray, Amen."

Her headaches immediately began to subside, she felt peace, and so She rested, with eyes closed, and Her heart open; ready to receive.

Those who don't believe in a higher power, perhaps have never been challenged by a testimony of faith. She was prepared to surrender Her life. Knowing from Her own experiences that life for Her would continue, beyond the boundaries created by Her living body. She understood that Her spirit would prevail any illness, she would be present eternally in a form unseen, but forever felt.

CHAPTER 42

It was late in the fall following Her supplication, that Her grandfather started to take long afternoon naps. She sat and watched him as he slept. His chest rising and falling with each breath, she thought it interesting how the human body required rest.

The intricacies of the human body were perplexing to Her. Her understanding of the basic functions was clear and concise. She had been programed to comprehend basic function, enabling Her to heal others, and accept change in Her own body. The manifestation of illness however was something that She struggled with.

She was able to see change in Her grandfather, his color was poor, he was consistently in need of precious sleep. She had been monitoring his caloric intake, a steady decline in consumption was cause for Her concern. She prayed over him while he slept, requesting from the Lord a healing.

The wind beyond the window blew hard, moving the leaves that had fallen from the trees to the ground below. She watched the leaves as they gust to and fro, a subtle reminder that as humans we are blown about by consequence. Lives mapped out by choice but controlled by the winds of change.

She stood, wiped away a tear that was falling from her lower lashes and vowed to pray each day. She was more than just aware that life can be easily changed, she was also cognizant of Her grandfather's sacrifice on Her behalf, his offering of his own life over the taking of Hers. She had heard his prayers that day, she understood why he had done it, and She appreciated the gesture. It was grand, and it was righteous, in keeping with his character. She felt profoundly unworthy but humbled by his integrity and his sense of honour.

CHAPTER 43

Her brother had not struggled with the transition into their home countries culture. There had been no adjustment period, no language barrier, no change of pace nor alteration to his speed of play. He assimilated easily, tweaking his own circumstance to fit his new environment. He adapted well. Or so Madam had assumed.

The school into which the children were enrolled had not embraced the style of teaching to which the children were accustomed. Her brother enjoyed a liberal method of teaching to which the children had been exposed in Mexico. The method being one of luminous and edifying empowerment, enriching and developing the mind, tapping into knowledge that is present from birth, tenderly cultivating and molding the child's mind into practicing self-development; rather than giving knowledge by book and instruction.

In Mexico, after a series of unfortunate events, their mother had sought out a preferred school for the children; shortly after She had been expelled by Lady Gonzalez from a school with a traditional education platform. Both children had done well in their new liberal school, and then they up and moved to Canada; very suddenly.

Her brother liked uniformity. He liked things to go his way, and he liked to have things lined up in a row, with order and structure. He also had a sense of humor and enjoyed playing games. He had a passion for knowledge and for filling his mind with information, he relished the concept of retaining and being able to express more knowledge than others. It generated a feeling of power from within in him that was gratifying. He delighted in it. He sought knowledge because of it, and shared that knowledge knowing that it made him appear intelligent and superior to his peers.

In his imaginary world, he created for himself a life of grandeur. He would become King, or he could easily rule the world by waving a wand or dictating to his people from a balcony window. He would preach the written word, pray for the ill, and feed the impoverished. By role playing with other children, he would enact his own inauguration and depict the events leading to his own canonization. He would be President; he was a Saint; he was the Pope.

The new Canadian school was not as liberal, and most certainly was not as welcoming of her brother's theatrical and self-gratifying behaviors. The educational system provided the structure that he enjoyed; columns, rows, neatly organized and identified daily requirements; but didn't engage in the encouragement of open-minded thinking or thought-provoking collaborative intellectual exploration where the child's interests were supported. Both children were comfortable in a school that supported a belief that all children should begin to understand themselves while applying a practical application of academics and gaining a wider and wider frame of reference.

The new school saw none of this, attempting to close off his imagination. Administration believed that by syphoning his supply of information, they would be able to curtail his theatrics, and his attempts to engage the other children in the classroom in drama and spontaneous talks of technology, ecosystems, and space travel. His mind began to feel stifled, he eventually began to act out in class. Using his intellect for entertainment rather than for enrichment. He assumed the role of class clown; savoring the daily attention while it lasted. His demeanor digressed.

Soon a Board Psychologist was called in, and specialized testing was done. His behavior was not only unacceptable, but not found to be normal; for the classroom setting to which he was exposed to daily. His teacher was not prepared, not willing to deal with him. And so, Madam agreed to the testing of both children, for peace of mind, for resolution, for sanity and for her son's self-preservation.

For weeks, he and his sister met with Dr. Altman, a psychologist specializing in early childhood behaviors, and giftedness. Dr. Altman presented various examinations, readings and assessments evaluating their cognitive abilities, behavioral mannerisms, emotional development and language comprehension. Indices were calculated such as verbal comprehension, visual special abilities, fluid reasoning, their working memory and processing speeds. From this a defined Intellectual Quotient was formed for each of the two children.

Both children had a desire to do well and participate wholeheartedly, however She paid little attention to the assessments, or Dr. Altman. His unruly hair, his wire framed aviator style glasses were not suited to his face shape and bothered Her. His cartoon depicting neckties were tiresome and rather childish; she wondered if he was attempting to relate to children while wearing them, or if instead he was childish himself? Regardless, she found him a bore.

Her brother however, engaged in the examinations. He viewed them as an outstanding opportunity to express himself and to show the world just how smart he in fact was. It was competitive in nature as he had been placed head to head with Her, he had occasion to shine. He vowed to do well, and to exert himself above and beyond. He would come out on top.

CHAPTER 44

Jorge Alvarez continued to obsess with Madam's husband. The police chief's focus had changed from the woman that he had once loved so deeply, to the man that had destroyed her life.

The chief sat in an internet café with a cup of cold coffee, and a dried-up blueberry muffin, searching the web for information on the whereabouts of the man that he had learned to despise. He knew from his own experience that Madam's husband had been placed on a greyhound bus from Puerto Vallarta to Matamoros. Matamoros was on the North-Eastern most tip of Mexico bordering Texas at Brownsville.

Jorge was very familiar with the Mexican side of the border and had a fondness for the Gulf of Mexico. As a child, he had spent a great deal of time playing the waters of the Gulf, having grown up in Vera Cruz.

The city of Vera Cruz is a major port of Mexico, primly located within the Gulf of Mexico in the Mexican state of Veracruz. The city is located along the coast in the central part of the state, exhibiting the some of the most pristine beaches on the Gulf of Mexico.

It is the state's most populous city. Developed during Spanish colonization, Veracruz was Mexico's oldest, largest, and historically most significant port. When the Spanish explorer Hernán Cortés arrived in Mexico in 1519, he founded a great city which he named Villa Rica de la Vera Cruz, referring to the area's riches of gold and dedicated to the "True Cross", because he landed on the Christian holy day of Good Friday, the day of the Crucifixion of the Son of God.

It was the second Spanish settlement on the mainland of the Americas but the first to receive a coat-of-arms. During the colonial period, the city had the largest mercantile class in the country and was at times wealthier than the capital of Mexico City. The cities vast treasures and immense beauty attracted the raids of 17th-century pirates, against which fortifications such as Fort San Juan de Ulúa were built.

In the 19th and early 20th centuries, Vera Cruz was invaded more than once by France and the United States. During the 1914 Tampico Affair, US troops occupied the city for seven months. For much of the 20th century, the production of petroleum was most important for the state's economy but, in the latter 20th century and into the 21st, the port re-emerged as a main economic engine. Vera Cruz became the principal port for most of Mexico's imports and exports, especially for the automotive industry.

Jorge had enjoyed his childhood. He grew up in a loving family with five boys; with all brothers and no sisters there had not been a lot of cuddling or subtle niceties. His father had been born in the late 1920's in Germany and had settled to Mexico after the Second World War. The family never spoke of why, never asked how he had found his way to Vera Cruz, and never questioned his decision to take a young Spanish bride. It was a topic that had gone unspoken of. Jorge respected his father's wishes to remain silent but knew that there had to be a significant story to his quiet and solemn father, Hugo.

The Alvarez family was a strong one, both in the physical nature and intellectually and emotionally. The boys had all been trained to succeed, and all had military backgrounds. Jorge relied on this training to circumvent the justice system that he respected and worked for; for so long.

He sipped on his cold coffee, dipping through websites, in search of a clue to the whereabouts of Madam's soon to be ex-husband. He stayed until he could stand it no more, went home slept and then went to work the next day, performing his duties as Chief of Police, as was expected of him. He didn't miss a beat. When his shift was done, and after he had eaten he returned to the Internet Café with a few clues that one of his detectives had managed to dig up without cause.

Jorge entered the information into the search engine and waited patiently for the page to load. A smile formed on his face when he saw the image appear, and then an address where the man he sought was located. He then purchased a ticket for commercial flight to Vera Cruz the following week.

He was once again on the hunt; Jorge Alvarez, Police Chief extraordinaire, man by day, superhero by night.

CHAPTER 45

With the onset of the academic examinations she approached Her mother with news of a clear head. Her pain had completely alleviated, Her appetite and Her abilities were returning. She had seen Mary Mack for the first time in months and was relieved to know that Her companion was not lost forever. Trust had bound them together, she depended on Mary Mack as a life force. A source of goodness and encouragement. In the months that She was disabled with the headaches, she had lost the ability to physically see the young apparition but knew by faith that her presence was still inevitable.

Madam was shocked by the news and questioned the validity of it. She wanted nothing more than to experience a healing for her daughter but was uneasy about the potential disappointments that may lay ahead.

A simple telephone call was made to their Doctor, and a series of tests at the Children's hospital were scheduled for the following week. An MRI confirmed that Her tumor was in fact completely and totally absent. Her brain tissue appeared as fresh as newly fallen snow, with no scaring, no blemish or mark where the tumor had once been.

Madam shook the hands of the medical team that had been assigned, and Her doctor hugged Her tightly. He had never experienced such wonder, this was the first time that he could claim to have witnesses a miracle. He bent forward after hugging Her, and whispered in Her ear, "To this world you have come to teach us great things. Hold steady in your faith little one, for we shall see the very expression of divinity in your face."

She looked up at him. Grateful of the acknowledgement, pleased that in Her he saw the divine. "It is His will that I have been healed, for His glory He shall be seen. I am but a vessel of hope for humanity."

The doctor remained still next to Her. His own desire to move away frozen. He looked in the eyes of the child and saw a profound depth, the dark chocolate of Her iris captivating him. He saw himself as a child, in a flash his own childhood played on his memory, her eyes a screen for his own movie. He touched her auburn hair, indebted for the opportunity to have known Her. In that moment, with Her; his life changed. He became a believer not only in the science that made his profession possible, but in a higher power that permitted change to occur without human intervention. In Her he saw faith, raw and inviting.

He released Her, his hand lowering to his side, then raising to his own face where he wiped tears that were falling effortlessly down his cheeks. As She began to move away, Her tiny hand in Madam's; She smiled at him. Her radiance penetrating to the depths of his soul. He was forever changed, a scientist by design, converted by Her presence to a believer in a higher power.

CHAPTER 46

With Her headaches now alleviated, and Her strength returning to Her more and more each day, she returned to school as any child Her age should. Her body still physically smaller than most of the other children's, she appeared frail.

She jumped off the school bus with an exuberance that she had not felt in quite a long time. Her hair neatly cut, in a shoulder length bob, she believed she looked fresh, fun and fancy. Just as the hairdresser had suggested. She carried Her books and Her lunch in a small backpack slung over one shoulder. She felt oddly comfortable as she entered the grand double doors at the front of the elementary school.

From behind Her, a small group of children giggled. She opted to ignore them and continue moving towards Her hook, strategically placed in the hallway outside of Her classroom.

"Hey freak!" Came a shout from behind Her.

She was certain that the direction of the shout was intended for someone other than Herself, and so continued walking.

"I'm talking to you freak show!"

She turned around slowly finding Herself face to face with a native boy, much taller than Herself, dressed in jeans and an old t-shirt that may have been his fathers.

"Pardon me?" She questioned him.

"I thought you died." He nudged Her shoulder pushing Her backward. "What do you think you are doing coming back here? We've had enough of your kind."

She shook Her head. "No, I didn't die. I was very sick though."

"What kind of sick? Sick like I am of looking at your stupid red hair? Or sick like I am of how you know all the answers to everything?" He sneered at Her, some of his front baby teeth missing.

"Sick like I had a brain tumor." She attempted to move past him. "Excuse me please, may I pass?"

"Fuck no freak, I'm not done with you yet. Where do you get off? 'May I pass?' Who says shit like that?"

She took a deep breath before speaking again. "I don't like your choice of words. There are literally millions of choices in the dictionary, that are far more effective than the ones you are using; you should learn some of them. You might then appear as though you have perhaps half a brain."

He shoved Her again, this time Her back smashing into the hooks on the wall. "I don't like you, you are a know it all. You should have done everyone here a favor and died. Your hair looks stupid. You think you're better than everyone else, you are a loser. And where did you get that shirt? Who do you think you are? A fashionista or somethin…? I'm asking you a question freak."

"I don't feel like I need to answer your questions. You are being mean." She felt trapped, Her back against the wall, with no help in sight.

"Ya well I think ya do freak. I'm coming for you." He began to back away, moving towards the doorway for his classroom which was next to Hers. "Lunchtime, I'll be looking for you. We're not done. Not even a little bit done."

She watched him as he disappeared through the doorway. Her hands shaking, she retreated to the waiting classroom, taking a seat at Her desk, with tears brewing and fear of the lunch hour billowing in Her gut. She tried fruitlessly to maintain focus on the project and materials presented by Her teacher. She watched the hands of the clock sliding past ten and then towards eleven. She knew that by ten minutes to twelve she would have to face him. She anticipated that the confrontation would be much like it had been in the morning. Perhaps he would take Her lunch, he would belittle and berate Her, pull Her hair, push and punch Her. She thought about telling Her teacher that she was ill, so that she could go home. The thought although intriguing, would concern Her mother. She knew that the school secretary would call Her mother at work. That was not an option that she believed would benefit Her in the long run.

The sound of the clock ticking made Her queasy. Her stomach was in knots, Her heart fluttering between each beat. She placed Her head on the desk in front of Her. The smooth surface of it feeling cool on Her cheek.

She felt a gentle touch on Her shoulder. "Everything okay dear?"

She raised Her head to meet the gaze of Her teacher. A tender man with gentle eyes and a soft voice. "Fine. Just feeling a little sick."

"Okay, well take a moment. Deep breaths should help, in through the nose, out through the mouth. Do you feel like you should see the nurse?"

She processed the thought quickly. "No, she wouldn't be able to help me. That's fine, thank you Mr. Jones."

"Okay dear, if you change your mind let me know." As he moved away she watched him, his tall lanky body moving between the small desks. She wished silently that she could change Her mind, that he could help Her. But she knew that interference from adults would only worsen the situation. She looked up at the clock, quietly praying for deliverance from the tyrant that would be seeking Her out in less than ten minutes.

The ringing bell shook Her into action. She stood, pushed Her hair back behind Her ear, and moved quickly towards the door. The hope of beating him to the playground was all that she had. If she could move faster than him, she might be able to outsmart him and hide. Protecting Herself from the physical and mental abuse that she anticipated would ensue.

She found a spot to hide near the teachers parking lot. The school's garbage bin was surrounded by a wooden fence, about six feet high. She snuck her tiny self into the space between the fence and the brick wall of the school. Sat down and felt pleased with herself. She opened the top of Her lunch bag, interested in seeing what delights awaited Her. Hummus, rice crackers, carrots neatly cut, cucumbers sticks, snap peas, strawberries, and lemon water. "Barf." She knew that other kids ate left over pizza, with meat on it. She wondered how it would taste, how it would feel in her stomach. Or a sandwich, with doughy bread and loads of mayonnaise. Cookies were a delight never indulged Her. She would like to have a bag full of them in Her lunch; full of chocolate chips, or ketchup flavored potato chips. Simple pleasures for some, but taboo to Her. She seemed to want them more than ever. An extreme violation of Her agreement with Her body, an infringement of Her own understanding of self and Her choices. She ate Her hummus serenely taking refuge in knowing health was a primary concern, one that she respected and obliged.

"Hey Freakshow, what's for lunch?"

She rolled Her eyes before answering. "Nothing that would be of any interest to you what so ever."

"Yeah? Why don't I be the judge of that? I didn't get a lunch today, so yours will do me just fine." He grinned at Her sitting in the grass between the fence and the school. "Were you hiding from me? Oh my God, you were! Weren't you!?! Scared, are you?"

"No, I'm not scared of you." She held on to Her lunch bag, hoping he would lose interest in Her and in Her food.

"Gimme, gimme your lunch." He held his hand out towards Her. "Now freak. Give it to me or I am going to beat the crap out of you. You picked a good spot, no one will see."

She fought the urge to pee. Her bladder screaming, she squeezed Her legs together. "Fine take it. What am I supposed to eat?"

He laughed out loud. "I don't' care. I don't care if you ever eat, actually. On my give a shit meter you do not even register. You are nothing. You are a loser. You should have given up and died."

She saw Her brother approaching and kept quiet. She watched her bully as he ranted. "You are an ugly fucking grunt. I bet your parents even hate you. You probably cut your own hair it looks so bad. Look at you, pathetic, red ugly hair, skinny legs, and your lips are too big for your face."

Her brother grabbed the boy from behind, pulling him in one swift motion to the ground. His fist found the boy's face, pounding him over and over again until blood began to spew from the boy's lip and nose. She stood to Her feet.

"Please stop. Don't hurt him." She saw in a flash the pain suffered by the boy in his own home. The nattering and jabs from siblings, the physical abuse perpetrated by a parent. She saw him cowering, hiding in a closet, fearful of pain, afraid to show his face.

Her brother looked up at Her still holding the boy's t-shirt in his left hand. "Stop?"

"Yes. Stop now."

Juan Maria de Salvatierra watched the children without being seen. He made a mental note of the anger in Her brother; and also, of the compassion of Her towards Her oppressor. Empathy deeply rooted was rare.

Her brother spoke. "He was hurting you. I have to protect you."

"How did you know? How did you know where to find me? How did you know he was hurting me?"

"I don't know. I just did. Are you okay?"

She smiled. "I will be. You need to get off him before someone sees."

Her brother stood, letting go of the boy's t-shirt, noting the blood running down his face to his chin. "What are you going to say happened here?" He asked the boy.

The boy stood. "I'm going to tell the truth. That you beat the shit out of me for no reason."

She spoke. "But that's not the truth! That's a lie! You have been picking on me all year!"

"Who do you think they are going to believe? Hmmm? I'm covered in blood."

Her brother brushed off his pant legs. "We all do what we need to do. Don't come near Her ever again. Are we clear? You are leaving Her alone."

"Clear as you can imagine. You're going to pay for this. You haven't even seen the beginning of this fight."

Her brother stood his ground. "Your fight is with me. Leave Her out if it. I can take anything you are able to dish out."

The boy began to walk towards the entrance of the school. "We'll see, we'll see about that! My dad is going to kick your ass."

"I welcome it! If he's as easy to take as you it will be entertaining for all to see, cuz I can dance like a butterfly, but sting like a bee!" He bounced from left to right foot and back again, as Muhammed Ali would do himself.

Juan beamed with pride at the bravery shown by Her brother. The instinct to protect Her, the desire to ward off enemies was often ignored by humans. Instinct set aside and rationalized away. He was proud of Her brother. Pleased that he had followed his gut, answered the call and went to Her rescue. Juan stepped in front of the boy as he walked back towards the school, creating an unseen physical obstruction in the boy's path. He fell to the ground. Instigating laughter on the playground. As the boy attempted to get up, Juan pushed him down again. The second time he tried to stand, Juan shoved him hard, the boys' face planting in the gravel on the ground. To the other children on the playground it appeared as though his bleeding face was rendered by him tripping over his own feet. Juan moved on, leaving Her and Her brother by the garbage dumpster wondering what had overcome the boy who had been mistreating Her, causing him to fall flat in front of everyone, and what the punishment would be for the wounds caused by Her brother.

CHAPTER 47

Rohan's diligent efforts in school continued. His friendship with the janitor grew with each passing season, his relationship with Father Raul was based on a mutual respect for one another, and for the creator of the universe. His studies were becoming easier and easier for him, while he stayed focused on building friendships with the boys who had once antagonized him. He had decided that the best way to earn their admiration was to stay strong and unwavering in his beliefs.

Nigel continued to be a pain in his butt, however Roh could not be responsible for the actions of others, and he was learning to accept the good and the undesirable in all things that he came in contact with. Jealous of Roh's academic prowess, Nigel did his best to always be confrontational and pessimistic about his adversaries' educational gains.

One spring evening, when they had both been at the school for nearly six years, Nigel corned Rohan in the boy's communal shower.

"Roh, I need you to do my physics homework."

Rohan was busy with the task of washing his own hair and was surprised and disturbed by the request. "No, Nigel I cannot do that, and you know it."

Nigel was intrigued by the strength that had been growing in Roh over the past five years. "Excuse me? I said I need you to do my physics homework and I think you said no. Is that what just happened here?"

Rohan was tired of the theatrics, he turned off the water in the shower, and grabbed his towel. "Nigel, I was quite clear when I said no. the answer is no. No, I will not do your homework. I am certain that I was clear."

Nigel poked at Rohan who refused by his own will not to poke him back. "Roh, finals are coming, and I need your help. If I don't pass my physics, then I will have to repeat this year. I can't do that. My father will kill me."

Rohan if nothing else, was compassionate and empathetic. He nodded at Nigel. "Okay, tell you what; I will help you to study for the exam, and if you need help with your homework I will help you. But I won't do it for you. I can tutor you, be your study partner whatever you need, but you will learn the physics well enough to pass yourself."

Nigel had always been one to take the easiest road to his destination. Studying himself was certainly not the easiest road, but he saw merit in it. He saw the value in learning, and he saw how it might benefit him in the end. He decided to take a chance on Rohan and agreed to allow him to help with his studies. In his heart, he knew that it was the right thing to do, and Nigel was driven by a need to achieve his own father's acceptance. He perceived this a way to fit into his father's heart and grow closer to him. "Okay Roh, okay. When do we start?"

The two boys began to study together daily, with the primary intent to master the art of physics. A quiet understanding between the two, kept both of them from sharing their new found understanding, with others. Nigel feared appearing needy, and soft towards his sworn enemy. Rohan chose not to look like an enabler, and he most certainly didn't want to give anyone the impression that he had a fondness for his bully. The two worked diligently, some days into the wee hours of the morning.

From the agreement grew a new regard for each other's strengths, and weakness'. The two began to share intimacies of their childhoods, likes and dislikes. Both were drawn to women, but their chosen life path would keep them celibate. They shared a fondness for the outdoors, and for their rich Indian culture. The full-bodied flavors of the cuisine, the music and the colors of the tapestries. Most importantly the two shared with on another a great love for their maker, an understanding of a power greater than their own will. And the Lord was pleased with them.

CHAPTER 48

Giftedness has been defined as showing exceptional or extraordinary capabilities and potential with respect to intellect, creativity and task commitment. The ability to perform well, with a wide range of knowledge and skill in one or more of the following areas: general intelligence, specific academic applications, creative thinking, social tasks, musical applications, artistic expressions, and kinaesthetic. Combined with high performance levels in these areas the observance of an Intelligence Quotient in the scoring range of a minimum of 130 is optimally found, and in some gifted children can be as high as 170 points.

Madam prepared herself for the meeting with Dr. Altman, her hair in a bun, her black cardigan sweater neatly buttoned to the top. She wore a mid-calf black pencil skirt and simple black pumps, plain hose. Her skin bore no tint, no make-up of any kind what so ever, except for a glimmer of tinted gloss on her lips. She remained a classic dresser, she thought herself refined, subdued and un-noticeable.

Dr. Altman entered the room, his gait quick, but his feet dragging slightly, old weathered brown Mophestos in much need of polishing shuffling across the floor at the pace of a quick two step tempo. Madam observed him crossing the room, his gold rimmed glasses slightly dusted with dandruff. The remainder of which had fallen onto his shoulders. His salt and pepper hair was parted in the middle, which Madam found oddly feminine.

Their gazes met, and he extended his hand.

"Good Morning" said Dr. Altman. "Nice to meet you."

She stood from her chair, gracefully as always, the air lifting her, not a sound was made as her body rose. Madam reached forward with a neatly manicured hand and met the doctors, taking his cool hand into hers. "Nice to meet you Doctor, thank you for taking time from your busy schedule to meet with me. I appreciate the effort that you have put into the assessments on both of my children."

The doctor was taken aback at the warmth that radiated from her hand, and the power that exuded her. He felt at awe in her presence, and yet subtly at ease. "It has actually been all my pleasure to be honest Madam. Both of your children are quite remarkable, and unique…. Individuals…. they are. Their results are quite astonishing as you will see, and if I may just say, I have had moments with both that have been monumental in my career. I would like to ask, if I may be so bold, to write a research paper on the very assessments that I have just done. My findings here may be helpful to other psychologists, and psychiatrists; may open doors that have only been knocked on so far. We need to explore, to develop these ideas more, and honestly, I think your children hold the keys to many of these doors for us. When I say "us" I mean the medical profession; science. I mean your children possess many answers that we have been looking for."

Madam sat quietly in her chair, she heard many sounds around her. She heard from an office down the hall a woman speaking on the telephone, she heard from somewhere else in the building the sound of a photocopier making copy after copy; she heard also the sound of an electric pencil sharpener eating away at an HB pencil chewing the ecosystem away one tree at a time. She could hear the snapping of gum between someone's molars, the deep methodical wispy breathing of an asthmatic; her senses heightened by the strain she felt on an emotional level.

Madam disliked the very thought of testing, examinations, and assessments to begin with. Furthermore, to parade results and scores of said testing seemed boastful, show boatish and not something that she was willing to participate in. "Doctor, why would you be interested in writing papers, or researching further any of the information that you have gathered on my children? I'm afraid that I am going to need more information from you. Please, if you don't mind."

The doctor looked at her, pushing his glasses up his nose slightly. "Of course, I don't mind, Madam. Not at all. I think it would be of benefit if we discuss first the results of the assessments. Would that be okay with you? I think if you see the children's results, your children's results, you will understand better my position, Madam."

She nodded. "Yes, of course, if you wish."

The psychologist picked up one of the two files that was sitting atop of his desk, a manila folder, containing information that was integral the future of the child. It was stacked with pages of written information, data and his own notes. He opened it, on the top left corner of the folder was stapled a Polaroid photo of Her. "Shall we start with Her?"

"If that is what you feel is best, certainly." Madam took a deep cleansing breath and prepared for what she believed would be the most interesting of the two reports. She was quite aware that the information the doctor was about to present would be mind blowing. She sat slightly forward in her chair. Her heart beat calm, her breath steady, she felt prepared.

The doctor's nerves seemed jagged, he was nervous in the presence of the children's mother, he struggled for proper diction. "Well, Madam where to start? Language comprehension? Processing speeds? Behavioural mannerisms? Academic Prowess? Visual Reasoning? The reason that I am at a loss is because Her scores are almost identical in every category; which is unprecedented. The variance in scoring is less than a tenth of 1 percent, and I am of the opinion to be frank that she put zero effort into the examinations. Her intellectual quotient score is superior; would you like to know what it is?"

Madam took a moment to think before answering. "Will it change my life in any way? Alter how I should treat Her? Or will it in any way change the way that she sees Herself?" Madam was processing the information that had already been provided and was preparing for the remaining information that was forthcoming.

The doctor was quick to respond. "All of the above are possible, yes. Of course, there is always the option of not sharing the information with Her. There would not be any harm in that. For now, anyway; I suppose there is always the chance as you suggest that yes, you may treat Her differently, knowing that she is capable of great things, there may now be an expectation. She may fall short one day if she doesn't realize your dreams for Her."

"You are assuming Doctor, that I have dreams for Her already. That I have planned Her life for Her." The clock hanging on the wall behind the doctor was ticking loudly.

"Most parents do, it may be an assumption, but it is an educated one. I did not mean to offend; I was simply responding to your statement."

"Of course, no one ever means to offend Doctor, and yet by expressing one's opinion it is rarely difficult not to, isn't it?" Madam held her breath for a moment. She waited for the doctor to process her comment before continuing. "Please do not misinterpret my intentions, I appreciate your work, and I am quite interested although I would not use the word excited, to see the results. I am disappointed to hear that she did not however: apply Herself. I am guessing that Her brother did?"

The doctor placed his hand again onto the manila folder in front of himself that bared a Polaroid photo of Her. He glanced at the picture and thought how stunning the little girl was, Her dark eyes deeply penetrating, wise and knowing; Her smile engaging, welcoming. "He did well, yes Madam, shall we discuss his assessment results?"

"Before we do, I gather that you have drawn a comparative, and that for some reason you believe one child to be superior? That would be the reason for wanting to prepare this paper? This study or research paper that you have asked about writing?"

The doctor picked up his coffee cup to which the coffee from earlier in the morning was cold and unpleasant, but wet; soothing his parched throat, allowing him to speak. "Madam, I assure you that although it appears that a comparative is drawn, it is only slight, and please may I show you his results before we jump to conclusions about what my intentions might be?"

"Doctor, I am not jumping to conclusions about your intentions, I am protecting myself from making my own assessment of my children's intellectual potential. If I don't possess the information you have gathered; I cannot compare them, cannot push them to limits that they are unable to achieve, I will not be able to crush their spirits. Please understand me, my hope is always to love them for who they are, not who they might be, or what they might do. The data you have compiled might change that."

Doctor Altman responded. "May I ask Madam, why you allowed the examination to occur in the first place? I do hear what you are saying. And from a spiritual perspective I can appreciate your intent. I wonder however if the parents of Albert Einstein felt the same way, or Sir Isaac Newton, Alexander Graham Bell, or the Wright Brothers. People who can do great things Madam have great parents who support them. All of them could pursue their dreams and to grow as individuals. I would challenge you to not stifle what these children are capable of."

Madam pushed back. "An interesting and yet slightly narrow-minded response doctor. Let us please consider that none of the individuals that you have identified would have been subjected to the type of assessments and testing that my children have been through. This testing is not the first time for Her. It is however for Her brother. What is interesting for me, is that you assume that by rendering the results, and writing your paper; the children will suddenly be compelled to do great things. That's not how it works though. From what I understand, and I will admit that I am a rookie-this is my first-time parenting and the children in fact did not come with an instruction manual"

She paused for a brief moment before continuing. "Doctor, the will to do great things comes from a sense of need, an instinctual passion, a gut feeling, or a natural gift. Whether you are artistic like Frank Carmichael, Arthur Lismer or A.Y. Jackson of the Group of Seven, the great painters of canvas, athletic like Pele, Bobby Orr, Muhammad Ali, or Babe Ruth. All who overcame adversity to succeed in their respective sport. Great scientists as you mentioned, Einstein, Newton, Maria Curie, Bell, and inventors such as Ford, Phelps Jacob, the Wright brothers, and Crane. Writers the likes of Hemmingway, Shakespeare, Poe, Woolf, and Fitzgerald; great world leaders and activists like Nelson Mandela, Sir Winston Churchill, and Mother Theresa. There are so many great individuals' doctor, who by choice, by free will did great things. Not because of a test, or a research paper written by a member of the medical profession."

"Madam, I agree with you on many points, however, the results I am holding are perhaps the most incredible the world has seen in centuries. I believe it would do yourself and the populous in general a great benefit in just hearing what I must say. Please? And Phelps Jacobs?"

"Mary, Phelps Jacobs- the brassiere." Madam smiled coyly at Doctor Altman. She resigned herself to at least agree to hear what he had to say. Her points had been acknowledged and respectably received. She succumbed to his wishes now. "Yes, Doctor Altman, please I would be although not pleased to hear what you must say, I am open to hear it."

The doctor smiled at her before responding and engaging in the sharing of materials. He was nervous and thrilled at the same time. A Board of Education Psychologist, he wasn't one who would normally come across profound greatness. Often, he would see the likes of children who were from broken homes and were neglected, battered or worse were exposed to lives of crime, prostitution or the drug trade. He saw children who knew nothing different than welfare, and social assistance, the food bank and community service. These two were different. Both were uniquely beautiful, striking and picturesque. They were regal in appearance, with good posture, impeccable grooming and discriminate diction. Their mother paid attention to detail. Every little thing that made a difference; that made the children stand out from the rest, had been attended to. He thought it very intriguing how she missed nothing.

The clothing always neatly pressed, and fresh scented. Never a rip or tear in the pants, never a zipper in need of replacement. No elbows worn in the sweaters, no fraying on the collars. Mittens always matched the toques and scarves.

The children's hair was always neatly done; Hers curled or in a bun or braid. Her brothers always cut and trimmed, he never had a blond hair out of place. Doctor Altman wondered how it was possible. He knew that she was a single mother, and that she in addition to working full time was working on an additional degree. How she found the time was baffling.

He began. "I'm glad Madam. Okay well as I said earlier, Her testing results were abnormal, scoring equally high in all categories, Her brothers scores were a little more discriminatory, with variances slightly higher than Hers. However, results were still remarkable. His assessments showed a tendency towards ADD, Attention Deficit Disorder, and a tendency towards Asperger's, the ADD can easily be medicated to appeal, his intellectual quotient is off the charts however. What is most interesting to me from these assessments Madam is that again I must stress that I believe that she put little or no effort into them, and her cognitive abilities are as I indicated, unprecedented."

"So, Her brother has ADD? Asperger's? And what is his IQ Doctor? I suppose that I may as well know at this point. And can these numbers that you are assigning change?"

The doctor seemed excited to be moving on. "Well to answer the latter of your questions first, yes, they can of course change. You can of course improve your IQ, or intellectual quotient by providing your brain with sustenance; or information, however we are talking about a point or two. What is relative with these scores is the processing speeds, the working memory, long term memory and cognitive reasoning in general which refers to specifically the ability to accomplish tasks-. I'm just giving you Reader's Digest here, so we can get to what's important."

Madam nodded. "I see."

"So, the IQ although can improve slightly, to answer your question; no, it's pretty much there from birth. We think. Anyway. Her brother's score was slightly higher than Hers, at 168. Hers was 156, but again, she didn't apply Herself to the assessments and what was remarkable to me about Her scores was that there was no variance on any of the testing modules. Both children would therefore be considered genius' Madam."

Madam looked at the doctor from where she sat and said nothing.

"So, to finalize, for the intent of this meeting, we should consider alternate placement for the children, schooling wise. Both would qualify for the GATE program and could be placed for the new school year, although I could arrange to have one moved immediately, there isn't room for the two children as of today."

"What is GATE, Doctor?" Madam began to breathe through her nose. Inhaling air that was needed to process information.

"Oh, I'm sorry, I assumed you would have known, Gifted and Talented Education. A program designed specifically for children such as yours who have special educational needs." The doctor placed the pen on his desk that he had been playing with.

"And so, this is a special school? They would be moved?"

"Yes, indeed, the school itself is centrally located, you would be required to provide transportation to and from school daily, but the benefits would be outstanding."

Madams head was swimming with questions. "Which child would they take now? If you were to place one child now Doctor, which one would you send to the school?"

Doctor Altman didn't need time to think about Madam's question, for he had prepared for it, he had anticipated it. "I would send Her Brother Madam. His scores are higher, he would be considered, as would She, in the top one percent of intellectuals. A placement in a school such as GATE would allow his mind to cultivate and problem solve, seek the information and answers that he desires, he will be encouraged to grow intellectually, and they can deal with his ADD should it manifest in adolescence, which is what we would typically see. If not present from a young age, we see the condition establish with the onset of puberty."

"How many children his age attend the school? My concern is for his social well-being; he is a social person. Isolation is not something that would benefit him at all." Madam began to twist the side of her skirt in her hands, a frustration building in her.

"Class sizes are small, which is advantageous for the children, teachers are better able to provide for the needs of the gifted in small settings. Actual class sizes differ by grade, but my guess would be ten to twelve children per classroom. Many of these settings also include an aide. I can call for confirmation. And of course, I can arrange a tour, and if you are seriously interested we can speak to potential teachers, and other parents that have their children enrolled, the principal, whatever you need. He will thrive, his mind will develop and flourish and intellectually he will respond almost immediately to them stimulus that the school provides."

"And you would suggest we leave Her here? Behind in this school? Alone? In a different school than Her brother?

Here where she is bullied? Where he can no longer protect Her? And where She would potentially be left to the wolves?” Madam seemed more than agitated and slightly alarmed at the idea of separating the two children. She appeared to the doctor to be frightened of the concept of it, almost angered by it.

“Madam, it would be in Her brother’s best interest, and it may just serve Her well too, to develop Her own friendships, to begin to interact with the other students at Her grade level. I don’t presume to tell you what to do, and I cannot and will not interfere. I have no idea what you are attempting to protect them from, but I can for certain tell you that the both are smarter and more independent than you give them credit for. Shielding them from the world Madam is not doing them service at all.”

“Is that what you think Doctor? That I am shielding them? Protecting them from the world? If you think it’s the world that I fear, then Doctor your science has rendered you more ignorant than you appear to be. And I apologize if that makes me sound arrogant, however it is not the world and what we can see, that we should *all* be fearful of. It’s the things that we cannot see that are the most harmful, the things that lurk in the shadows, and the ideas that hide in our minds. Doctor I would suggest to you that you might do some reading. Open your mind beyond the basics of your science, navigate into the concept of Indigo children, reincarnation, and spiritual transcendence. Just to begin. Then factor in the divine, and evil and the war between the two. Once you begin to have a basic understanding or minimal comprehension at least of any or all of those, then we can discuss why I insist on having him protect Her. There is a reason why he is Her brother and not mine, or yours. These things do not happen by chance Doctor. So, no they will not be separated."

Doctor Altman lowered his gaze to the desk top, his thoughts on Madam, her comments, the children, and her suggestions he kept to himself for the moment. Normally he would have found the concept of divinity absurd; however, in the presence of this woman he was willing for some strange reason to consider it. Was it the children themselves, the way they had conducted themselves during the assessments? Was it Madam and her arguments? Well-constructed, informed, articulate? Was it her presence or was it a combination of all three of them? There was something about the trio that had him perplexed. "Madam, if you wish. I will then leave it to you to decide what to do. The door is open; my door also will be open to you should you need additional information or if you would like to investigate other alternatives. If you would like also to place the children on the list for the fall, you will need to let me know, and the sooner the better. I would just stress to you the potential, and the application of their intellectual greatness to which we have not seen in so long, I would beg you to consider the need for proper nurturing, proper guidance and care in their education."

Madam stood from her seat, she had all the information that she needed to make her decision and was exhausted from talking with the doctor. She extended her hand towards him in gratitude, they shook as a formality. As Madam always took the hand of a newly introduced person, it allowed her an opportunity to tap into the essence of the individual. She could better identify the spirit with physical contact. "Thank you so much Doctor, I appreciate everything that you have shared, and I value your opinions, truly. I have tried to establish in both children the concept of gratitude and service. I believe that true giftedness reaches beyond the complexities of science and history, mathematics and language comprehension. I consider kindness and generosity gifts, I take pride in the fact that they comfort the lonely, think of others before themselves and share whatever they may have. They look for good in everyone, and when it's not there, they pray for it. I have attempted, to raise them well, to be respectful of others, and to acknowledge a power greater than ourselves. I would definitely be concerned with the idea of either one of the children being in an environment where there is little or no social interaction. Both thrive on the engagement with others-especially Her brother. However, I will oblige you and as you said, think about everything." She let go of his hand, which had felt cool to her. A sign of courageousness, he was not a person easily abashed. But she couldn't be certain if he was trustworthy. She saw in him pools of dark water. She shook it off and let go of his hand.

"You will let me know then? You will be in touch?" The doctor made one last attempt before Madam exited the room.

"For sure, yes."

And with that, Madam left Doctor Altman's office, she walked the long corridor past doorways and windows, back to the building exit where she had come in. There was a wind blowing outside, brown dry leaves left from the passage of seasons, gust around in small funnels apparent of small tornados. Whisking away memories of autumn, obliterating any hues or facades of summer. Winter was upon them once again, the cold would chill Madam to the very cusp of her bones, drying her skin and leaving her parched and withered; frozen to the very core of her being. The snow would come, the ice would build on the buildings and the roadways, the trees would freeze, covered in abundant white sheets of snow.

For months, the climate would be frosty white with sub-zero temperatures, Madam thought of her children's future, the idea of training for greatness rather than trusting that faith would provide for it. She watched the leaves as the wind gust passed her, her hair pulled from her neat bun. In the absence of planning, which she thought, life rarely provided consistently, one might think, that training would be a beneficial alternative. A strict scholarly choice might be in alignment with God's will. Yet she believed with the entirety of her heart, that the intent of faith itself was present in the absence of our planning. For if in the absence of faith, she herself would then have nothing but doubt, regret and pure sadness. She would be like a bowl of half eaten cherry Jell-O, ready for the trash after Sunday dinner.

She walked to her car, and temporarily dismissed the idea of special placement, special schools, special papers for medical journals and separating the children. She saw no need. Not at this point. If the school was to be then she was certain that He would make it clear to her.

CHAPTER 49

She sat alone, windows closed drapes drawn. The room was dark, cool and placid. On Her knees beside the bed She knelt, with Her hands held in prayer. Her tiny face looking up at the figure on the far side of the darkened room She spoke out to him. Not fully aware of his motive, nor of his origin, destination or needs.

"For what have you come to me?" She questioned, Her tiny hands quivering slightly, a natural fear rumbling from within Her.

"I don't know. I don't know why I am here. Who are you? Where am I?" He was not an old man, middle aged, in his mid-fifties She would guess. He was physically fit, not overly tall, of average height. He was average; he was not thought provoking, nor memorable, but as She looked over at him, she thought to Herself that he had been someone's superhero. A father, a good one, a husband, a brother; there was loss being experienced, this man would be missed. His hair was cut short and had been neatly combed.

"I can help you. You need not be frightened." She waited for engagement from them before She revealed much of Herself. It wasn't often that they came to Her. Mary Mack had helped Her with the first few to come. She was cautious of Her words, deliberate in the delivery of them. "Do you remember what happened?"

He touched his chest. "I was running, I think, I think I was running, with Joe, I think we were in the park, that's all I remember. And then there was a darkness that came, I still feel a tightness in my chest. It feels heavy. Like someone is sitting on it. I'm having trouble breathing."

She smiled up at him, Her hands still in prayer, his feet hovering slightly off the floor. "Yes, I see, I can see the park. I can see your friend. He cares for you very much. I can feel everything that you are feeling right now; your physical pain, your emotions. Try to calm your breathing now, take shallow breaths, in and out through your nose."

He ran his hands through his hair. "So, what is this? What has happened to me?" He looked at the young girl, her long auburn hair pulled into a neat ponytail, her pyjamas crisply pressed, white with small pink bows covering them.

The room immaculate, the white down quilt on the bed-fluffy and inviting. He felt a need to lay down, he felt tired, the bed was crying out to him.

"I'm here to help you. You are having trouble understanding. It's okay. It's not uncommon."

He tilted his head to the left. "Understanding? What am I having trouble understanding? I was at the park, I know that. I was running with Joe."

"Yes, you were."

"And now I am standing in the bedroom of a little girl that I have never met before." He moved towards the pink velvet chair in the corner of the room and sat. The wide expanse of the seat consuming him, his back-end disappearing.

"You are indeed in my room, I was just saying my prayers, and preparing for bed. It's that time for me. Time for bed I mean. I have school in the morning." She stood and then sat on the side of Her bed. Pulling on a large cozy blanket that hung over the footboard and wrapped herself in it. It was pink and fluffy with knit tassels that hung long, nearly touching the floor.

"Why? Why am I here and not with Joe? How did I get here? Who are you? What's your name?"

"I can answer some of your questions, some of them you already have answers for and you know what those answers are. I can help you to accept them. It's not important what my name is."

"Am I dead?"

"Dead is not what you might believe it to be, and really not something we should ever fear." She paused, watching for his reaction, waiting for his next prompt.

"What happens to me now?" He seemed calmer, less agitated.

"Your spirit continues on, the physical body that you inhabited for a time, that you were using; has now expired."

He continued to sit in the chair, processing information, strangely beginning to feel at peace. Her presence tranquil, he looked for more. "My family? My children? Joe? What happens to all of them?"

"They remain."

"And so... I just move on?"

"Yes. That is exactly so." She had become by the age of eleven, advanced in what she considered Spirit Transition. She divulged the least amount of information possible, to answer the questions needed in order to ease the worry created by the change. Not every spirit was troubled, or had difficulty with the process, and it wasn't often that She was needed. She was grateful for that.

"Is this heaven then? Is that where I am?"

"No, you are in my bedroom. I am human."

"Oh, okay. When do I go there? To heaven?" He was beginning to accept, she was pleased, she was doing well.

"I am not at liberty to answer that level of questioning. I do apologize. Your chest is no longer hurting you though. Your breathing is not laboured. This is good. We are making progress. The pain is gone."

He placed his hand on his chest once more, nodded at Her and smiled, "Yes, you're correct. All the pain is gone, I can see so many things, I remember now too, I can see what happened; in the park; I was with Joe, we were running. I think I had a heart attack. I know that my knees gave out, and I fell to the ground. And Joe, he had his phone with him, he called 911, I could hear him making the call, telling someone where we were. I remember thinking that he should call my wife, I remember feeling so much love for her, and then everything faded to dark."

She knew that he was ready; She took a deep breath in, filling Herself completely with the gifts She had been given and blew the air from Her lungs towards him.

"Receive it…. In Jesus name, I pray."

A flurry of activity surrounded his spirit, his mind became clear, his heart settled, his misgivings resolved. A sense of peace descended; and then he was gone.

CHAPTER 50

Juan Maria de Salvatierra and Mary Mack travelled together one cold winters day with the intention of speaking directly to the Dark Angel himself. Juan believed with his whole heart that if a problem arose, it was in everyone's best interest to direct all inquiries to the source of the conundrum, rather than fishing around and wasting time.

Juan was quite certain that the dark angel was behind the turmoil in Her life, as he always was. It was for this reason that the two of them had made the trip together, not under the pretense of battle, but rather of proclamation. Their travels had been for the sole purpose of declaring and negotiating a truce.

Juan spoke first with great animation and clarity. "When our leader created Her, He had great intentions for Mother Earth, she has a plan, He spent superfluous time in adding context to Her programing, and allowing Her access to certain, shall we say insights that would normally not be human traits." He paused, took a deep breath for courage and continued. "She will not be overturned, she will not under any circumstance be destroyed."

The angel asked." Why spend so much time on Her? What was all the fuss about? I am at a bit of a loss Juan. Could you please help me to understand? Hmmm? I thought we had it all with the Son?"

Juan spoke on the Lord's behalf and answered. "Have you been watching the world? Mankind? They continue the same path, of self-destruction, but it's much worse than in the past. They cannot control themselves anymore, the planet now is in a path of devastation, Mother Earth is dying; the Lord is suffering, so He crafted Her. Have you seen all the specifications He had to meet to form Her? She is capable of functioning in all kinds of situations, she can embrace several at the same time, she can heal anything from a bruised knee to a broken heart simply with a word, a prayer or sometimes a touch or a simple smile. She is fortified with the spirit of goodness. She is truly remarkable. "

The angel seemed impressed but gave nothing of his secrets away. "I have been watching Her, she is remarkable, no question... but it's impossible Juan, you know it, I know it.

She cannot be. He has created such before but always as a male, never a female, and never quite like this. Tell me more."

The Angel looked down through a magnifying glass to where he could see Her interacting with Her friends; laughing and talking. In controlled enjoyment. He began, "But the Lord also made her so soft; She is very vulnerable Juan, I'm not certain that this will fare well for you. She might be too 'human'. You could be in trouble Juan."

"She is soft, and she is vulnerable," said Juan, "That is why He has assigned us to protect Her. We will stay with Her, potentially forever. But She is also one of the strongest to have ever arrived. You can't imagine what She can endure and overcome. Her powers are only beginning to manifest.""

"Can she think?" The Angel of Darkness asked.

Juan was quick to answer. "Not only can she think, she can reason and negotiate well."

The Angel touched his own cheek, the leathery feel of his own skin pleasing to him. His own agelessness had become a pleasure, of increasing intensity with the passing years.

"It seems that the Lord's special creation is not immune to sadness! You have put too many burdens on Her."

"She is not overburdened...it is just a tear, she is capable of all human emotion; unlike the rest of us. She can feel, she can love, she feels loss, she can cry." Juan corrected the Angel.

"What's it for? Why would He do that? " Asked the Angel.

Mary Mack believed that She knew Her best and spoke. "Tears are Her way of expressing Her grief, Her doubts, Her love, Her loneliness, Her suffering and Her pride. I remain with Her, Her servant, faithful and by Her side. She is wise, she is compassionate, and temperate. She is more than we expect for Her size."

This made a big impression on the Dark Angel, he had fought the Lord for power for many centuries, his own ego growing stronger with each passing decade, his clutches on humanity fiercely remaining. He had seen many things, destroying the likes of many great individuals who by choice had succumbed to his commands. "Will She ever break? Can I win Her over?" He fluttered his wings and winked at Mary Mack.

Mary Mack looked at Juan, both shook their heads, Mary again prepared herself to speak, the silver buttons down her back glistening in the light that penetrated the window. She thought of every soul to which each button represented. She wanted to believe that by faith and with knowing Her, she had in fact learned herself how to feel love, how to empathize, how to console and how to cry. She believed that by knowing Her, she had become a better soul, a stronger soul; a more divine spirit. Mary mourned the loss of those represented by her silver buttons, she held one in her hand, rubbing the back side of the button, remembering the face of the one she had hoped to save.

The dark angel spoke to Mary Mack directly, "Like the silver bullets all down your back aren't they Mary? Those you could not save? Those who were too weak? Those who were too feeble to stand strong for *your* God. Those that were not able to live up to the rules? Why do you insist on wearing those buttons Mary? Are they not too heavy on your back? Too much for a little girl to carry? And that rhyming? Isn't it time? Can't we just put it to rest? "I'm Miss Mary Mack, with Silver Buttons all down my back," Good Lord, if they only knew what it was that you had done to get the damn things there in the first place! Isn't that right Mary Mack? Couldn't we just for today, please Mary stop with the games?"

A single tear rolled down the cheek of the beloved Mary Mack. She reached up with her left hand and touched it. A smile breaking over her face, she looked back to Juan; for it was true, she was able to feel. She had learned to cry like a human. "I like to rhyme; it brings me pleasure. I have learned from Her to feel. Which had been taken from me. Wiped away, scrubbed from me like my memories. I appreciate that you were able to cleanse me of the unclean, the misery that haunted my dreams, the torture that I was exposed to before death; but could you not have left some of the beneficial? Some of the niceties of life? Of my life? Could you not have left me a sliver? A shard? Not even a fragment of my life to hang on to so that I may remember and hope for tomorrow?"

The dark angel shook his head, his hands in his lap, Juan noted that the angel was ringing his hands tightly together. "Mary please, you knew what I was offering was not going to be pleasant for you, you cannot have one and not sacrifice the other. That is not how it works. You understood my terms when you accepted the arrangement. I am sorry that you are not happy now that your Lord has assigned you to Her and you would like to "feel" more. *Tsk tsk*, perhaps you shouldn't get so attached to your projects."

"I also enjoy my silver buttons, and the heaviness that they represent. The weight on my heart, reminds me every day of the poor souls that sacrificed themselves. I feel terrible that they were not able to make it to their destinations. I wish that the assignments would not have had to suffer. In their haste they made poor decisions, but the

Lord allows them to reconcile; I wish that like Her I could save them all. That is Her plan; to save each and every one of them; the old and the new. I pray that one day, when this war is finally over, you too will be freed of your chains enabling you to free all of those who have fallen, free them to the kingdom of heaven. And then I will happily give you all of these silver bullets that you used to slay them."

The dark angel laughed at Mary Mack before speaking, his breath sour, his skin old, wrinkled and aged. His hair was grey and falling forward on his head, it was thick and wavy. His wings protruded behind him, long and black, feathers reaching far beyond where he sat. "Well, well, she really, really has done a number on you hasn't she? Do you two honestly believe the lies that have been spun? Juan? All that's written in His Book? All the stories and the history? All that He's been pumping into everyone's head for all these years? I thought we had an understanding Mary? I thought we had a deal? I thought when we made our agreement that things were changing; that you would for appearances sake continue on His path, but that you would be recruiting members FOR me!" His teeth were exposed, gnarly and gnashing, froth rolling and spilling from beneath his tongue, excreting out the sides of his mouth.

Mary looked to Juan, and then looked at the dark angel, her own fears dissipating, a new strength growing within her. "I stand with Her. I am with the Lord."

"Lord, you are a genius." The angel clapped his hands together, "You thought of everything with this little one. This little gift that you created, the one you sent back to save the planet. She has then converted you Mary, you are once again a child of the great leader. I can see it, entirely. She is indeed marvelous."

Juan responded. "Indeed, she is. She prays without ceasing, and for souls that are not always worthy. As a man of the cloth, I am honored to serve Her. You know I have never wavered, I faithfully have served my Lord, all of my days, and She is the way, she brings new light, the truth. She has a strength that amazes men. An internal strength, that could move mountains, and tame the grandest of monsters, she is capable of warding off all forms of evil with only a wave of Her hand or with the slightest tilt of Her smile. She can handle misfortune and carry heavy burdens, even for the likes of others. She exudes happiness and love and holds her opinion close to her chest, she holds her tongue when others cannot. She smiles when she feels like screaming. She sings when she feels like crying, alas when turmoil and conflict prevail, she fights for what she believes in. Her love is Her bounty and is truly unconditional."

The Angel asked: "So She is a perfect being then? She is the one?"

CHAPTER 51

Jorge determined it was best to stop in Vera Cruz before heading to Louisiana in search of Madam's husband. He hoped for a visit with his parents and some much-needed rest. The drive there provoked in him reminders of his childhood, of surfing and swimming in the ocean, enjoying fresh mangos and avocados from the trees on the family plantation. His mouth watered at the thought of devouring a meal of red snapper freshly prepared by his mother and sipping on tequila with his father until the wee hours of the morning.

His arrival was grand, his mother waiting at the gates of the property for him. Her kitchen apron tied snuggly around her waist, adorning brightly coloured apples and oranges, with a ruffled hem. He smiled at the sight of her. His jeep pulled up beside her, her dark hair now turning grey, her olive skin darkly tanned. She opened the door and climbed into the passenger seat, reaching across the stick shift for her son.

"Jorge, hola my baby, how are you? You look tired."

"Mama, hello, I have missed you. You look well." He was pleased to see her.

"You ignore me my love, you look tired." She reached for his cheek.

"I'm fine Mama, a lot of things at work on my mind, you know how it is." Jorge turned away from her towards the driver's side window. He was very aware that he was never successful in the art of transparency when it came to his mother.

"It's a woman then?" His mother looked at him, certain that there was something different about her son, he seemed to her to be more vulnerable, he was changed.

"No mama, there is no woman. I just have a lot of things on mind. It's nothing for you to worry about, really." He appreciated her concern but wished that she would drop the subject. "How are my brothers?"

His mother was pleased to have a change in the subject as well. "Oh, they are all fine. The grandbabies too are just wonderful. I do enjoy them you know. One of life's great blessings, children. When do you think that you might get on with that? With having children? You would be such a wonderful father Jorge."

Somehow, she had managed to bring the conversation full circle, back to himself and to the woman in his life; or lack thereof. "Mother I would need first to have a permanent type of relationship with a woman to have children, as we have already established that I do not have that; I am bewildered as to how you think that I might in fact be having children soon?"

"Well it was just a question, really Jorge you don't need to be so sensitive. Come on then, grab your things, your father is waiting for you in his study, and I will have dinner ready in a couple of hours. Go say hello and have a rest if you like. A nice siesta might do you well. You do look frightfully tired." She climbed out of the Jeep and moved towards the house. Her hair neatly pulled into a bun at the nape of her neck, grey strands falling forward around her soft face. Jorge thought his mother to be the perfect image of motherhood, knowledgeable, kind, soft, and strong. To the best of his recollection she had been a pillar of strength while they were growing up. He knew that his brothers felt the same way that he did, they all appreciated her, and if anything, ever happened to her, the family would suffer greatly.

Jorge found his father Hugo in his study, watching football on the television. He stood when he saw his son enter and embraced him. "Jorge, my boy, I have missed you! How is my crime fighter? Hey?"

Jorge was always touched by his parents' interest and enthusiasm in his work life. He had chosen his path wanting to save a part of humanity that he believed may have been lost. He had a profound belief that people turned to crime from the depths of despair and desperation; rarely from desire.

"I'm well Father, how are you?"

"Very well! Your mother is still feeding me, and we have the Lord to be thankful that she is still going to bed with me every night. After fifty-one years I suppose myself to be a lucky man."

Jorge smiled at him. "You indeed are a lucky man father. I wish I had your luck, or at least a fragment of it." His face was solemn, in his eyes his father could see a multitude of history.

His father looked at him from the side, he realized that his wife's instincts were correct, and that there were likely woman troubles in his son's life. "So, tell your dad what's going on…is she special?"

"Is who special? To whom are you referring dad?" Jorge felt like he was in the middle of an interrogation. He preferred to be sitting on the opposite side of the table, asking the questions, performing the interrogation however. "I told mama, there's no one, I just have a lot of work stuff on my mind."

"I see, so you think that we don't know you? That we don't notice a difference in you? I can see it plain as day, as soon as you walked into the room."

Jorge was hesitant but resigned to having been found out. "She is not someone that I can ever be with. I have to walk away Dad, I cannot ever be with her. I am doing my best to block her from my mind."

Hugo was uncertain what to say next. He knew that his son needed something from him. As he often did, he thought of Mary Mack, the young girl that had visited him within the walls of the concentration camp. Her black dress neatly pressed, with silver buttons all down her back. "For what reason do you believe that you can never be with her?"

"She is complicated. Very complicated. And her situation is more so. Pursuing her is not something that is permitted of me. I cannot choose to be with her. I must not seek her out, ever."

"Your happiness is important too, if this is a one-sided relationship and she has determined that you must not seek her out, then it's not a relationship, but you were merely infatuated. These things happen sometimes."

Jorge was embarrassed that his father would think of him in such a way. "No, you have misunderstood me father. She is married, with children...her situation is changing but never the less, I have been warned to stay away."

"Warned? By who have you been warned? The husband?"

Jorge laughed, "Good heavens no, no, not the husband. It's complicated."

Jorge's father picked up his glass of tequila and took a sip. "For Pete's sake boy tell me what it is then, I feel as though you are dancing circles around me. Just tell me what it is."

"The thing is Dad, I don't think you would believe me if I told you. It's too far- fetched. The story is a bit crazy and wild sounding. I haven't told anyone, and I don't think that I should."

Hugo again thought back to Mary Mack, and of how he had kept her a secret for all these years. He had never forgotten her riddles and rhymes, her hidden message, her not so subtle instructions. He pondered the thought of sharing the memory of her with his son and decided that it would benefit him to know more about his father's life.

Hugo embarked on the story of his young life as a member of the Third Reich. As an officer of the holocaust he hated what had been done during the war, as a man he was subject to the reality of living with decisions that had been made so long ago. One day he would have to answer to a higher power for his own actions during his life as a young officer.

Jorge listened intently for over an hour as his father shared his most secret part of his life. Jorge's mother knew nothing of the past, nor did any of his brothers. Jorge was surprised, but relieved to finally share in his father's memories of his life in his twenties, before he had met his mother. His recollection of the camps, the women and the children; of their suffering, was moving.

Finally, Hugo began to tell the story of his visitor. Of the freezing temperature, the wind and the ice on the day that she had come. Jorge stopped him "Dad, so you believe that a young girl who was a ghost or an angel of some kind visited you, bringing a message?"

Hugo poured himself another tequila and offered the same to his son. He nodded at Jorge. "Yes, I do believe that. I believe it with everything that I am. She was clear on her message and told me specifically what would happen if I didn't follow her instruction. And so, I did; I did everything she told me to. I was lucky enough to find your mother after the war. Just as my angel said that I would. I did my best to be a good servant, we escaped Europe and settled in Mexico not because we thought it was an ideal place to live; but because the move simplified my disappearance. I was terrified after Germany surrendered that I would be hunted. I found great fortune in the fact that I was able to come to Vera Cruz and live a quiet and tranquil life. I followed her instruction and crossed the ocean."

Jorge pondered the idea of telling his father about Juan Maria de Salvatierra. He decided that there was merit in sharing his story with his father. And so, he did. He unraveled from the beginning of the romantic endeavor, he revealed details of how and when he had met Madam, their short but steamy affair, the rapid and reckless way that he had fallen desperately in love with her, and the late night visit in his own office by a man that had been dead for well over two hundred and fifty years.

Hugo Alvarez looked sadly at his son, "I cannot be clear enough to you that you mustn't mess with her, if the intent was strong enough to send you a messenger the likes of Juan Maria de Salvatierra, then you must obey Jorge. You know who he was? Do you?"

Jorge stood, moved towards where his father was sitting, and poured himself another tequila. "Yes Father, I do. I know that he was the Apostle of California. I've done a little research, but mostly I know what we learned about him in school. Jesuit Priest, from Italy I think, settled on the Baja California and preached the word of God his whole life. From what I understand he died in the Church quarters. Totally devoted to God. A true servant."

"Exactly my son, yes, and he was powerful. Very powerful and connected, in Italy and here in Mexico. His family was well to do. His time was the 1600's, I believe that he basically ran away to become a Priest." Hugo was impressed that his son remembered the basics and had taken the time to learn what he could on the impressive visitor that he claimed to have had. He was concerned as well, for if it was true that his son had encountered a spiritual visitor the likes of Juan Maria de Salvatierra, then Hugo had to assume that the woman that he had fallen in love with, was exceptionally important.

CHAPTER 52

Rohan enjoyed the new alliance with Nigel. He felt stronger as a man, and believed his tutoring was genuinely helping his new friend. He was grateful that the bullying had stopped, feeling more secure and less anxious now.

He approached the end of his final year of high school, preparing for exams and applying to Universities. Contact with his family had been eliminated; with the exception of a letter from his father once in a while. News of his mother was positive, her release from the hospital forthcoming. Rohan was elated that she was finally well enough to return home, to the comfort that she knew and created for all the family.

The country was changing, Indians felt the pressures of ensuing unrest. In 1974, the Allahabad High Court, found Indira Gandhi, the first female Prime Minister guilty of misusing government machinery for election purposes. She had not won the popular vote, she had manipulated it.

Opposition parties conducted nationwide strikes and protests demanding her immediate resignation. Various political parties termed Gandhi's rule a dictatorship; leading strikes across India that paralyzed its economy and administration, Jaya Prakash Narayan; an independence activist called for the Army to oust Gandhi from rule.

In 1975, Gandhi advised acting President Fakhruddin Ali Ahmed, to declare a state of emergency under the constitution, which allowed the central government to assume sweeping powers to defend law and order of the great nation. Explaining to the President, the breakdown of law and order and threat to national security as her primary reasons, Gandhi suspended many civil liberties and postponed elections on national and state levels. Non-Congress governments in Indian states were dismissed, and a thousand opposition political leaders and activists were imprisoned. A program of compulsory birth control was introduced. Strikes and public protests were outlawed in all forms.

India's economy benefited from an end to paralyzing strikes and political disorder. India followed by announcing a twenty-pointe program which enhanced agricultural and industrial production, increasing national growth, productivity and job growth. Many organizers of government and many Congress politicians were accused of corruption and authoritarian conduct. Police officers were accused of arresting and torturing innocent people. Indira's son and political advisor, Sanjay Gandhi was accused of committing gross excesses. Sanjay was blamed for the acts of the Health Ministry; carrying out forced vasectomies of men and sterilization of women as a part of the initiative to control population growth. And for the demolition of slums in Delhi near the Turkmen Gate, which left thousands of people dead and many more displaced.

Indira Gandhi's Congress Party called for general elections in 1977, only to suffer a humiliating electoral defeat at the hands of the Janata Party, an amalgamation of opposition parties. The leader of the Janata became the first non-Congress Prime Minister of India. This new Prime Ministers administration established tribunals to investigate emergency-era abuses, and Indira and Sanjay Gandhi were arrested after a report from the Shah Commission.

But in 1979, the coalition crumbled, and Charan Singh formed an interim government. The ruling Janata party had become intensely unpopular due to its internecine warfare, and a perceived lack of leadership on solving India's serious economic and social problems. Indira Gandhi was quietly planning a return to power, she would overcome the shame she had once faced, and would once again rule the six hundred and eighty-three million people who worked the lands of her heritage.

Rohan being a scholar was acutely aware of the potential consequences of a prolonged stay in his beloved India. With the population continuing to grow exponentially he viewed his potential opportunity in his volatile homeland to be limited. He thought back to a time when his brother, had suggested moving to New York. The United States of America, the land of opportunity and Disney Theme Parks.

Instinctively he knew that he would need to escape to survive and to thrive in his chosen career. By faith he would continue his studies, and once completed, he would fly over the vast and expansive ocean to where he believed he could best serve the Lord.

CHAPTER 53

Hugo Fromm was sad to see his son leave the ranch. They had enjoyed tequila together along with similar stories of incredible visitors. Late day meals had been enjoyed in the warm night air, on the patio overlooking glorious sunsets.

He worried about Jorge, just as he worried about his other boys. Jorge though was a lone soldier, defiant and introverted. Hugo saw in Jorge much of what he himself had been as a young man. A strong soldier; loyal and dedicated to the cause. What differed between the two men however was Hugo's resignation to the message he had received from Mary Mack. He succumbed, he surrendered, and he altered his path. He worried that his son was not able to let go of the woman he had fallen so deeply for. Concern bread in his thoughts of Juan Maria de Salvatierra, the implications of Jorge's quest to find her husband, and the consequences that may result.

Hugo had said good bye to Jorge on the morning that he left for Louisiana, hugging him tightly he reminded his son of Juan's message to cease and desist. "Please be aware that the message bears a heavy load. Don't look the other way son, thinking that you can change the world on your own.

There are plenty of women in the world, many of whom would be thrilled to pair with you."

Jorge smiled at his father. "Thank you, father, I appreciate your compassion, this trip has been amazing. I fear that you don't understand me completely however. I cannot let her go. I can't. It's impossible. I have tried and have been unsuccessful. She imprinted on my soul. I fell hard because she and I were meant to be together; she is my soul mate."

"Jorge, how can you be certain? The finding of a soul mate doesn't include so much pain, so much suffering. I am afraid that I believe otherwise. I can't agree with you." Hugo held his ground, he had found an immense love and a great passion with Jorge's mother, having never questioned or second guessed the concept of soul mating.

"I know it in my heart. You must understand that father. You have been with mother for so long. You must know that you were meant to be together."

Hugo looked off to the distance, he thought that he saw the image of the little girl that had visited him so many years ago in Germany. A reminder to him that the messages were real, the deliverance of them imperative to the survival of the race. "When I met your mother, I knew that she was the one for me. No question. But there were never so many obstacles in our way. I believe that we had the blessing of the universe. Everything fell into place so easily; our relationship was and always has been effortless."

Jorge decided not to argue with his father. There would be no winning, and he didn't want to board the plane to Louisiana knowing that his last words with his dad had been sour. "Fine, Dad I will find another, happy now?"

Hugo shrugged at his son. Disappointed with his response and able to see through his misleading comment. "No, I'm not happy, because now you are not only a hopeless romantic chasing wild and crazy dreams, you are a liar as well."

CHAPTER 54

Winter fell, and subsequently Christmas arrived again in Canada with a full bounty of snow and freezing temperatures. She was feeling well about Her headaches that had disappeared, the absence of Her tumor, and about the rigorous testing that had been completed. She was thrilled that Her mother had determined special placement was not in either Hers nor Her brothers' best interest. She would remain in the same school to which she had transferred to upon their return from Mexico. She would maintain Her same routine, limiting the amount of change that she would be exposed to. Change was of course uncomfortable, and therefore, unwelcome.

Her grandfather was becoming more and more tired, the color of his skin seeming to be more and more grey. His eyes looked weathered, his speech was deliberate and often yielding messages. She knew his time was drawing near. She approached Her mother with a head full of questions.

"Mother, is grandfather going to be okay? He doesn't look well to me."

Madam chose her words carefully, not wanting to alarm her child. Madam also had seen him deteriorating, his strength and energy fading, his need for rest increasing. She had watched while he napped on the couch, his breathing laboured, raspy and profound. "I hope so Sweet-heart, I really hope so."

Days were passing by, she was growing and maturing as most young girls do. Her burdens were however much heavier than most children Her age. She was aware of the implications of Her grandfather's failing health, she was preparing Herself for the inevitable. He seemed so old to Her of late, with his diminished color and need for sleep. He had not so long ago, been a vibrant and exuberant soul, his spirit never wavering, a desire for help never apparent. He now seemed to Her to be smaller, his physical weakness making him appear frail.

She dove into Her studies, and into Her training time with Mary Mack. She used academics and theology as distractions from Her reality. Visitors came needing attention, and assistance with crossing into their new realm.

She happily, but cautiously helped them to accept their destinies. She continued to evolve.

One morning as She was preparing Herself for school, a spirit appeared to Her that She had seen before. This was the first time that a soul had returned, to Her it was alarming and slightly unsettling.

With a smile on Her face She inquired. "Hello, I remember you, how can I help?"

The spirit smiled at Her, beautiful colors radiating from the core of the spirit, shades of gold and orange, with splashes of fuchsia; She suddenly remembered who the woman was. "Hello Dear, how have you been?"

The old woman who had lived under the stairs when She was a child; was no longer dark and scary, she was beautiful, shiny and full of love. "I've missed you! I've missed our meetings, our talks, your direction. I am doing fine."

The old woman looked at Her, reaching forward to touch Her hair. "You have grown, you are incredibly beautiful. The Lord has done well."

She relaxed with the woman's touch. Her hands stroking Her hair without making actual physical contact. "I feel lost most of the time, I don't understand why I am different, why things happen to me differently than to others. I spend a lot of time frustrated and confused. I would prefer if the Lord would just tell me why I am here. I have searched for answers, but I am afraid that I have none."

"Do you remember a time, when you were very young.... I told you that you would love many but hold few?"

She nodded before speaking, "Yes of course I remember. I was just little, I think I was still wearing my breastplate for protection back then."

The woman couldn't contain herself, a song of her laughter filled the room. "Yes, you were indeed, and you had those little foil covered Easter Eggs in your basket that you shared with me."

"Yes, you're right, I did. I thought that if I shared with you, you might be more accepting of me. It was a peace offering."

"It was, and I did accept. It was all part of your training. From the very beginning we have been protecting and preparing you. Your heart is clean, you are doing well."

"Can you tell me why I am here?"

"No, I cannot. I am not able to share with you that information. You will do wonders. Achieve much and care for many. I cannot tell you much more."

"My grandfather? Is he near his end?"

The old woman reached into the pocket of her cardigan sweater, in it was a foil covered Easter egg from years past. She took it out of the pocket and held her hand out towards Her, a momentous gesture that bore a profound message. "Would you like this one, this is the last of what I have, this is all that I have left; but I will give it to you, because I think that you need it more than I."

She looked at the woman, tears spilling down Her cheeks, she understood. She accepted the Easter egg, and that her grandfather had shared his life for Her; knowing that She needed Hers more than he needed his. She carefully peeled the foil from the egg and placed the milk chocolate form on Her tongue, closed Her eyes and gave thanks. The smooth and creamy texture was pleasing to Her. "Thank you for coming to me today. I appreciate your honesty. I will begin to prepare for his departure."

She returned to brushing Her auburn hair and wondered how She would tell Her mother.

CHAPTER 55

Jorge landed in New Orleans with no plan, no formal intent or reason to be there. He was hunting for purpose, searching for reason, looking for answers. He managed his way effortlessly through customs and immigration and left the airport terminal hopeful.

He checked into his hotel, which he had reserved ahead of time, dropped his bag on the king-sized bed in his more than adequate room, and set off on foot, unsure for what he was seeking. He walked aimlessly until he suddenly felt a need for nourishment.

He saw across the street a subtle sign, inviting him to cross. "Café du Monde", with its emerald green and white striped awnings enticing visitors and locals to enter since 1862. The French Market coffee stand was serving powdered sugar-capped beignets, French doughnuts. Jorge had a soft spot for a sugar doughnut and thought it would be best served with their chicory-blended coffee. He took his sweet treat and java in his hand, embarking on his walk down the river banks of the mighty Mississippi. He marveled in the taste, as the powdered sugar melted on his tongue, and the smooth and rich taste of the coffee in luxurious contrast with the doughnut.

He meandered the French Quarter and immersed himself in thought. He was determined to find Madam's husband, but wasn't sure why, or what he would do if he did find him. He had no idea what he wanted to say, confirming that there was no purpose to the trip.

He had never smoked, devoting his life to his health, fitness and nutrition. But as he walked he craved the smell, the sensation that he believed to be so unbecoming. It was the one thing about Madam that he found disturbing, and uninteresting. He vowed to himself that he would help her to give up her desire for the cigarettes that did nothing but harm her. He had good intentions and would do everything he could to change that one thing about her.

Jorge turned the corner and approached a cemetery. The entrance gates were unlocked, begging him to enter. He pushed open the heavy black wrought iron barrier and pushed his way into the burial ground. Antique tombstones and articulate limestone and marble grave markers flanked the daunting walkways. The hair on Jorge's arms stood up, his skin felt a chill.

A brisk air blew past him, his head turned from left to right, looking for the cause of the sudden change in temperature. He saw nothing.

Juan watched Jorge from behind a tree, his arms crossed tightly in front of his chest. Once again, he donned his formal robes and cassock, with sandals. His hair flowing freely, long and grey. He was disappointed in Jorge, he had been certain that the young Police Chief had heard and understood his message. He was clear and concise on his delivery and was surprised by the determination of the man with the wounded heart.

Juan Maria de Salvatierra stirred the wind once again, alerting Jorge to his presence in the cemetery. The young officer looked behind him, catching a glimpse of Juan lurking in a shadow behind the tree. He saw long white robes, and a man with long hair and a beard.

He turned quickly and started walking towards where the man stood. His pace quick, a near jog, crushed gravel that covered the walkway crunched under his feet. In his haste and instinctual need to contact the man in the robes, he tripped over a marker on a freshly lain plot. Jorge tumbled recklessly to the ground, his knee smashing on the gravestone. Pain surged up through his leg and into his hip. His hands scraped and bleeding, thrust to his lower limb, holding the joint that had cracked on the marble slab.

Juan watched him, chuckled to himself, and then vanished. His work was done. He was quite sure that Jorge had recognized him, and if not, he was now questioning himself and his decisions.

Jorge stood, grimacing as he put weight on his injured leg. He was drawn to the area behind the tree, which now bear nothing but blue sky, green grass, and rows of tombstones. He turned on his heel, thinking in his fall he had altered his direction. His eyes searched the landscape for the man in the robes and saw nothing.

He moved on, again uncertain of his direction. Unclear of his purpose. The tree continued to call out to him, its hanging branches lush with green leaves, full and robust in its breadth. He lowered himself to the ground, after making his way to it, and sat in the grass leaning himself against the trunk of the magnificent creature protruding from the ground. He closed his eyes for a moment, only to see her face, and hear her laughter. He imagined the alluring scent of her, her soft lips and her tousled curly dark hair.

His body ached, his leg was throbbing from his fall. He kept his eyes closed, slowing beginning to drift into a subtle slumber. With his thoughts still focused on Madam, and his consciousness slipping from his grip, he heard a discernable voice.

"You mustn't pursue her. You have already been warned, contact with her would be disastrous and mustn't happen. He is not pleased with your actions."

Jorge remained still, his eyes still closed but his body acutely alert. He shouted to the sky, only hoping to be heard. "I am not pursuing her, I seek revenge on her behalf. In her name I will claim vengeance and destroy the beast that drove her from me."

It was quiet for some time. Jorge listened to the rustling of the leaves on the trees, and the chirp of birds above him. He waited for a response, but nothing came. Eventually, as the pain in his leg began to subside, he drifted off to sleep, with a prayer on his lips and anger in his heart.

CHAPTER 56

Madam continued to fear for her father's health. She stressed about the children's placement in school and worried about her husband seeking the three of them out.

The gravity of being a single parent was weighing on her, when her mother approached one Sunday morning after a scheduled visit to a routine church service.

"Darling, I'm worried, you seem on edge, and are rather withdrawn."

"I'm fine mother, I just have a lot on my mind. I am struggling with my load at work, and I'm terribly concerned for Dad."

Her mother touched her daughter's hair. The long dark locks in profound contrast to her own smooth blonde bob. She looked deeply into the dark brown eyes of her child and wanted for her to be settled, content and free of burdens.

"I am worried as well, but I am also concerned for you. Your father will be fine honey, he too has stress at work. I'm sure that's all this is. Just stress. He is strong, there's nothing to worry about."

Madam reached up and touched her mother's hand as it stroked her own hair. Her mother's hand was soft, the skin lightly fragranced from her hand lotion. Her nails expertly manicured, she was to Madam an icon of parenthood. "I wish you would make him go to the doctor, he's getting so thin, and he sleeps too much."

"I do agree with you there. But he's stubborn, you know that. It's always a challenge to get him even to go for a basic annual physical, which he just had a few weeks ago. I am certain that he's fine, otherwise we would have heard from the doctor."

"Okay then." Madam wasn't convinced, "I guess I am worrying about nothing."

"Not nothing Dear, but don't stress about things that we cannot change. It won't make any of it better and in the end the only change will be a loss of sleep and some weight. Of which my Darling, you cannot stand to lose. You too are becoming far too thin yourself."

Madam brushed her hands over her hips, she could feel bones protruding slightly from beneath her skirt. "A little too thin, I agree Mother. But I eat, it's not like I have given up on that."

Her mother sat, making herself comfortable in a chair by the kitchen table. "You need a rest; maybe you should go on a vacation. The children will be fine with your father and me. Take some time to relax, you have been through so much. Find some sunshine to knock the alabaster off your skin. I miss seeing you with some color."

She contemplated the idea of a break from reality. "Maybe I should, I don't know Mom, where would I go? And alone? I would feel awkward."

Her mother retaliated. "Don't be silly. You are a grown woman. There would be no reason to feel silly, or awkward. People travel all the time. You know you could go to Puerto Vallarta, see some of your friends. Enjoy the heat and get some much-needed rest."

Madam's thoughts immediately drew to Jorge. The idea of seeing him was very appealing to her. "I guess I could."

"I will pay for it myself Darling if it means that you find some peace."

Madam hugged her mother, nodding. "Okay, I will go. When?"

"There's no time like the present. I would go sooner rather than later if I were you. Take a leave from work. The children will be fine. She is well now, thank God. Go. Book a ticket and get on a plane."

And she did. She contacted her boss the following morning who agreed with her mother. She needed a break. She booked a ticket the next day for a flight to Puerto Vallarta and planned to leave her worries behind, if only for a short time.

CHAPTER 57

Mary Mack and Juan sat unseen, watching as Madam prepared her suitcase for the trip. Both were concerned for potentially hazardous reunions between parties which were not to ever meet again. The risk was great, and both warriors were prepared to intervene.

"Mary Mack, why do you think she wants to return? For what purpose really?" Juan was frustrated with the amount of care that was becoming necessary to protect Her. Disturbances never seemed to cease.

Mary Mack knew, as she hadn't left Her side for years. She saw in Madam a gentle love, and a great passion that had been lost. She knew that Madam was searching for a part of her soul that had been left behind. Mary Mack was aware despite never having a romantic relationship that love cannot be lost and doesn't dissipate due to geography. Mary understood the longing and the need to find him.

"She's in love Juan."

"Well that cannot be. We cannot allow it. You know that, it's not part of the plan. It can't happen; *they* can't happen." Juan looked at Mary Mack, seeking acknowledgement of his statement.

"Mary Mack…you do understand? You understand that Madam cannot be in a relationship with the Police Chief? You understand why?"

Mary Mack nodded, "I do understand Juan, I understand the reasoning. I understand the rules and I understand that we are assigned to protect Her and ensure execution of Her plan. I am sad though, that this cannot be. Her heart will be broken, as his already is."

Juan played with the rope that held his robes at the waist. "He will survive. Trust me, he will get over her eventually. It just cannot happen Mary, and in time she too will find love, elsewhere."

"You know Juan, I really don't think you understand as I do. I have learned a lot from Her, I see love in everything she does, it is genuine and heartwarming. And I feel compassion for Madam. Let's face it, neither one of us has any right commenting on the foundation of romantic love. The very idea of us having an opinion is ludicrous. A young girl, and a Priest? Please. I am hopeful that the plan can be altered. Why can love not win? Why can love not for once come out on top Juan?"

"You know love always wins. Take off the rose-colored glasses for a minute. Love wins, but romantic love is not what we should be talking about. Don't confuse the concept of romance with the principal of love. The two are very different. His love will win. He will be victorious. Love will conquer the darkness that gets in our way. Romance and lust however have no place in Her plan."

Mary Mack decided to back down. "Fine, that's fine Juan. Do what you need to do. I will follow my orders and stay here, with Her. You do whatever type of destruction and intervention that you see fit. I don't want to be a part of it."

Juan looked away from her and swallowed hard before responding. "You know I will now have to report your conduct. You have lost sight of what's important Mary. Your assignment is not to fall in love or help another to do so, your assignment is to protect and train. I would suggest that you do exactly that….and please don't slight me by suggesting that I know nothing of romantic love. Quite the contrary my dear, for I loved so deeply once that I waited for a woman to return for decades. Or have you forgotten?"

Mary Mack was taken by surprise. "I'm Miss Mary Mack, Mack, Mack, all dressed in black, black, black with silver buttons, buttons, buttons, all down my back, back, back. I saw your face, face, face, in that very dark place, place, place, and I wore white, white, white, that starry night, night, night, I did not know, know, know, that your love for me would grow, grow, grow."

Juan held his friend, his confident, his partner on this assignment. The two of them so different, by design they had been brought together with the security of Her in mind. Hundreds of years of planning, and creative implementation of plans had resulted in a profound relationship based on true love. A love provided and cultivated from a shared comprehension and appreciation of the Lord. Juan released the remaining fragments of his secret, "I have loved you from the first moment that I set my eyes on you. Your spirit touched the very core of my soul, reaching to depths never before penetrated. I cannot imagine having lived and not known you. And I would never want to lose you now that we have found each other. I believe that He always wants us to have what we desire, but that sometimes, our desires are unbecoming. In those circumstances, He intervenes. We are from different times Mary, you and I were not meant to be, as Madam and Jorge also cannot."

Mary Mack nodded in agreeance. "I understand now the point of view that you were attempting to have me see.

My heart breaks for Madam, as her love will never be, with time she will heal, her soul mourning from the ordeal, he will move on, a new love he will find at dawn; the Lords message understood, I will protect Her as I should."

Juan stood from where he had been sitting. The hood of his robes, he pulled over his head. "I will go, to ensure that they do not meet again, be brave and move with clarity Mary Mack."

The two prayed together for the success of their mission, for humanity and for Her; and then Juan was gone.

CHAPTER 58

Madam packed a small suitcase, with only necessities in mind. Arrangements had been made for accommodations, with passport in hand she was ready to head south to the exotic land that had been home to her and her children for so long. Butterflies brewed in her stomach as she closed the case that held her belonging required for the week in paradise.

Her thoughts kept returning to Jorge, the notion of seeing him was thrilling and filled her with immense pleasure.

She entered the room, looked at Her mother with the suitcase in her hand, and spoke. "Mother, why do you have to go? I don't think this is a good time for a vacation."

Madam sighed, she had known that the separation, if only for a short time would be difficult for Her. "Sweet-heart, you are going to be fine, Grandma and Grandpa are excited to have some quality time with you, without me being in the way. And it's only for a week."

She wasn't pleased with Her mother's response. "Why though? Why do you have to go? I need you here. And Grandpa, he needs you too."

"Your grandfather is a grown man, he does not need me every second of every day. And you need to start learning a little bit of independence. This will be good for you, you'll see." Madam looked at her wrist watch and bent forward to kiss Her. She had to say her goodbyes if she was going to make her plane.

She was growing angry with Her mother and didn't understand the feeling. She knew anger, she had learned coping skills to apply when the emotion surfaced, but the feeling had never before been directed at Her mother. She fought back tears, for the thought of not being near her, not having her support was daunting. A moment would feel like an eternity, in desperation she muttered. "What if Grandpa dies while you're away?"

Madam's head turned quickly, making eye contact with Her. "What did you say? Why in heavens name would you say something like that?"

She let go of the tears that had been threatening to emerge. She no longer could hold them back, nor the secret that had been harboring in her consciousness for weeks. The message delivered by the old woman was harsh and bore consequence more than She was able to carry. "It's true, I know it to be true, what if something happens while you are gone."

"Listen to me, nothing is going to happen. Everything will be fine. It's only a few days, and although he seems old to you, Grandpa is a young man, and he's very healthy. He runs every day, which gets him more exercise than most people my age can manage. You don't need to worry about this, okay Sweetie? Try to focus on happy thoughts, see the good."

She knew Her mother wasn't going to listen. She knew that she wouldn't understand. She needed comfort, she longed for a different time, when things were complicated; when activity buzzed; and people were scurrying about Her, a time when things were more controlled in the confusion, when things felt manageable. She had been fighting so hard for so long, she wanted nothing more than to be the one going on a vacation. She yearned for Lupita, for her still and understanding nature. "I will try, I'm going to miss you mother."

"I will miss you too, I love you. Be nice to your brother, and do your homework, and don't forget to say your prayers."

She laughed on the inside at this. Absurdity. Her mother had no idea that She was in continual prayer, her mother knew nothing of Mary Mack, or Her visitors. Her mother didn't know that she assisted the dead in their passing, that she was able to see into the souls and minds of the living. That she was able to communicate not only verbally in many languages, but that telepathy was now second nature to Her. Her mother was in the dark. Her mother was simply not as exalted as She. "I will Mother, I promise."

CHAPTER 59

University study was well structured and allowed for the expression of free will. Rohan and Nigel applied themselves, reviewing and writing daily papers, speaking to other students in study hall, and cramming until wee hours of each morning. In the Monastery, they had both learned to apply themselves.

The boys had decided that their college of choice would be the Vidyajyoti College of Theology or commonly known as the 'Light of Knowledge' College, found in Delhi India. The University, an institute and faculty of theology run by the Jesuits. It was started in 1879 in Asansol, West Bengal, as a modest 'Saint Joseph's Seminary'. From 1889 to 1971 it developed in the mountains of Kurseong near Darjeeling where it was renamed Saint Mary's College. From 1972 onwards, it flourished on the campus of the University of Delhi after being relocated.

Theology is the study or understanding of God. It is true that by its transcendence the Divine is beyond the scope of human rational study. There are other roads to contact the Mystery at the root of all existence. Religious sectors within their own belief systems have given testimony to it. The study of religions and supplementary ways in which the concept and the reality of the Divine has impacted human history, forms the specific field of the study of theology. Theology includes the study of the great Scriptures, and the way in which the respective communities have understood their message. For believers of the Christian Faith, the Bible is primary, but the study of Theology does not exclude other Scriptures. Theologians also study religious history of humanity, of our own community and of the multiple expressions for the Divine found in history.

Theology is necessary if religion is to avoid the pitfalls of irrationality and narrow fundamentalism. Rohan found it important to study his own faith by using the gifts of reason and understanding, and the sense of the higher values, which nature, or which God, had given him. Theology is not a rationalization of religion or of faith. It helps faith find its truly human form, flourish and be fruitful within the complexities of life.

Rohan was in heaven. Surrounded by equally minded intellects, loving life and appreciating all that the word of God presented, he flourished.

CHAPTER 60

Madam's flight landed, and she cleared customs and immigration quickly and without incident. Friendly exchanges with immigration officials intrigued her and invited the impression of being home. The heat sweltered outside of the terminal but was welcomed on her skin. Humidity filled the air and made her hair curl immediately. She breathed the air deeply into her lungs. Feeling relieved to be back, and anxious for what the week would hold.

Her taxi dropped her at her hotel, with one simple suitcase she breezed through the check in process and was escorted to her room. The bellman slid the room key into the lock and swung open the door. "Madam, after you."

Madam entered the hotel suite, both appreciative and in awe of the upgrade provided by hotel management. Yellow and red hibiscus blossoms were strewn across the expansive king-sized bed, tempting her to take a nap. A luscious fruit bowl, filled with mangos, guavas, bananas and pears sat on a table in front of the window next to an ice bucket filled with ice and a bottle of Moet & Chandon. Two glasses flanked the bucket, on a pewter tray. Madam tipped the bellman, and bid him adieu, "Gracias, que tengas buen dia!"

"Gracias a ti, Madam, nos hablamos si necessitas algo." He nodded and moved to the door. Madam was comforted knowing that she had arrived safely and that the hotel staff were both accommodating and receptive. With a head full of thoughts and a heart bursting with gratitude, she lay down on the bed, and took her much needed nap.

CHAPTER 61

Louisiana appealed to Her father. He enjoyed the sights, the music, the food and the ladies. He had settled on the New Orleans area for two reasons, he had always wanted to see it, and he had agreed when he left Mexico not to get too far from the border. His services in the United States could be utilized and would be of great benefit to the organization that was determined to protect him.

For many years, he had operated without his wife knowing it. His secret had sometimes weighed heavily on him, but the rewards were so grand he opted not to let it bother him. There was no denying the fact that Madam herself worked hard, and that she provided well for the family. Had she not, he might not have been at liberty to save as much cash as he had.

He had heard many horror stories of men who took brides with looks and no brains. Their abilities to earn not only limited by their gender, but often non-existent due to apathy. A deeply rooted lack of interest in the creating or managing of wealth. Many of these women preferred to be kept in the dark with regards to finances, just so long as they didn't have to work. In replacing a career, they chose the nail salon, the hairdresser, shopping and exercise classes to fill their time. Bearing children and caring for them was a cursory affect and solidified their position within a marriage.

Not his Madam though, she not only made her own money, she managed it. Often questioning his own resources or what she believed to be a lack of resources. Unbeknownst to her, his holdings were all off shore. Safely hidden from her, and from the very organization that kept him employed. He sipped on a mojito and considered his past, his decisions and his potential moving forward. He weighed the risk reward, and there was no question in his mind that he would continue on his same path.

When he had been just a young man, he had escaped his home country to Mexico on a whim. A spontaneous and fulfilling get away that had altered his life path. He chose to accept an offer that had presented and had never returned to Canada, until he met Madam. Her sultry ways, the allure of her was more than he could resist. He had run to her, hiding from those that depended on him for service.

For four gruelling years he had managed to disappear, hiding with her and their children in Canada, always pretending to be something that he was not. It had been difficult for him, always a struggle to engage in and maintain relationships. The idea of friendship was foreign to him, for he trusted no one. Just as he should. He knew by experience that the concept of friendship and trust was something that he could not afford. It was too risky; his safety was contingent on him keeping his secrets.

When Madam had pulled the carpet out from under him, exposing him to the Feds; he had been instructed to disappear for a while, but not to go too far. She had thrown a wrench into his business, making more than just himself upset. Her disregard for discretion had resulted in him spending time in the underground prison of her beloved Police Chief. He was appreciative that those in higher up positions of the organization that employed him, had managed to pull some strings. Pay offs had happened, those who needed to be paid received envelopes of cash in dimly light bars; resulting in his release from the clutches of the Police Chief, without a scratch. Somehow any evidence the

Chief may have had; had been completely destroyed, leaving Jorge Alvarez nothing to support his crazy theories.

Her father found humour in the entirety and complexity of events. He questioned Madam's interest and attraction in the Police Chief, granted he was a good looking, strong man, his earning potential however would be limited by municipal government restrictions. But he honestly didn't care what she did; he would never allow her a divorce. Her upset had resulted in him taking an extended vacation. Eventually he knew that he would be called back, once the dust had settled, and Chief Alvarez had lost interest in his day to day activities.

For now; he was left to his own accord, drinking and abusing the expectations of loose women while he waited anxiously to get back to work. Back to throwing money on his pile, creating for himself a massive wealth that would ensure his own happiness.

CHAPTER 60

She sat in the park, watching a group of girls about Her age. They played on the swings, they raced up the slide and slid down. They played tag; they laughed and had fun. When one of the girls pulled a piece of pink chalk out of her pocket, and drew a hopscotch board on the pavement, she gave in. Resistance to playing a game that she loved was futile.

Mary Mack watched Her from the swings, unseen by anyone, quiet and intense.

"Hi there, can I play with you?"

The girl with the chalk looked up at Her from where she was crouched near the ground. "What's your name?"

She responded, smiling. "Her."

The little girl giggled, "That's a funny name, I'm Kalila, say it like Ka-Ly-la. Simple but extraordinary, just like me."

She thought it strange that someone with an odd name like Kalila would think Her own name was peculiar. "Hi Kalila, is it okay if I play with you?"

Kalila looked at the others in her squad, all neatly dressed, some in Mary Janes, others in sneakers, the group nodded. "Are you any good?"

"Well yes of course, I'm well practiced, and I know all of the history of hopscotch as well, I would be quite happy to share with you, if you are interested in expanding your mind."

Kalila frowned at Her. "Look here's how it works, I always win. You do not. So, the correct answer would have been, 'no, I suck at hopscotch, but I would love to try.' I don't care about the history cuz I'm making history right here, right now. If you understand my rules, then you can play."

She thought for a moment before responding. "Why do you always win? That's not playing together; that's a sort of dictatorship. That's not fair to anyone. I should have the same opportunities as everyone, do you girls always let her win?" She looked towards the rest of the squad, who were all shocked at Her reaction to Kalila's rules. A couple of the girls looked at the ground, the rest looked away. And although they had not verbally answered Her, she was able to discern their response through their actions.

Kalila was also taken aback, not certain where to go next, she instinctively reacted. "I win because I am the leader of this group! That's just how it is. If you want to play, then you play by my rules."

She took a step back, looked to Her left and saw Mary Mack standing near. She found comfort and strength in having Mary Mack close for support. "I want to play but I won't let you win. If you win fairly then I will accept that you are leader of the squad, if I win, then I get to be the new leader." She swallowed hard, uncertain what Kalila's reaction would be to Her challenge, and almost definite that She had made a mistake. She had thrown caution to the wind, exploring Her own strengths and Her desire to be accepted.

Kalila took a hair elastic from her wrist, reached up and pulled her dark hair into a ponytail. She stood, brushing her hands off on her jeans. "Fine, let's do it. But if you don't win, you're out. You don't get to be part of my squad at all. I can't risk having any type of revolution behind my back."

"Okay, I can live with that." She looked at the ground around Her, searching, and picked up a stone. She looked over to Mary Mack who was smiling at Her. She was nervous but felt confident that She could win. If She won, she would suddenly be the leader of a squad of girls. She had never had a close friend other than Mary Mack; friendships were an abstract idea. She wasn't clear as to what the leader of a squad was to do.

She had spent an unprecedented amount of time playing alone, as a girl of nearly twelve now, she was treading on ground that was unfamiliar; panic brewed in Her chest, stirring butterflies in Her stomach. She moved closer to the court, eying home base. She felt a faint brush of air touch Her skin. She looked to where Mary Mack had been standing; Mary was gone.

She heard Mary Mack's voice run through Her mind; *"For you, this will be a breeze, toss your stone and skip the court with ease."*

She took a deep breath and set on to win. For Her, this interaction could change everything she had come to understand about Herself, about friends, about values, and about competition. She had to be victorious or she would forever be stuck in the house with Mary Mack, who although was Her best friend, kept Her stuck in a place that she wanted to leave. She called it Solitude. And she filed it away in Her green box, for it had provided Her immense growth and understanding of the human character, through meditation and prayer, but there was still room for Her to grow further in different areas that she hadn't explored yet. It was Her time now to grow into Herself, to learn expression, and to nurture friendships. Green, for she had always envied the very girls that may allow Her now to be a part of their squad, green because she was totally new to the idea of camaraderie.

The two girls executed 'rock, paper, scissors' to determine first stone; Kalila won. Kalila's stone was placed on the first square, she skipped through the court with the edge of a highly seasoned performer. Kalila smiled at Her, "See how easy it is? Any lame butt can do it...or at least hope to. Let's see you Her, it's your turn."

The girls took turns tossing, hopping and skipping. She remembered the day that Mary Mack had come to play with Her. So long ago now it seemed as though it hadn't happened. She had learned the craft of hopscotch and had mastered it by playing every day. For three years She tossed and skipped at lunch time, having no one but Herself to talk to, no one but Mary Mack to play with.

Kalila tossed her stone towards home base, the smooth grey rock sliding just outside of the chalk drawn lines. Her face took on a contorted look, twisted and maligned. Her cocky smile disappeared, the sarcasm now quieted by intense anticipation. Kalila had overthrown the half circle at the perimeter of the court.

She stood at the end of the court, her red Chuck Taylors, tightly laced around Her tiny feet, she remained behind the line that clearly marked the start of the court. She closed Her eyes, silently praying for an outcome that would be pleasing to the Lord. She didn't pray to win, nor did she ask for favor. It would have been wrong to request that an opponent lose just to gain advantage, so she did not. Her palms were sweaty, and Her stomach felt a little ill at ease. She contemplated what Her new life would be like, being the leader of the squad, and having real friends. Friends that everyone could see, friends that could sleep over, friends that she could laugh with and play Monopoly with. She thought of Mary Mack and knew that Mary would want this for Her.

She opened Her eyes, placed the stone between Her fingers and Her thumb, and lightly tossed it towards home base. In the second that the piece of rock was in the air, it seemed to Her that time slowed down. The stone flew in slow motion, turning and flipping as it vaulted towards the other end of the chalk drawn hopscotch court.

The other girls looked on, their eyes glued to the court. The stone hit the ground and all of them gasped. It landed dead center in the middle of home base. She had won.

In that instant, she felt elated, she had utilized expertise, previously gifted to Her by Mary Mack. The knowledge had benefited Her; leaving Her victorious. She swallowed and lifted Her eyes to Kalila.

"I'm sorry." She felt grateful to have won, but guilty that She would be taking the place of the squad's leader.

Kalila smiled at Her. "Don't be, you won fair and square. You're cool." Kalila removed a necklace that she had around her neck. "Here, this is the leader ribbon. You must wear it all the time and lead us with honour and integrity."

She was taken aback at the forwardness of Kalila. She shook Her head. "No, I will not do that to you. You are the leader of this squad. Your girls don't even know me. You are the best to lead. You keep it. Keep the necklace, I would like to be part of your group though. If I can, I just live over there." She pointed towards Her house. "If you don't mind that is."

Kalila reached forward and took Her hand. "Are you sure? Because you did win. I will step down."

She nodded. "Yes, I'm sure. If I can hang out with you and stuff, then it's okay, you can still be leader. But I want to be YOUR sidekick, your best friend."

Kalila thought it through, she nodded at Her. "Yup, that works, I have never had a best friend, so this might be cool. I like you. You've got a good vibe about you."

She looked over at Mary Mack, sitting near the swing set. She smiled at her confidant who was smiling and nodding at Her.

Mary Mack was pleased, pleased that she had applied the physical properties of Her training, and had won the challenge; and ecstatic that she had applied the intellectual and spiritual lessons of hopscotch as well. In daring Kalila to the game, she had staked Her ground establishing Her place. She had managed not only to win, but she had been gracious and forgiving in Her victory. She had shown compassion to Her opponent, a quality very rarely found in young women.

However, Mary Mack also found herself melancholy, for in Her victory on the court she found happiness and fulfillment with the squad. She had a new best friend, leaving Mary Mack once again on her own, watching from the sidelines. A warrior for the Lord, seeking nothing more than to be a girl again herself.

CHAPTER 63

Madam rose from her siesta, put on a bikini and
headed to the beach. She planned to spend a few days
sunning herself and relaxing before she might find the
courage to endeavor on her mission. Finally, she showered
and chose a simple white dress. She wasn't pleased that it
hung a little loose. The stress had taken its toll, and she was
just like many thoughts; too thin.

She stood in front of the mirror and put on some
lipstick, mascara, and thought how frightfully pale she
appeared to be. Instead of the white dress, she switched to a
black one covered in small rose buds. She would save the
white for later in the trip, once the sun had kissed and
toasted her skin to a slightly darker shade of golden brown.

As she waited for the cab to take her into town,
Madam reminisced to a time when she was very young, and

exceptionally naive. She had met her husband when she was on a spring getaway to Mexico. Reading week for all Universities drove students and the likes to hot destinations. They had met in a nightclub, she had had too much tequila and was like the rest of the patrons, dancing on tabletops. When he entered the room, she was immediately drawn to him, he was handsome, charismatic and suave. He was also 13 years her senior. She had fallen into a whirlwind of activity with him; dinners, sailing trips, shopping expeditions. When at the end of her week-long vacation he had asked her to wed, she jumped in; anticipating that the lifestyle would continue.

Wedding planning had happened at the same pace as their romance, fast and furiously Madam's mother had put it all together. Securing the best venues, buying the grandest dress and inviting all the necessary people. By the time she had found out that he was a fraud, she believed herself to be in the mix of it too deeply. Shame overcame her thoughts when she had realized that it had been greed that had drawn her to him. Greed that was her own. Greed that made her feel ugly. Greed that separated her from God.

They were only moments into the marriage when she had uncovered the validity of his complex and vile character, and it was then that she felt that the keys to her cage had been thrown away. She was trapped. In chains and shackles, she dismayed.

"Madam? Excuse me Madam? Your cab is here." The bellman hated to interrupt her thoughts, she was strikingly beautiful and poised. Regal in her mannerisms.

She acknowledged him. "I'm so sorry, thank you."

"You're welcome Madam, have a nice evening."

Madam instructed the cab driver as to her destination as they headed out of the resort complex. She watched the buildings passing by her window from the rear seat of the small cab and became quite moved by the scenic views and colorful flora. Bougainvillea's flanked the roadway in colors of bright pink and salmon. The air to her smelled humid, and salty.

When they arrived at the destination, the cab driver turned to her, "Here we are Madam, that will be fifty pesos please."

She took a deep breath, uncertain of what would be waiting for her. "Would you mind waiting? Just for five moments, please. I will then need to go into el Centro."

He nodded in acknowledgment. "Sure thing. No problem at all." He turned off the engine and turned up the radio.

Madam entered the building, dark and dingy. The floors were barren, the cement walls had been erected from cinder blocks on the solid dirt ground. A man sat behind a small desk, his glasses grimy and held together at the nose bridge with masking tape. His dark hair was neatly combed, parted on the left side. A short-sleeved shirt with tiny pinstripes and sweat stains, held a pocket protector filled with pens. She was amused.

"Good evening, Madam, what can I do for you?"

"Good evening, I hope that I have come to the right place, quite some time ago, I had a cabbie take me to the airport, his car was number 3447, I didn't get his name, but as it turned out, I was in quite a bind, and he was not able to make change."

"I see, how long ago? How many years ago would this have been?" He tapped his pen on the pad of paper in front of him.

"Well, it's been a while, I am guessing that it's been five, maybe six years."

"And what brings you to us?"

She looked at the man that was in charge of the dispatch office. She strained in the dark to see his name on his tag but wasn't able to make it out. "I would like to pay him his fare."

The man with the pocket protector shook his head. "You come back five years later, and you want to pay a fare that was not paid?"

She nodded. "Yes, exactly."

"You crazy or something Lady? Nobody does that. You just take the charity and go. Move on."

"That's not who I am. I would really like to find him."

"I dunno if he would even be in town still. You didn't get a name?" He rubbed his hands through his hair. Madam shook her head no. "Do you remember what day? And the time? Maybe I can look through the logs...but it's going to take some time, you know, and I can't guarantee anything. But if you know, it was worth it for me, I could at least look."

Madam was very aware of what he needed. "And what exactly would make it worth it to you? Hmm? How about an American fifty?"

"If you can make it a hundred, I'll be finding the time to look into it tonight." Madam nodded at him, he continued. "What hotel you staying at lady? I can have him contact you when I find him."

"I'm staying at the Westin, but, I prefer to maintain my privacy. Why don't you call me, here's my number?" She wrote her cell number on his pad of paper and slid it back towards him.

"Okay lady. Buena's nochas, I call you as soon as I find something."

Madam turned and walked out of the building and back to the waiting cab. She told the driver her next destination as he lowered the music. He asked her if everything was okay, and then they were off.

CHAPTER 64

Rohan worried not about the intricacies of relationships, he focused his time and effort on his studies and prayer time. Nigel however felt differently, he thrived on interaction with others. For Nigel, idle talk was a manner in which to recharge his soul battery. He became energized and enlightened through conversation.

University life was proving to be quite enjoyable for both of them, each one of the two had eased into the culture without difficulty or hesitation. Roh observed his friend, who had originally started as a foe when they were just young boys. He was aware that he could benefit from Nigel's easiness around people but was always reluctant to engage himself. He watched how Nigel talked to people, he surveyed how Nigel approached them, and how he listened to them. He exuded a confidence with people that drew them to him and kept them close. Rohan believed this to be one of the greatest qualities Nigel had. Listening. He wondered how many people could actually do it well. From his own experiences; he believed that most people preferred to do the speaking. Preferred to lead interaction themselves drawing attention to their own triumphs and woes. He took note of the necessity of compassion in their chosen fields of work. The priesthood would for sure prove to be a role of leadership and public speaking, but also required would be Nigel's gift for hearing people. He vowed to master the craft himself. Instinctively knowing that one day he would need to use it. For many are called, but only a few are chosen.

CHAPTER 65

Jorge Alvarez had been hunting Madam's husband for three days and virtually had no leads. He had exhausted all the original tidbits of information that he had gathered, nothing had resulted in finding him. He was on the verge of giving up, he would return to Mexico, return to work and try to forget about the entire lot of it. Frustration brewed in him. His belly filled with anger and loathing for the man.

He entered a small pub, bearing bright neon signs on the store front. Inside was dingy and smelled of moth balls. He sat at the bar and ordered a beer, hoping to cool his mood with the crisp and clean ale. He sucked the foam from the top of the poured beverage, paid the bartender, and thought about his father. His father had been correct, and he should have returned home. The expedition was futile, a hunt for a man that may be innocent. He really didn't know why he was even in Louisiana. He questioned his own motives and wondered how he had gotten so far from home. So far from what was real, and who he was.

His brief interlude with Madam had resulted in months which lead to years of unrest, and a feeling that he sought revenge from a man that he barely knew. She had so magically hypnotized him. The concept of having her for his own was all that he could think about. And he hadn't seen her in many years now.

He sat sipping his beer and watching the news on an overhead television. Between clips the screen faded to dark, a reflection in the darkness provoked him to turn around. He stood quickly from his bar stool and ran towards the door, leaving his jacket and phone on top of the bar.

CHAPTER 66

She completed the list of words provided to Her by
Her teacher, with ease. Spelling tests for Her were a chance
to relax. She need not think about the spelling of words in the
English or Spanish languages, French for Her too; had
become second nature. The complexity of letters and sounds
were only difficult, she thought, if one didn't listen to the
manner in which they were being delivered.

She aced her spelling test and then headed outside
with the other children of the class. She had come to enjoy
recess, using the time wisely for observation and reflection.
She watched the other children as they mingled, their short-
lived fights, and disagreements were entertaining and
provided subtle insight into human interaction.

The joyful play that also occurred was intriguing to
Her on many levels. The flirting and mockery that she

believed was unnecessary and yet it happened in many circumstances, between the boys, between the girls, and also between the boys and girls. She was aware that this was the beginning of courtship, but it saddened Her that both genders found it necessary to start so young.

For Herself, she imagined being alone for a long time. She wasn't certain why she felt so strongly about this, but without question she would not engage in any type of relationship with a person of the opposite sex. She needed them not as friends or companions. She was independent and was comfortable with that. She watched one of the girls across the playground flipping her hair and laughing while the boys played tetherball. It seemed ridiculous to Her. So unnatural and in no way genuine. She hoped that the boy saw through the white knee highs and bouncy hair. She hoped for him that he would overcome her restrained advances and see through her. The girl was not authentic. She was playing a game, acting a part. She was willfully seducing an ignorant, but hormone filled mind with nuances of her sexuality. Totally fake ones, but none the less this girl was playing him.

She saw Her mother, in many ways similar to the young flirtatious girl that was Her classmate. She perceived Her mother's misgivings as weakness. She knew, even though it had never been announced, that Her mother fancied a man in her life. She watched Her mother as she ate less and less, hopeful to lose weight. She presumed from this action that Her mother was desirous of eventually attracting another man. She wondered why.

With the absence of Her father in Her life now, she questioned the necessity of the male female relationship. Her father had disappeared, having no contact with either Her or Her brother. They knew not where he was, or of what he was up to. She had grown to be fine with that. She understood now that his time was needed elsewhere, and that to him both she and Her brother had been an obstacle to his success and happiness.

She found the essence of a romantic relationship to be a hindrance to one's own personal growth. At least for now. At least while she was attempting to gain understanding of Her own reason for being.

On the other side of the playground, she saw a small group of girls who were smoking, leaning up against the chain link fence, enjoying the fresh spring air, and the numbing sensation of nicotine on their brains. Their hair dyed dark, almost black, their clothing dark and strategically ripped in areas that presented a less than polished look. She had heard someone call their style 'Grunge'. She felt it appropriate.

She laughed silently at them. Then She wondered why they felt that they needed to numb themselves, she wondered what they could need to hide from. How bad could things be that one would choose to alter their appearance and hide their personality behind a filthy cigarette. She laughed to herself again. *"Grunge"*

The taxi cab arrived at the destination that Madam had requested. The driver braked to a stop and then turned to her. "Madam, we are at your requested destination."

"Yes, I see, thank you. Would you wait again please? I'll only be a few moments. I promise." Madam had her hand on the door ready to step out.

The driver turned off the ignition and again turned up the radio. "No problem, I gonna have a little siesta, just nudge me when you are ready okay?"

Madam found the man amusing. "Of course. Muchas gracias."

Madam climbed the short flight of stairs to the entrance. With her hand on the door knob she took a deep breath and then pulled on the door. She wasn't certain how she would be received and was nervous about the unscheduled meeting.

A bell jingled as she stepped through the doorway, alerting the clerk. Madam's eyes darted from left to right, searching for her target. She saw her sitting behind the counter, a romance novel in her left hand, she looked up.

Rosa gasped. "Oh Dios Mio! Madam! It's been so long!" She stood from her wooden stool and moved around the counter to where Madam was standing. Rosa embraced her richly.

"Hola Rosa. How have you been?" Madam asked.

"The same, glory be to God. Madam good heavens; you are a sight for sore eyes." Rosa was beaming with excitement to see the woman that she had helped so long ago.

"Rosa, you look wonderful. How are the children?" Madam chose to be cordial, to engage Rosa in conversation. To show an interest in her life. A life that had at one time shown sacrifice for the benefit of herself. Had Rosa not helped her, she may not have been able to leave Mexico when she did.

"Fine. Fine, the children are growing, most of them in College now. You know how it happens Madam. So quickly they leave us. Alone and grey. I was quite lovely once, now

I'm just a lonely shop keeper. But oh, I love them so! They kept me on my toes for so many years."

"Of course, I understand. Rosa, I have something for you." Madam reached into her handbag and took out an envelope. In it were six one hundred American dollar bills. One for the original one-hundred-dollar bill that Rosa had graciously provided without questioning Madam's need on that day so long ago, and one for each year that had passed since they had seen each other.

Juan Maria de Salvatierra watched from the shadows of the small grocery store where he had once purchased mangos. He couldn't help but smile, touched to his very core by the unselfishness of Madam. Her generosity and appreciation of what had been provided to her was apparent. "*Lord be the blessing in her life.*"

Madam placed the envelope into Rosa's hand, "Madam for goodness sake, what is this?" She pulled open the envelope and a lump rose in her throat, hindering her ability to speak.

"Rosa, it's for you. Not for Raul, not for the children; I want you to have this. For yourself. Buy a dress, and some shoes, a new purse or a lipstick; save some if you feel so inclined. Keep it though for yourself." Madam placed her hand on Rosa's. It was warm, and her skin was leathery from years living under the hot sun.

Rosa responded. "It's too much, I can't take this from you Madam. I would feel obligated to you forever. This isn't right. It's just too much."

Madam decided to take a firm stance. "Rosa, please. You must. You are deserving of this in more ways than you might know. I insist. Really."

Rosa's mind wandered to the magazines that she flipped through regularly, pages and pages of the dresses and make-up that she couldn't afford were so eloquently depicted on pencil thin models. She secretly longed for some of what she had never been able to have and said. "Well, if you insist Madam, then thank you. And bless you woman."

Madam hugged her friend and bid her adieu. She retreated to the cab, nudged her driver and addressed the next stop on their route.

The driver looked at her in the rear-view mirror, "You sure lady? This address is where you want to go?"

Madam turned and looked out the window. "Absolutely. Thank you."

He started the engine again, placed the vehicle in first gear and started off towards the destination that made him nervous for her.

CHAPTER 68

Jorge ran from the bar, believing that he had sighted Her father. He pushed his way through the crowded street, dodging strollers and sidestepping small children. He could see over the heads in front of him, what he believed was the back of the head of his prey.

A marching band was moving down the street, playing the theme song from '2001 a Space Odyssey'. Jorge paused for just a moment thinking of how ironic their choice of music was. It struck him as strange considering his current pursuit of his enemy in the very street that they were playing. He couldn't help but chuckle, as he leapt once again into action.

He pursued the figure that he could only see from behind for what felt like miles. They had moved twenty blocks from the bar, when they finally they arrived at the gates for the cemetery that Jorge had been at just a few days earlier. His knee still bore the bruise from his fall. It was throbbing.

Jorge slowed to a turtle's pace, not wanting to be seen just yet. He was now certain that it was Madam's husband, he wanted to take a moment to prepare what he would say. He had anticipated this moment happening for so long and he had been certain that his search had been futile. Jorge needed catch his breath and to process the idea of finally finding him; he dodged behind a tree to avoid alerting the man. He lost his footing on a jagged edged rock and stumbled forward. Into plain sight.

Madam's husband turned with the noise from the commotion behind him; saw Jorge and stopped moving. He was surprised to see the Police Chief in New Orleans. He stumbled for words. "Well...what do we have here?"

Jorge moved towards where Madam's Husband was now standing. Disappointed with his inability to remain quiet. "Surprise, surprise stranger; we meet again."

"Are you following me Chief?" Madam's husband had lost weight. Jorge could see that he was significantly thinner than he had been when he was released from the jail. So much time had passed Jorge wasn't certain why he was even here now.

"I have been looking for you for quite some time. You are hard to track down."

Madam's husband rubbed his head. "I'm hard to find for a reason Chief, what the hell are you looking for me for?"

"I know what you did. I know who you really are; I need to set some things straight. The feds might not have been able to hold, you, but I can hold you accountable."

"I see. So, you have been looking for me for what? For almost five years now? So, we can chat? Is that what you are hoping to do? Cause if that is what you want, I'm not interested. And I might add; that if anyone should have something to say about what has happened between the two of us Chief, it should be me."

Jorge looked away, shame filtered through his thoughts, he knew deep within his gut that Madam's husband was right about that. He had betrayed the sacred marriage vow by entering into a relationship with her. And even though it was consensual, he should have known better. He did know better. He knew it had been wrong and yet he hadn't been able to help himself. He hadn't been strong enough to resist her.

Juan Maria de Salvatierra watched from the sidelines. Pleased with his accomplishments today. It had been a challenge to have the two men finally cross paths. It had taken quite some time to effectively execute, but this timing now seemed to Juan to be just perfect. Alerting Jorge, having him turn at just the right moment when he sat on the barstool in the dark and dreary watering hole; having the husband pass by the window at just that precise moment. He believed himself to be a master of his trade. He had placed the marching band in Jorge's path, distracting him enough to entice him to re-engage the chase. He had placed the rock under Jorge's foot causing him to stumble. He really had done well. Now he waited while they talked about her. He would whisper in an ear with suggestions if it was necessary. Offering thoughts, never being seen. Suggesting to the intuitive receptors of each brain; allowing for instinctual reactions, gut feelings to manifest.

Jorge responded. "You're right, I should have stayed away from her. You of all people must understand how I couldn't though. You must get it."

Madam's husband shook his head. His grey linen pants hung loosely, draping neatly over his Salvatore Ferragamo oxfords. "Once a long time ago I could have agreed with you, or at least understood. But that was before Madam became Madam. I fell in love with her when she was just her. It was a more; shall we say, simple time. She was young, and innocent. She was forgiving and understanding then; I can't say that I get it no, not the Madam that is now. And you had no right. She was my wife, how dare you, and then chase me around like I deserve to be hunted?"

"You stole from her, you hurt her; you deserve everything that is coming to you." Jorge began to feel enraged.

Juan whispered without being seen into the ear of Madam's husband. *"How does he know that you stole from her?"*

"What do you mean exactly that I stole from her? And even if I did; how would you know that?"

Jorge spoke before thinking. "The blue bag, the one you had at the airport when we arrested you, it was full of Madam's money."

Madam's husband smiled at Jorge. "And so, you came upon this idea...where? How? You believe it was Madam's? That's ludicrous. It was my money that I had saved and planned to give to her. Some detective you are. You should get the facts straight before you speak out Chief."

"No, that's not how it was; I know it to be true; give it up. Stop the lying, it's just you and me now, so it doesn't matter anyway right? She's gone. It was hers. I know it, and you know it. You're going to pay for what you did to her. I'll make you pay."

Her husband laughed out loud. "Oh my, she really has put a spell on you, hasn't she?" He looked at the Police Chief, normally strong and in control, now weak and vulnerable. "Look, Chief, I can see that you think you've fallen in love with her. Obviously. Or you wouldn't be here. The thing is that I'm still married to her, and I won't ever divorce her. Not ever. She knows that. She has always known."

Leaves on the trees rustled in a light breeze that gave only a very brief relief of the stifling heat. Both men were sweating. The blazing sun beating down on them where they spoke.

Jorge responded. "So, what if I do? What if I do love her? So, what? I bet there are a hundred men that would feel the same way if they knew her the way that I do. I can't live without her, I will find a way. I have to have her in my life."

Madam's husband laughed. "Oh, you do? Is that right? Let me tell you something Jorge, you know and understand Madam exactly the way she needs you to know her. She is not what you think. She is full of mystery and secrets. I know, because I fell for her once myself. But forget about having her or keeping her for your own; that will never be. That won't happen. It simply cannot. You can't possess her; no one can. She is like the wind, or the sunlight on your face. When we need it, we crave it, and when it comes to you it feels oh so nice, it's soothing and a delight to your parched and hungry soul, and so you want it to last forever; but it never does. Without it; you sometimes suffer, like we are doing now. In this heat, a cool breeze would be nice right about now. We long for the wind to refresh us; we enjoy the heat on our skin until we can no longer bear it. Madam is just like that Jorge, like the sun that warms us, and the wind that cools us; but she belongs to someone else though Chief, you can't have her. She is more valuable than anyone knows."

He paused, took a pack of Salem's from his pocket, and a silver lighter, and lit one. He held the pack out towards Jorge who shook his head no. "Don't smoke? Look, I get it. I understand what you are feeling. More or less. But forget her. Find someone else Jorge, someone that you can share a life with, or whatever it is that you want. And stay the hell away from me. You've got nothing on me, and you never will. I am completely innocent." He laughed again. "At least where you're concerned. So, tell me how did you find out about the money anyway? Hmmm?"

Jorge started to back away, glad that he had brought his firearm. He should just finish him here and now. Be done with it. He knew that Madam's husband was messing with him. Manipulating the situation to escape, filling Jorge's head with crazy ideas. He put his hand on his gun, resting neatly in the small of his back, held firmly in place by his belt. "You don't know her like I do, she is more than the sun, more than the wind. You never understood her. You never took the time, never gave her the time. You are nuts. You know that? You had her, and you didn't appreciate her. You didn't know what you had." Jorge pulled the weapon from where it sat and held it up towards Her father.

Madam's husband shook his head as he took a long drag on his cigarette. "No Chief, I'm not crazy, I'm a realist. I'm no angel, granted...but I'm not crazy. And if either of us didn't know what we had; it was you Chief. It was you. You have no idea."

Juan continued to watch, entertained, and very interested in the conversation that was unfolding in front of him. He decided to stay on and watch this through to completion. Finding excitement from the interaction. He wondered if he pushed a little harder, would the chief snap? Would he resort to killing the husband? Should he let it happen? He thought not. He saw no benefit in allowing the Chief to carry such a burden.

Juan moved forward, unseen, next to Jorge and whispered in his ear. *"Walk away from the trash, leave it on the curb for someone else to deal with, it's only a matter of time until someone else takes it out. No point in putting your life at risk."*

Jorge turned on his heal, looking back at Madam's husband, he said. "No, you are one crazy assed bastard. But you're not worth me risking my life, or my career for." Jorge returned his pistol to his belt in the small of his back. The fabric of his shirt damp with sweat.

Madam's husband called at him as he walked away. "So, I'll be seeing you around then? Hey Chief? I'll catch you later?"

Jorge walked towards the gates of the cemetery looking down at the tombstones and grave markers as he made his way. He saw names, and dates, none of which had any meaning to him, but he was aware that all of them had meant something to someone; at some time. They were all important people, they all deserved being remembered and cherished; he presumed that they had all been madly loved at one time, as he was now in love with Madam. Each one of them had lived a life that unfolded, exciting and theatrical, serene and plentiful. One day something occurred in each of their lives turning a page in their story; and then their time had ended. And so, these stones, bearing their names, were what was left of what had once been.

Jorge walked on, replaying the words of Madam's husband in his mind, searching for meaning, searching for the reason. He didn't understand. That much he knew for sure. He was in the dark. He really didn't know her; not like he had once thought that he did. He didn't understand why her husband continued to hang on to her. He might never grasp why he refused to divorce her. And he knew for sure that he didn't understand the blue bag, the old smelly knap sack, Juan Maria de Salvatierra, and why Madam had married her husband in the first place. He was still in love with her, that he was not able to change. He knew clearly now however; that his time, with Madam; was finished.

She sat with Kalila on the couch in the basement of her grandparent's comfortable home. Her mother was still away on vacation and had not had the good fortune of meeting Her new best friend yet. She knew though, that Her mother was going to be very happy for Her.

The two girls, as it turned out had many things in common. Both had parents who were divorced or in the middle of divorce proceedings. Both had a brother, both were seasoned hopscotch players, and both loved to watch movies on the television. They liked similar foods, Kalila was being raised a vegan, to which many choices were in alignment with the dietary restrictions placed on Her.

Kalila's dark hair was cut in a shoulder length bob, with fringe bangs. Her blue eyes expertly framed by the shape of her haircut. Her vocabulary and intellect like Hers were vast, lending to interesting and elevated conversations.

"How long do you think it would take you to travel around the earth in a hot air balloon?" Kalila looked at Her.

She was not certain, and so thought for a moment. "I do not have any idea. I bet you could do it in a week? Maybe more. I dunno."

"It would be a challenge for sure. I wonder how many stops you would need to make. Wouldn't that be a cool adventure?" Kalila was intrigued.

She was less so. The idea of flying untethered and unprotected was frightening to Her. "How would you fuel it? I mean you couldn't stay flying for more than a couple of days without landing. I don't think. You would need to very carefully plan all of your stops."

Kalila nodded. "And you would have to maintain a constant altitude. Not sure if that would be possible for a hot air balloon. At least not the kind that I have seen anyway."

She was pondering the idea, if only in jest; it was entertainment for the two of them. "Maybe you would use helium, you know because it floats.... like a combination of hot air and helium. That could maybe work."

Kalila giggled. "Okay let's pretend that we can fly around the world. Where should we stop? Where's your globe?"

She got up from the couch to retrieve her globe from her bedroom. "It's not about where we would want to stop, it would have to be strategic, like you would have to know the distances that you could fly each day. Between fueling. And then from there you would pick your flight path. And depending on the time of year would determine whether you flew in the southern hemisphere, or the northern."

"So, when do you think we should try this? In our summer I guess?" Kalila took the globe from Her and started to spin it.

"Summer would be ideal Kalila, no school, warmer weather, more opportunities."

The two girls sat, munching on popcorn, sharing the globe and lofty ideas about air travel around it. They exchanged compassion, and subtle nuances that fortified their friendship. They were both eager to learn, and easy to forgive and accept. Their relationship blossomed into something that wasn't expected, but was profound, and heartfelt. They had become best friends. Her prayers had been answered, and to Her, Her faith refreshed.

When the two settled down for the evening, she said Her prayers, and gave thanks for Kalila. She gave thanks for life, and for the abundance of grace in Her life. She prayed for Her brother, Her new friend, and for the safety of Her mother while she was away. She prayed for the "Grunge" girls at school, for enlightenment, and realization of their value. She gave thanks for the trees, and the wind, and of course for Her confidant, Mary Mack.

CHAPTER 70

Hugo sat on the expansive deck on the back of the ranch house. His view was that of his fields, and the mountains off in the distance. A warm breeze touched his skin, the sun just beginning to threaten its departure for the day.

He sipped on a tequila, while he waited for his beloved wife to return from inside the house. He closed his eyes for a brief moment; taking in the evening air. It was moments like this that he thought of his five boys, of the war, and of how richly he had been blessed after leaving Germany. The faces of the women that he had tried to help, were now a distant memory, memories of each one of them were still sprayed within the vast expanse of his mind. His physical strength was starting leave him now, he wasn't the same man that he had been during the war. His mind was just as sharp, he could still remember the dress that his bride was wearing the day that they had met, he could recall the look on the face of each one of his five boys as they learned to drive, and he had never forgotten the sound of the voice that had visited him that cold winters day within the walls of the concentration camp.

He took another sip from his glass of tequila, looking out over the horizon. He wondered if there were many who had been blessed as richly as he had been. If many were shown compassion for their sins or shortcomings. After that memorable day he had never questioned the presence of God, and although he never spoke of his experience with the beautiful young girl named Mary Mack, he knew that his wife felt the same way about the Lord.

He remained concerned for the well-being of his son Jorge, and silently prayed for his perfect mate to show up one day soon. He hoped for him a love as great as the one he shared with his own wife, a love that could survive change, a love built on trust, compassion and respect; one that would last the tests of time.

His chair was still, his long and slim legs outstretched. He wondered when his wife would return with his evening snack, and then suddenly she appeared. It had been so long; so many years had passed; that he had believed she would never come back.

She leaned against the railing in front of him, her black silk dress shining in the early evening light. Her hair appeared to be gleaming, dark ringlets hanging loosely, filled with diamonds, shining brightly under the setting sun. She smiled at him and reached her hand out towards where he was sitting. He reached forward to her, a bright light shining from within her. Their hands touched.

"Hugo, it's time." She whispered.

"I have waited for you, I knew you would return to me." Hugo feared nothing, for his plate had been full his entire life. He knew little of his family in Germany, but had built his own family on Mexican soil, none of them knowing anything of his past; until he recently had shared his story with his son Jorge.

"You have done so well, you rose up, helped the weak, when others fell. He is pleased, your descendants will for nothing need."

Hugo Fromm was pleased to hear that he had done well. He was content to know that his children and theirs would be protected by the covenant that he had with the Lord. His sacrifice had provided for them a security blanket. Protecting the innocent within the wall of the concentration camp had been risky for him. At times he had feared for his life. In the end, he had sacrificed a relationship with his birth family to survive, leaving his country of origin to create a new life in unknown territory.

The air was still warm on his skin, humid and comfortable. A magnificent sunset painted the sky with colors of yellow, orange, and pink over wispy clouds of white. Blessed. He felt blessed.

"Come with me now Hugo, it's time to go." She waved her hand at him, beckoning him to follow her. Her smile bright, a glow radiating from her that invited peace. As she turned her silver buttons glimmered, catching the sunlight, exposing the face of each soul that had been lost. Hugo saw each face, and instantly prayed for their salvation.

Hugo stood, shaking off his body. Relieving his soul of the skin that kept him bound to the earth, tied to the life he had created. He longed for one last sip of tequila, but Mary Mack shook her head no. He took her hand and they disappeared into the night, his empty body still in the chair, appearing to be enjoying the evening air.

CHAPTER 71

The taxi cab stopped in front of the police station on Juarez, the driver now turned to Madam and asked if he should wait once again. "No, that's fine, it won't be necessary this time, but thank you for offering. And thank you so much for driving me tonight. I really appreciate your patience."

"No problem lady. Two hundred pesos, please." He looked at her in the rear-view mirror again. Her dark hair shining in the moonlight.

Madam handed him the cash and stepped out of the vehicle. "Buenas Nochas amigo."

"Buenas Nochas Madam. God Blesses you." As she closed the door of the taxi cab Madam pondered the ways in which He did; The Lord really did bless her in so many ways, and for that she was grateful.

"Thank you for noticing kind sir, may God also be with you." She raised her hand in a wave, as the driver pulled away, leaving her to her thoughts, and to her own design in the warm evening air.

She pulled on the front door of the main entrance to the Police Station. The air escaping the building was fresh, cool, from an air conditioner blowing at full speed. A portly officer in whites nodded at her. "Madam."

"Officer." She nodded back acknowledging him. The lobby of the building was clean and designed in a very classic European style. The floors were highly polished Carrera marble, a wide staircase provided access to the mezzanine level, which overlooked the vast lobby.

"Can I help you?"

"Yes, please, that would be best I think, I am looking for Chief Alvarez?" She responded.

"Oh, he's not here. Vacation time for him Madam. Someone else can help you?"

Madam's heart sunk. "Vacation?! Oh dear, where did he go?"

"I'm sorry but I really couldn't say. That would be wrong you understand I'm sure. Would you like to see someone else?" The officer adjusted his belt.

Madam was at a loss. She hadn't anticipated that he might not be here. It had never occurred to her that he would take a vacation, or that she should have contacted him in advance. She looked down at the fabric of her black dress that she had so carefully picked out for the evening and felt a deep sadness. "No, no one else can help me. Thank you. When do you expect him back?"

"Oh, I'm not sure lady, maybe a couple more weeks I think. He had personal things to tend to. I really shouldn't say anymore. Listen, would you like to leave a message? Maybe a note?"

Madam struggled to find words, she felt her head spinning, her feet no longer felt as though they were tethered to the ground. "Yes, I would actually, I would like to leave him a note, thank you."

The two walked down the hallway to a reception desk where another officer sat. Madam's hands were trembling when she reached to take the paper from the officer that had greeted her. "Jeu okay Madam?"

"I'll be fine, thank you." She removed the lid from the pen and put it to paper. Within a few moments she had completed her note and folded the paper neatly into thirds. The officer handed her an envelope, into which she placed her carefully written note and sealed it. She wrote 'Jorge' on the front of it and handed it back to the officer.

"I'll make sure he gets this as soon as he gets back Madam. You are a friend then? No one uses the Chiefs first name Madam, so I am assuming that your visit is of a personal nature?"

Madam's eyes were filled with tears when she responded. "It will be too late in a couple of weeks, but I appreciate that you are willing to take care of this for me. Yes, I was a friend. Thank you, Officer."

She left the building and wandered down the Malecon surrounded by loneliness. The consequences of not planning her trip well, and in advance, were heavy on her heart. She came upon sand mannequins and stopped to watch them for a moment within a crowd of people. Juan Maria de Salvatierra watched her movements and was pleased that he had been successful so far in keeping the two of them apart. But he had to admit that he empathized with her pain in this moment.

Madam left the crowd of people, seeking somewhere to stop for a glass of wine, or a margarita. She wandered north, enjoying the night air, her thirst building. The restaurant bar Las Palomas invited her to enter, with its lush palm fronds and open windows beckoning her from across the street. The ocean air penetrated the busy restaurant with a cool ocean breeze calming and soothing the cajoling patrons. Glimmering gold lights and table top candles brightened the space; making it more appealing to her than the rest of the drinking holes and nightclubs along the crowded Malecon.

Madam ordered a tequila and sat alone at the bar. The crisp taste of the savory liquid soothing her to her core. She had wanted for nothing more than to see Jorge again; disappointment in her decisions and more so with her lack of planning poured over her thoughts and into the very core of her soul. She questioned his interest and wondered if he felt the same as she did; or if he had finally moved on. Leaving what the two had shared behind him.

She stayed planted on the bar stool, perfectly content to enjoy the night air, and her own misery. Wishing silently that she hadn't waited so long to return and hadn't risked losing her love to the means of time.

She sipped on the tequila, wallowing if only for a moment in her own self-pity. Feeling lost and betrayed, tricked by her own desire, lost in a past that could not be brought forward to the present. She hungered to be cared for, longed for a time when she felt carefree. She had been certain that this trip was intended to reunite her with Jorge, and now she felt remorse for her own misguided aspirations. She was now certain that he must have moved on, and that for only one day, a long time ago the two had crossed paths. She would return to her home, where her children were waiting, and make a life on her own. Of her own accord, to fulfill her own desires and dreams.

Madam paid the bartender for the tequila, and as she did he smiled at her kindly. He saw many people cross his path, many travelers and tourists, some alone, some in groups. Most of them by comparison to the life of a Mexican national wanted for nothing but were void of love. Their own strive for success and pleasure manifested into feelings of sadness and profound disappointment in themselves and their accomplishments.

In this woman, he saw something else. He couldn't be certain what it was, but her face was memorable. She appeared genuine, and authentic, her subdued manner made her seem candid and transparent while she sipped on the Don Julio he had provided her. He wondered from where she had come, and to where she would be going. Why she was alone, and if she had been waiting for someone. He was certain that he knew her from somewhere but wasn't able to place her.

Her hair was magnificent, long and dark falling down the center of her back effortlessly. Her skin was olive, but not dark, she hadn't been in town long, that he was sure of. Often, movie stars and famous people would sit at his bar, and he would be completely in the dark in regard to their accomplishments. He didn't believe himself ignorant, but not interested nor intrigued by the likes of them. He was at peace with himself, and the life for which he had created. He was what many consider to be an old soul, he had seen many things in his time, experienced more than he should have. What made him stand out from the rest though was a feeling that people got when they were around him. He felt wise, he exuded strength and was peaceful in his nature. His eyes were dark and penetrating, pools of imagery from lives past. He loved his wife and their children, relishing in the time that they spent together when he wasn't working. The life he managed to create for them was modest, but he afforded the luxury of having his wife at home with the children, she had never worked a day since their marriage, and he was proud of his ability to provide her that indulgence. The family spent their Sunday mornings at Mass, and then enjoyed lazy afternoons at the beach. Chasing waves and eating fresh caught fish; grilled over an open flame. When he had been a young boy, he had prayed for the life that he now had. In receiving it he was blessed and very grateful to the divine. He was aware that a higher power was present in his life and that His hand worked in ways that were often unseen. He acknowledged that unbeknownst to himself, he was an active participant. Making choices and decisions that altered his direction. God worked in profound ways manifesting in manners that intrigued the mind, and then when needed healed broken hearts.

As Madam stood from the barstool, she received his smile, and when returning the favor; she turned to pick up her purse from the stool next to her. As she did so, he saw a radiance in her, luminous and golden in color it streamed from the ceiling to where she stood. He took pause, and silently said a prayer of thanks. For he was now certain of where he knew her from and was grateful to have been in her presence.

CHAPTER 72

Mary Mack had watched Her with Her new best friend for days, in the absence of reason she felt envy for Her. And although she was pleased for Her and Her new-found friendship with Kalila, Mary Mack missed the closeness that she had felt with Her for so many years.

Mary Mack had spent many years in service and was grateful for every interaction that she had had with her assignments. In her appreciation, she maintained a steadfast and humble devotion to His cause. Her service for over one thousand years had resulted in the saving of many souls from perish. Only once had she herself succumbed to the power of the dark angel. Only once had she self-destructed un mediated. She knew that her mistakes had hindered her dearly, and that the gift of free will had been the source of her near demise. She prayed.

"Dearest Father, who took from me the darkness, and replenished my soul; my oldest friend. I've come before you to plea once again. My desire for life has been softly waking me, stirring seeds of a vision that was so long ago planted in my mind. Of vibrancy and life, of grace and the will to live. For You; I have so often walked alone, on narrow planks and on cobblestone, over nations and across waters; beneath a halo that you bestowed, strong in my faith, ever true in my appeal to serve you. I ache to once again live, to feel and to be loved. My faithfulness to the cause will not cease, my never-ending adoration for you shall carry on. My gratitude to you Lord is unwavering, leaving me with the burning desire to once again live as She does. To experience the life that only you can give. Lord take from me these silver buttons that fall down my back, a heavy burden of my fall from grace. Save these souls and free me Lord. Free me to the world."

A shift occurred in the heavens, as her prayer drifted towards the divine. Mary Mack had provided a great service; for a greater number of years. Her cries did not go unnoticed, her voice was not unheard. No longer would she whisper rhymes, or speak in riddles, for her prayer had broken through the sound of silence.

CHAPTER 73

Jorge prepared to depart Louisiana, packing the few things that he had brought with him to New Orleans into his small suitcase. He placed his passport and his visitor visa into the pocket of his navy sport coat, and then slipped on his loafers, his feet void of socks. As he was about to pick up his cell phone it began to ring. He considered not answering the call, as he preferred to arrive at the airport early for his flight rather than late, but instead instinct forced him to answer.

"Bueno, hello, Alvarez here."

He heard his Mother's voice through the cellular device, creating in him a sudden panic. "Jorge, Jorge is that you?"

"Yes mother, what's wrong, why are you crying?" Jorge's stomach suddenly felt uneasy. He moved towards a chair in the corner next to a small round table the housed a book of Louisiana Tourist information, and the room service menu.

"Jorge, it's your father honey."

"What is it mother?" He felt a lump rise in his throat.

"Jorge, I went inside for just a few moments to do the supper dishes and gather him an evening snack; and when I sent back out to him on the porch he was gone." His mother was openly crying now, he could tell that she was having a hard time speaking.

"Mother slow down. Where did he go? What do you mean he was gone?"

"Oh Jorge, he's gone, he has left this place. He looked like he was watching the sunset, with a glass of tequila resting in his hand."

The sudden realization that his father had passed on, hit him hard. Jorge pushed his dark hair back from his forehead. Shock, not grief overtook him, he was at a loss for words, he lost direction and any sense of reason that had been present before the call. "You're sure? Mother? Are you sure?"

"Jes, Jorge, the doctor is here now. There's no doubt. Your father has passed on."

Jorge quickly left the hotel room with his suitcase, and took a taxi to the airport, his return to Puerto Vallarta however would be further delayed. He would return to Vera Cruz. He knew his mother needed him, his brothers would be expecting him to return home, he couldn't think about returning to work until the arrangements were settled.

His mother wept quietly, alone in Vera Cruz, for the man she had loved nearly all of her life. She knew no other, she had given herself only to him, and shared with him every intimacy imaginable in a fifty-two-year marriage. She knew of nothing else, her world had just shattered. She allowed the hole in heart to grow and overtake her temporarily.

CHAPTER 74

Juan Maria de Salvatierra sat waiting for Mary Mack. He had recently returned from the street cloths appropriate for the current time period; back to his formal robes in which he found a familiar comfort. Comfort that brought him a sense of security, and pride from his years of alignment with God and his service as a man of the cloth. He still worshiped on a daily basis, praising the works and accomplishments of the ever powerful.

Whenever he saw Mary Mack enter a space, his own heart skipped a beat, for her beauty was still both endearing and breathtaking to him. Her childlike nature was appealing on so many levels, for he knew all too well that a part of the human journey is to experience adult endeavors through the eyes of a child. Mary Mack was a master as she had nearly always remained a young girl. Her spirit was that of maturity.

A fully developed and intoxicating soul that he had been drawn to from the first time he had seen her. Juan saw the internal of the girl, the woman that she might have become. He saw her not as a child, but as a fully matured individual.

Juan wasn't one to question the plan, or the execution of such. He did sometimes ponder his own visitation with Mary Mack that time so long ago, when she appeared as a grown woman. To the best of his knowledge, it had been the only time that Mary Mack had ever taken the form of a fully matured female. Appearing to him, presenting herself in a manner that was captivating and irresistible. He understood, or thought that he did, the subtle test of his own virtues. But wondered if there had been more to it. More to the visitation on that starry night behind the church in Loreto.

He played through their interaction again in his mind, her riddles and rhymes still fresh as the day that they had happened. His memory had been electrified, it was active and alert to receive her message. The significance of her interaction with him had stirred an emotional response, making her unforgettable to him, the impact of her lessons bore such great weight that he had spent years waiting for her to return to him.

He sat alone, waiting for her once again, this time with a desire to discuss the demise of Hugo Fromm. Juan himself had not seen that particular diversion on his chess board and hadn't even consider taking out a family member. He did appreciate her craftiness, and the shrewd but effective way that she had managed to keep Jorge from returning to Puerto Vallarta while Madam was still an obstacle.

But he silently questioned the necessity of it. She may have acted too rashly and removed someone who was loved; without cause.

CHAPTER 73

Her brother played a handheld video game while She watched from across the room. His fingers moving quickly from left to right, jamming the tiny keyboard with manipulative hand configurations that he was certain would surge him ahead a level, or two.

She watched, and she practiced Her telepathy on him, hoping to gain a signal that he had received. After several minutes of them sitting in silence while he played, he looked up at Her.

"Why would you say something so mean?" He asked, she was smiling. Gratified that not only had she been successful in sending the message, but also that he had received it.

"What are you talking about?" She responded.

"Didn't you say something?"

She shook her head, she chose not to reveal herself to him just yet. "Nope, I didn't say anything. I was thinking a few things but there is no way that you could have heard that."

He looked up at Her, set down his Gameboy and paused. "You didn't say anything? Like maybe that you think I'm an imbecile, not capable of processing complete thoughts, and that I am proof that evolution did occur because I must be nearly half chimpanzee?"

She wore an expression of horror. She was aghast! He had heard every word! She was impressed with his receptive abilities, she wondered could everyone hear her? "I would never say anything so cruel! You know me much better than that."

He threw a toss cushion in Her general direction, not intending to strike her with it, but as an expression of his disgust. "I think I know you better than just about anyone, and I think you did say it."

"Didn't say anything. So sorry to disappoint you. I think it's your low self-esteem getting the best of you." Inside of Her own head, she was laughing hysterically. She had achieved on more than one level. She had verified that he was capable of hearing Her, but he had no idea that he was doing it, or that it was even happening. This meant that she might also be able to communicate with others. And as an added bonus, his own uncertainty had created an opportunity to place him in a submissive position. He would think about the interaction for hours, perhaps days. She took pleasure in the feeling of power that she was sometimes able to achieve over him.

"Hmmm, strange; it seemed loud and clear, in your voice."

She continued with Her deception. "Must be that voice inside your head that beats up on you. You know the one that tells you you're not good enough, not smart enough, not fast enough. The one that tells you that you will never to anything or achieve anything."

He thought for a moment. "No, I think you did say it and now you're trying to cover something up. But that's okay with me…I'm fine. I know I am not just one step from a Chimp; I must be at *least* two steps removed."

The two of them laughed. He invited Her to play with the Gameboy and he taught Her a few tricks that enabled Her to gain more points. His strategies were of high-level thinking; she was intrigued. Quietly she admitted to Herself that his intelligence level must be superior to most. She refrained from ever sharing this opinion with him however as she preferred to have the upper hand at all times. He was witty, and perfectly comfortable in social settings, at least from what she could tell. He managed mathematics and problem solving well and had an immense breadth of knowledge. He retained facts. His mind was like a sponge for trivia and tidbits of information that others would ingest and discard. He held on to data, enabling him to then refer to it later, or share with others. She believed wholeheartedly that she envied this about him.

She also knew that if he was receiving her messages, then his brain was in many ways developed as Hers was, but that he hadn't fully tapped into his abilities. She thought about sharing with him, as Mary Mack had done with Her, but decided against it. She believed that Her relationship with him would be better served in silence, at least where abilities were concerned.

CHAPTER 76

She set out to enjoy Her day with Kalila, spending time at the park, and exploring the many crevices of the ravine. The two had opted to construct a small lean-to with materials that they had found in the garage. Her grandmother had approved the scraps of wood for the project, siting that Her grandfather was resting and had not been feeling well. The two girls had placed all of the snippets of wood into Kalila's wagon and had set out for the ravine. An expanse of heavily treed land bordering the river bed, which was home to many rabbits, coyotes, deer and a plethora of bird life.

The Bow river runs the expanse of the city splitting the metropolis in two parts to the east and west. Along its path, the source of drinking water takes in the Elbow River near the city's core. The Bow begins flowing in the Rocky

Mountains and winds through the Alberta foothills onto the prairies where it meets the Oldman River, the two rivers then become one and form the South Saskatchewan River. These waters flow through the Nelson River and into Hudson Bay far to the east. For many years, the lengthy river was occupied by First Nations peoples who made varied use of the river for sustenance. Before settlers of European origin arrived, the natives used its valleys in the buffalo hunt. Today, she and Kalila used the river bed to cool their feet and quench their thirst.

She saw faces along the shoreline, dark skinned, and solemn; carrying bows and arrows their feet swathed in moccasins. She smiled at them, apprehensively at first, genuinely glowing once they had acknowledged Her. One, who appeared to be the most elderly and prominent of the group sent Her a message, which she received without alerting Kalila.

"The land, and the sky are our blessings dear child, from these we find a full bounty. Seek not lessons from the world but look unto your God. The world brings hostility, and an end to life. Such are we. From the depths of darkness emerges boundless light, unto you it shall whisper."

She nodded at him, accepting of his words, she found great wisdom radiating from him. She returned the favor of a

message that came from Her heart. "Shall I call you Chief?...
My path is unknown, but by faith I walk it; in reverence, and
alone. I have accepted these gifts, by the spirit who sent me,
to achieve the greatness He planned for His people; His
creation."

"*Fear not, for alone you shall never be. The greatness
planned be not for man, but for the soil, the stars, and the
boundless expanse of His land.*"

"And then what shall we expect of humanity? To dust
do we turn? A fading memory to be lost as the river flows
east?"

"*Trust in the prayer that leads you and hold steadfast
to His promise. The flow of the river never ceases, your answers
through knowledge shall be your key.*"

She nodded to him respectfully, ending the
interaction, acknowledging receipt and understanding of his
message. She pushed Her hair back behind Her ear, on the
left side of Her face. Exposing herself to the sun. Breathing in
deeply through Her nose, she allowed the images pass
through Her mind that He was sending. Images of
destruction and war; starvation and hatred. She understood
clearly that man may very well lead themselves to an end.
And that Mother Earth in their absence would survive
indefinitely.

The two girls had spent the afternoon building, playing in the sunshine and laughing; enjoying the tranquility of the river bed, taking in the sights of the ravine. All the while Her mind was set on two things; Her grandfather; and the survival of the human race. Her grandfather seemed to be sleeping more and more, and since Her mother had left on her vacation a few days ago, he seemed to be failing quickly. The human race continued on their path towards destruction, and so too; were also failing like her grandfather; on many accounts.

Hunger pains drove the girls to return to the house, the freshness of the air had invigorated them, both felt near starvation. The home was cool inside, the air conditioning blowing hard, a welcomed reprieve for both ravine explorers. They waited patiently at the kitchen table while Her grandmother made them lunch. When it was fully prepared, she placed in front of them a platter of roasted chicken, cucumbers, carrots, celery and watermelon. Kalila made a face.

Her grandmother prodded. "What's that face for my love?"

Kalila was quick to respond. "It's just that I don't eat meat. Totally vegetarian-I can't eat nothing with a face."

"Oh! I forgot! I'm so sorry! Well let's see what we can do about that. I'll have a look in the fridge." She moved back towards the kitchen, taking with her the platter of food.

"Grandmother, I will eat the chicken. I am so hungry I feel like I could eat a horse!" She felt badly for her dear Grandma who had taken time to prepare them a feast. "Can I ask you a question?"

Her grandmother was peaceful, rummaging about in the refrigerator for acceptable alternatives for Kalila. She took out some tomato soup left from dinner the day before and set to reheating it on the stove. "Of course, darling, ask me anything...except for how old I am or how much I weigh. Both are things that you should never ask a woman. Remember that, it will be important to you one day, mark my words." Her blond hair fell easily onto her shoulders, in deep contrast from her daughter's dark hair, or her granddaughters' auburn locks. She was a classically refined beauty, with green eyes and a straight nose. She liked to wear an apron in the kitchen, and always had a Kleenex tucked into her sleeve.

The girls giggled. "Ok then! I will remember never to ask, should I do the same about Mother? Not ask about her weight or her age?"

Her grandmother smiled. "Of course! Never ask and you shall always remain friends. What was the question you have for me my dear?"

"Well, do you know anything about the Natives and the Buffalo hunting in this area?" She munched on a carrot, waiting for the response.

"What buffalo dear? I don't think there have been buffalo or Natives in this area for centuries."

She nodded, "Yes, I know, but they must have been here at some point. Don't you think?" She pushed because She knew that they had been there, her curiosity was provoked by a profound knowledge of historical ignorance. If we pretended not to know, perhaps its history didn't happen. The horrendous way in which the natives had been slaughtered and manipulated was appalling to Her and hidden from view. She didn't intend to point fingers at Her own Grandmother per say, but she was curious.

"Well Dear, I suppose you must be correct. The ravine has always been full of animal life, and the trees down there have been around for hundreds of years, I would guess by the size of some of them. The Douglas fir trees have been down along the river banks for hundreds of years, they can grow to heights close to a hundred feet I think. And I suppose that we could conclude; that yes, First Nations people would have roamed the area as well. At some time anyway."

"They did, and you know how the river bank lays below the cliff on the other side of the river? That steep cliff? The river runs far below it? The First Nations people used to chase the buffalo off the cliff to their deaths. Then they would use them as a source of nutrition, and of course the hides were used for clothing and then later used in the fur trade when the Europeans began to arrive. I think that would have been around in the early 1800's, more or less. They were part of the Blackfoot Tribe I think, but I couldn't be sure. There are much greater cliffs than this one, but I was just using it as an example."

Her grandmother sat quietly, and then asked. "How do you know so much about the buffalo dear? Are you studying this in social studies class?"

She shook Her head. "Oh no, the Chief was telling me about it. How his people lived off the land, that is until the white man came to destroy." She stopped talking abruptly. She realized that she risked exposing Herself to both Her grandmother and Kalila. Who sat perfectly still, both being perfectly quiet.

"The Chief of what told you this Dear?" Her grandmother had stopped what she was doing, now focused solely on Her and Her story. In her hand was a tea towel, in her mind a multitude of questions for her granddaughter.

She took pause, realizing fully that she had entrapped Herself. "I just mean that when we were at the Agricultural Days Convention, there were a number of Native People there, and they shared a wealth of information with us. I think one of the men that I was speaking with was a Chief."

Kalila watched the interaction and waited pensively. Knowing full well the she had not spoken to anyone during the Agricultural Field Trip. Kalila remained mute, protecting her dearest friend, but intrigued by the knowledge that she had obtained from the Chief, and more so by the manner in which she seemed to have acquired it. She couldn't wait to see how this ended, wanting nothing more to save Her, but unsure how to do it.

CHAPTER 77

Rohan and Nigel completed their University studies in 1983, both graduating with honours in their respective graduate programs. Rohan had decided to double major in Theology and Sociology, with a minor in Religious Study. He was erupting with pride, which was evident on his face when he returned home for the first time in fifteen years.

The road was dusty, a haze of earthy powder billowing behind each vehicle as it rolled and jerked along making the long journey seem endless. It was dry, lacking humidity, and hot. The sun beating down from the heavens scorching any life that may have been left.

In February, near Nellie, one of the most horrific tragedies ever seen in India occurred beginning in the wee hours on the morning of the 13th day of the month. In a revolutionary effort, the All Assam Students Union demanded that elections be postponed until the names of foreign nationals were deleted from the electoral rolls. Indira Gandhi made a pre-electoral decision to give 4 million immigrants from Bangladesh the right to vote. The controversial decision to hold the state elections were opposed, in the midst of this Assam Agitation. The demand was to detect all the illegal immigrants and to expel those that were residing in Assam. When the demand was not met, the command was made; a massacre was unleashed.

As a result, the Muslim people of Nellie and neighboring villages were attacked and killed mercilessly. The blood of undocumented Muslims spilled into the streets, their cries and screams heard far to the south, to the Bay of Bengal, and as far to the west as Jaipur. Unofficial counts of the slaughtered were near ten thousand souls.

There was a feeling of uneasiness within the villages, people moved in fear, their decisions directed by an uncertainty in their elected government and their own safety. Rohan walked to his childhood home, uneasy, noting the faces of the local villagers; amazed and alarmed to see the increased number of motorized vehicles on the road. When he had left so long ago, to enter the monastery, most people moved about on foot, or by rickshaw. The passing of taxi cabs on this dirt road was foreign to him, he felt out of sorts.

He stopped to looked around, before he reached the gateway to his parent's home. He breathed in deeply, devouring the aromas creeping out of the kitchens of neighbors and friends. The smell of curry wafting in the air around him, he was pleased to have finally come home. He could see by the doorway of the house a rocking chair carefully placed where the sun wasn't able to reach. In the chair he could see a familiar figure, quietly rocking, enjoying the reprieve that the shade provided.

He picked up speed, moving from a saunter to a quick jog. From the profile, he recognized the face, the way that the grey hair fell, his mind raced to her, his heart would not allow him to wait.

"Mother! Mother!" He exclaimed. "Mother you are home!"

The woman turned and stood, a kitchen apron tied neatly around her waist, her comfortable sari falling effortlessly into place. "Roh? Rohan is that you?"

He had reached the yard and bounded into it, dropping his small suitcase as he passed through the gate. "Yes Mother! I'm home!"

His mother fell to her knees, emotion racking her body in sobs, tears flowing from her dark eyes she spoke.

"Oh, my dear boy, I thought you would never come back to me. I believed you had forgotten."

He took his mother into his arms, holding her as tight as he could. When he had last seen her, his hand had been small enough to fit comfortably inside of hers; now he towered over her, a fully-grown man. "I could never forget, I prayed for you each day, when I woke, and when I lay me down to sleep. I was so saddened by you leaving."

She patted his hand, noticing the great size of it now compared to her own. "I know, I know. But I am home now."

"I sent you letters mother. I wrote letters to you, and to father. I never received one in return."

His mother bit her lower lip before answering. "I couldn't Roh, I missed you so much, I couldn't write. I wasn't in the right state of mind. You understand."

"How are you now? How is your mind?"

"I am better now. I see the light of tomorrow, rather than only the darkness of today." She looked off to the left and lost herself for a moment.

"I needed you, I needed you to write to me. To acknowledge me. I needed you to love me." He was near tears himself, allowing her into a place of his soul that he had hidden and protected for fifteen years. For fifteen years he was gone to school. For fifteen years he had waited to hear from her.

"You only need God to love you my son. Don't hang on to things that just couldn't be. Let them go and walk towards the light that is planned for you."

"I wanted you to make my bed, or to iron my shirts. Like the other boys had their mothers do. I wanted to come home at Christmas, to share stories at Easter. I wanted a mother." He broke into sobs, releasing the pain that had been haunting him for too long.

"I was not able. I could not do those things for you Rohan. I wasn't able to care for myself. I had to let you go, and trust that God would provide for you."

Rohan nodded. He accepted her defence, and in reality, he was pleased that he had been sent away. He was a strong independent man, capable of many things. He never wanted to be alone, but he had learned to do so very well. Solidarity was familiar, and comfortable.

"Mother, I have come for only a day, and the purpose of my journey is to say good bye, to you, to father, and to my brothers and sisters. I have accepted a position in a faraway land. I will be leaving tomorrow."

His mother began to cry again. She took his face into her hands and kissed his forehead. "Oh, my dear boy! I do love you so."

The two of them entered the house. She made tea for them, and they sat in a comfortable spot and shared stories of the past decade. Rohan told his mother about life at the monastery, university and about his journey to Canada, and how he would take a position as a Priest. She was pleased for his success but saddened that he would be travelling so far from her. The separation of them again, it seemed would be for a very long time.

CHAPTER 78

The two girls spent the afternoon in Her bedroom, mulling over magazines with articles written about what one should wear for optimal success. Each of the young women found the magazines appalling but were so engaged in the beauty of the photos that they were not able to dismiss them entirely. The photos were of striking young girls, with perfect make up and wind-blown hair. Tall lanky girls looking directly into the camera, enjoying the feeling of fame. She wondered if there was a meaning or a purpose to the work that they did, if what they did on the pages of the magazine was done for more than just for money, or to sell product. She studied the face of one of the models, her eyebrows highly arched and much darker than her hair. Dark kohl eyeliner rimmed her lids, making the eye appear large. She wore red lipstick and had a perfectly straight nose.

At first glance the girl was the picture of perfection. But when She examined the eyes, she noticed that inside of the iris there lacked a spark. There was no twinkle, not a glimmer of shine. From Her own experience She knew that the essence of life shone through the eyes. The eyes are like a mirror of our internal battles. She could look unto the picture and see not only a deep sadness in this girl, but she was aware that the young model was searching for something that had thus far been unfound. She was a lost soul.

Her soul was trapped inside of a body that wasn't in tune with its purpose. She seemed to have achieved greatness, having her photo everywhere, all across the globe, on magazine covers and billboards. But realistically she knew that this poor girl was miserable. She could see it written in her eyes, playing on her face.

"Kalila, what do you think makes people happy?"

Kalila took a moment to think, as she usually did, before answering. "Well I think that there are various different metrics. All of which should be considered in the answering of that question. But I guess I think I it boils down to knowing what you're supposed to be doing and acting on that."

"Do you think it's possible to find happiness in another person? Or from a job? Like this model? Do you think if you have accomplished fame and fortune, you can find happiness in that?"

Kalila answered without thinking. "No. No I don't think so. I think that each person's happiness comes from within themselves, not from external stimulants or from gratification provided by others."

She took a few moments to ingest Kalila's response. "I think that I probably agree with you. But I'm not sure that there are many people who actually achieve happiness or even understand what it is. How would we define it? Like you said, if there are a number of different metrics to measure one's happiness then how can we discern which metrics are right for us, or if we should apply them to our lives? How would we ever know if we are on the right path or if we are just delusional?"

Kalila threw the magazine at Her. "Over-analyzer! Stop it! Just try to enjoy each moment. And be grateful. If nothing else be thankful that I am your best friend and you are permitted into my presence, and you are not spending time with some gnarly loser." Kalila laughed at her own joke and then rolled off of the bed. "Hey, I have to get home. My mom said my dad had some news to share. And apparently, I have to be there for that. He's coming over at four bells, so I guess I had better go. Oh, the joys of divorce!"

She helped Kalila find her jacket and waited while she put her shoes on. She hugged her friend good-bye and set on to her chores. While she swept the deck, she contemplated how deeply she had come to trust Kalila in just a few days. She felt as though the two of them had known each other for years. She was comfortable with Her new friend, they shared so many interests and in just a short time had come to have an understanding; a kinship. She was grateful.

She finished the sweeping, and as the sun warmed Her back, she noted that She had not seen Mary Mack for days. She had become so engaged with Kalila that she failed to notice the absence of her valued confident. She vowed to pray for Mary Mack later that day, after Her chores were complete, and once she had had time for a decent nap.

Juan watched Her from behind a gathering of trees in the back yard. He could see into Her bedroom, when she felt comfortable enough to leave the blinds open. He enjoyed seeing Her grow and relished in the fine development of Her as a person. He took comfort in knowing that the work they had set out to do, was resulting in a masterpiece of sorts. From all of Her trials, and the set-backs she had faced, she still remained humble, inquisitive and honorable. She was very different now as a young teenager than she had been as a toddler and then a young girl. He was able though to acknowledge that these changes were inevitable, and necessary.

He read Her thoughts and noted also that he had not seen Mary Mack himself for days.

CHAPTER 79

Madam returned to her hotel room, feeling light headed from the tequila. She enjoyed immensely the taste of the sultry liquid; a distilled beverage made from the blue agave plant. Tequila production occurred primarily in the area surrounding the city of Tequila, northwest of Guadalajara, and in the highlands of the central western Mexican state of Jalisco. Tequila was first produced in the early 16th century near the village of Tequila, which was not officially established until 1666. A fermented beverage from the agave plant known as pulque was consumed in pre-Columbian central Mexico before the Europeans arrived. When the Spanish conquistadors ran out of their own brandy, they began to distill agave to produce one of North America' s first indigenous distilled spirits.

Some 80 years later, near the year 1600, Don Pedro Sánchez de Tagle, the Marquis of Altamira, began mass-producing tequila at the first factory in the territory of modern-day Jalisco. By 1608, the colonial governor of Nueva Galicia had begun to tax his products. And soon after, Spain's King Carlos IV granted the Cuervo family the first license to commercially produce tequila.

Don Cenobio Sauza, the founder of Sauza Tequila and Municipal President of the Village of Tequila from 1884–1885, was the first to export tequila to the United States. He shortened the name from "Tequila Extract" to just "Tequila" for the American markets.

Tequila is served neat in Mexico; and as a shot with salt and lime across the rest of the world. Madam had enjoyed hers straight up; neat. She was sorry now that she had indulged as much as she did.

The light was flashing on the telephone next to the bed. On the nightstand stood a lamp, a trifold card for the hotel restaurant, and the telephone. The red flashing light blinking madly; lit the room. Madam moved towards the telephone and sat onto the bed. She reached forward to pick up the receiver, and then quietly replaced it in its cradle before listening to the messages. She was too tired to listen, and far too exhausted to deal with any of it. Instead, she lay her weary head on the pillow, pulled the sheets over herself, ignoring the fact that she was still in her black dress; the tiny rosebuds covering the fabric feeling wilted and stale.

She quickly fell into an alcohol induced slumber, full of restlessness, and awkward dreams.

A doorway opened, inviting her to enter the room, darkness covered every inch of the space, creating an abyss for her to walk into. Fear rolled through her, from her toes to the top of her forehead, a prickly feeling of anxiety that threatened her advancement. She took a deep breath and pushed onward, the great expanse of doubt and uncertainty set aside. This was where she was to be.

The door closed tightly behind her, her first step across the threshold allowing the partition to separate her from where she had come. Reaching her hand forward in the darkness she tried to feel her way around the obscure area. To her left she felt a wall, solid, and high above her head it soared. To her right seemed an unknown gaping expanse of nothing. Her mind urged her to stay close to the wall, with confirmation of security and stability. Her instinct, a quiet subtle voice in the underbelly of her brain directed her towards the uncharted waters of the open space. She let go of the wall, moving into the emptiness that surrounded her. The weight of fear lifted from her shoulders, freeing her of the anxiousness that was just a moment ago holding her back. Far in the distance she could see a small light. Like a pinhole, its luminosity penetrated the blackness that surrounded her.

Her feet moved quicker now, shuffling in the direction of the flickering light that sat on the very edge of the darkness. She felt an ease come over her, erasing the fear that had been controlling her movements. The light was within her reach now, a sense of accomplishment, and gratitude rushed about in surges, filling her with excitement.

From behind the light she could see the outline of an old window frame. The glass seeming to be partially open, reflecting the light shining in front of it. She continued to move closer, easing in on the light and the wooden window frame behind it. The light brightened as she drew nearer, illuminating the outline of a figure behind the window. She stopped moving, reeling in her thoughts, taking a moment to gain composure before continuing on. She no longer felt afraid, she no longer felt alone, nor isolated in anyway. The darkness that surrounded her became a blanket of security, easing her apprehension of the unknown. The light began to brighten, exposing a clear depiction of the figure behind the window.

She was small, with long hair that fell in ringlets down her back. Her skin the truest shade of ivory, her eyes dark like onyx. She reached her tiny hand up towards Madam, as if reaching out to touch her.

Madam moved closer to the window, the image fading as she did so. She blinked her eyes, attempting to bring the tiny girl back into focus. She reached the casement, and tried to open the window completely, wanting to release the girl from behind it. She struggled, the window refused to slide upward. She looked to the left and saw her own father. His calm demeanor apparent, his face shining from the surrounding light, behind him an expanse of fir trees. He nodded and then disappeared. She shoved the window with as much effort as she could gather. It released, moving upward with an awkward shrill. The youngster that had seemed to be so close behind the glass was now far off in the distance, but she could see her clearly now.

The little girl spoke, while holding her hands out towards Madam. "I've been waiting for so long, my voice only a song, the lost and the forgotten seek refuge in my rhyme, finally now I am free... it is my chance, it is my time."

CHAPTER 80

Her brother sat alone, contemplating the vastness of the universe. His mind open and alert to all the possibilities promised by a higher power. He sat cross legged, his hands laying lightly on his knees; eyes closed. He saw Her, and his mother together, himself to the side but within their reach. He saw his grandfather, transparent, and floating in the illusion that his own mind created. He saw a man, that he had never seen before, stepping into the picture, dominating the expanse, setting the tone. He felt uncertain at first with the new male addition to his picture, then frustration and anger. His grandfather disappeared, and the man moved closer to the group. His mind wandered, and he saw a beach, the ocean pulling at the sand in rushed waves as the sun beat down relentlessly. The sound of the water calming him, the push and pull of the tide caressing his fears into submission. He allowed the emotion to manifest and then to be erased by the waves of the ocean, cresting and falling into the core of his own energy.

He opened his eyes and stood, knowing that change was upon them.

CHAPTER 81

Jorge Alvarez called the airline from the backseat of the cab, wanting to change his flight while on-route to the airport. Disbelief of his father's passing filled his thoughts, willing it to be incorrect, hoping it to be wrong. He had always known that his father would pass eventually, and without question he knew that so too would his mother. Acknowledging awareness of inevitable passing however, did not obliterate the pain caused by the actuality of it. If anything, it only magnified it.

The airline was not able to change his flight on such short notice, and so Chief Alvarez would return to Puerto Vallarta before being rerouted to Vera Cruz. He thought it wise in the end, the short stop over would allow him to pack a suit and tie and make arrangements with work for an extension of his leave.

His focus was needed to be on his mother and aiding her through this transition. She would be frightened, she would feel a massive loss, the breaking of her heart was inevitable. She had dedicated her entire life to Hugo and to the children of their marriage. Her friends were their friends, her life had been their life. With the loss of her only love, she would need to recreate herself in her mourning, finding friends that were to be her own, a life that would be her own, an identity that would be just her own; for in the absence of the one, the pair of aces was now a single; struggling to make blackjack with missing cards.

CHAPTER 82

Juan Maria de Salvatierra placed himself comfortably into his robes, tied the waist with the rope that had become so routine to him that he felt uncomfortable without it. He noticed his long hair starting to thin slightly and found it odd that a human trait might still be manifesting in his state of existence.

In his hand he took the Bible from the place in which it lay, its leather casing worn with age, the pages marked heavily with notes and paper markers. His faith had grown profoundly since his father had given the literature to him for his eighteenth birthday, before he had entered the Jesuit ministry, and much before he had sailed the sea for New Spain.

Juan at times believed that he knew the Word from memory. However, there were experiences in his life that had shown him clearly that the meaning of the Word would change with the application and designation of principal. His understanding had never been in question, nor his devotion to his faith. What was sometimes altered was his own perspective, the message behind the Word, resonating to parts of his soul that were in much need of repair, that searched for comfort and that sought reason. He had no doubts, there was no room in Juan's world to question the validity of the Lord's message, or to question the reason for which it was sent. He knew that the Word brought hope, and on that he held tight, basking in the glory of the freedom that was provided.

With his robes on and his bible in hand, Juan walked the cobblestone street to where the dark angel resided. He walked alone, his staph held securely in the hand not clutching the Word of God. Today the pathway felt long, winding its way through a heavily wooded area, flanked to the left by a fresh water stream that flowed ever so quickly.

With his mind focused on prayer, he journeyed, searching not for empowerment or riches, but for answers to questions that could not remain unasked. His sandals felt secure on his feet, adding to the ease to the way in which he plodded forward. The fragrance of the trees filled his nose with a fresh and vibrant awareness of his surroundings, echoing a rich and pleasing scent of cedar and pine.

After a considerable walk, he came upon the dark angel, standing near the stream, watching the water as it ebbed and flowed. "Juan! Good heavens it's been a long time, to what do I owe this great pleasure?"

Juan stopped walking, his aging body feeling tired from the weight of the journey. His mind was full of thoughts and images, his heart robust with concern. "Where is she? What have you done to her?"

The angel looked upon him, resenting the accusation that he would have been involved in her disappearance. "Who Juan? What have I done with whom?"

"You know very well that I have come looking for Mary Mack, she has disappeared and hasn't come back."

The dark angel shook his head. "My dear Juan, remember her pleasure? Did you not listen to her as she spoke? Were you so busy that you didn't hear her? I thought that the concept of ignoring the pleas of a loved one stopped with your death. Your mother certainly cried out for you many times, did you hear her pain Juan? No? Hmm...I am afraid that I cannot take the credit in full or even partial for the whereabouts of the beloved Mary Mack. I can assure you, if she is gone; then she might never come back."

Juan was struck with an awareness suddenly. He remembered her supplication, he had heard without acknowledging her pain, and her desire. He nodded without saying anything else and turned to leave. He thought of his own mother, as he walked back the same cobblestone path that had brought him to this interpretation of his beloveds yearning for life.

CHAPTER 83

Soaked in sweat she woke from a deep and intoxicating slumber. She was initially unaware of her surroundings, holding the dream for just moments longer before She rose to Her feet.

She shook off the fogginess and started up the stairs to where she knew she would find Her grandparents and Her brother. The kitchen was oddly empty. The customary perk of coffee not occurring, the chatter of conversation, and the clanging of flatware completely absent. She wandered down the hallway to the bathroom and relieved Herself before continuing Her search for the comfortable people that normally filled Her day.

In Her grandparent's bedroom she found them, Her brother sitting on the bed next to Her grandfather who appeared deathly pale. His breathing was laboured, his movements limited. Her grandmother stood next to him, with tears in her eyes, nothing more than a weak prayer on her lips.

She moved closer to where they were, reluctant to accept the nature of their remorse. "What is happening Grandmother?"

"Oh, my dear, Grandpa isn't feeling quite himself today."

"Can I sit with him too? He needs me now."

Her grandmother responded. "Of course, dear, come on up, I'm not sure if he will know that you are here though, he seems to be in and out of sleep."

She rose to the bed and took a spot right next to Her brother. He moved over slightly, making additional space for Her next to their grandfather. She took her Grandfather's hand in Hers, and with the other took Her brothers. She knew that he too would be able to experience the transfer of energy and didn't want him to miss out on anything that might give him comfort later.

After closing Her eyes, she sent a message to Her grandfather, soft and gentle, like a whisper it left Her own consciousness and flowed through his. *I am here now. Take refuge in the Lord."*

She could see inside of Her brother's mind, running wild there were ideas and thoughts that were in grave need of harnessing. She resigned herself to speaking about this with him later. She saw great potential, his bold and untethered concepts of life and the mastery of such were alive with possibilities.

Within the cortex of Her Grandfathers thoughts were only memories. She watched and passed the memories through Herself and into the thought patterns of Her brother. She could see in him an alarmed sense of awareness, a rich and receptive acknowledgement.

The memories were vivid, colorful and full of energy. He had lived so abundantly, she silently thanked him for allowing Her to see into his private and delicate space. His life had been lived to the fullest, with enjoyment, engagement, and edification of others; his soul was so full of love, and so entirely prepared to share with anyone who had crossed his path.

She watched a memory of him playing as a child, with his own mother watching over him. She saw him playing football with a large group of young men, all wearing the same jersey. She hadn't known that he had played on a team. But she wasn't surprised to see that he was the captain. He was the leader, the organizer, the orchestrator of excellence there. Then he allowed Her to see his wedding day, and to feel the love that filled his heart beginning on that day and never ending; swelling up and pouring over and touching all that knew him. She saw him waiting in a hospital room, while Her grandmother was giving birth. She and Her brother were privileged to see his great courage and a protective nature that saved his children from demise. All of them safe and thriving adults because he and Her grandmother had provided a nurturing environment. And then their grandmother entered his memory book, the pages filled with laughter and the incredible gift of each other. She could see clearly that they had been connected for centuries, the pages of this book including more than just one lifetime's worth of keepsakes. He treasured his union with her and knew that it would continue. Their time together was not ending, they were only entering a temporary pause.

Her brother gently squeezed Her hand, in awe of all of the greatness that the two of them were so privileged to see. She sent to him an almost silent message. *"Be subtle in your thoughts, as you are now able to see into his, so too can he see yours."*

She held fast, knowing that the end was drawing near. She took a moment to share with Her grandfather a moment of tranquility and appreciation for all that he had been for Her. He took pause and then channeled unto Her a message before passing. *"It is my time to fly, I fear nothing for I know that I have lived well. I can see a light, glowing bright, don't leave me yet."*

"The light will overcome you, it is alright. I can stay with you." She continued to hold his hand, his soul becoming light, daring to leave his body behind. *"Allow the energy to take you."*

As he left his body, his soul whispered to Her. *"You will do great things, don't fear the darkness, but revere the light. From it bears all truth, your path is protected and right."* She had Her eyes closed, as he moved from the living to the spirit giving world. She watched as he was met by others who had already crossed over. His spirit glowing, his mind which had been held captive by his body, now at liberty to see his life and his actions through eyes unshielded. She wept as She watched him, transparent, and free. His heart bursting with gratitude, and the love that he was now receiving as told in the promise. He turned back to Her, Her slight frame and tangled curls blurred by the presence of the light. He understood now why She had come, why Her presence was necessary. Her spirit was so grand, so illuminating, it left him yearning to return, wanting to share with Her the secrets, the truth. She gave him one last smile, Her own energy glowing and alive, as he moved on. His spirit leaving the world that he once believed had known, but not leaving any of his loved ones behind.

CHAPTER 84

Madam woke to the sound of the telephone ringing next to the bed. She was in a fog, caused partially by the tequila, and partially by the lucid dreams that she had had.

She reached forward, taking the receiver into her hand. "Hello."

She heard the heavily accented voice of the hotel operator on the line. "Madam? Call for you, from Canada, may I put it through now?"

She assumed the children wanted to talk, to share tidbits of their week's endeavors. "Of course, yes thank you, go ahead and put it through now."

"Gracias Madam." There were a few subtle clicks and then a moment of silence before she heard her Mother's voice. "Hello."

"Honey, it's your father…" She started to cry. "He's gone honey. This morning. He went quickly."

Madam was in shock. "He's gone? How could that be?" Her mouth was dry, the tequila had dehydrated her; her eyes felt as though they were covered with a blanket of sand.

Her mother responded. "Since you left, he just deteriorated. I didn't want to call and bother you. You deserved a few days away, but you should come home now. I need you to come home now."

"Of course. Of course, I will be on the next flight. Have you called anyone else? My brothers?"

"I am going to call them now. I called the funeral home, they are making arrangements to come for the body, then I called you."

"And Her? And Her brother?"

"They are fine honey, they were with him when he passed. Both are fine. They are just having a quiet moment now."

"I'm so sorry Mom." Madam choked on her own saliva. Tears erupting from her tired eyes the reality of the situation hitting her harshly.

Her mother answered her. "I know honey, just come home…please."

CHAPTER 85

Rohan took the last of his things and placed them carefully into his small suitcase. In his mind he had accomplished so much in just a few years, and yet he was able to fit his entire life's belongings into one small bag weighing no more than twenty-five pounds. He had neatly folded his shirts, and placed his socks, an extra pair of black pants, a pair of comfortable shoes, pajamas and a robe, a raincoat, and his toiletries into the bag before laying his Bible on top and closing the suitcase.

He placed his glasses on his face, picked up his hat, and pondered the concept of moving to a country that bore cold weather for a vast part of the year. He was ill prepared for sub-zero temperatures and icy winds. He had heard from a fellow student who had vacationed near where Roh was being sent, that snow was prevalent for four months of the year. As he had never seen snow, he was uncertain as to what one would wear for clothing to protect oneself. He assumed that someone in the new country would educate him on the requirements and traditions of such unfavorable weather.

Rohan took one last look at the space around him, knowing that a great amount of time would pass before he was able to return here. It had been so long that he was away, it now felt awkward, and to him a little strange to be in the house where his brothers and sisters grew up. He was more than pleased that his mother had finally returned home; he had been assured by his father that she was well, and that she would not need to return to the hospital any time in the presumed future. This provided a sense of peace, that enabled Rohan to proceed with his adult life unencumbered. The weight of having her in a hospital somewhere cared for by strangers had been lifted. He was free to move on, free to pursue his dreams, free to preach, and to heal the sick and the lost, himself. He was free to perform the duties lain before him, and free to do as his brothers had never thought possible of him. He was free to take a flight across the globe. Free to make a life in a country other than the one in which they had all felt so oppressed. He was free to do as they had only dreamed that they would do.

He chose freedom, and said goodbye as he moved through the doorway, and into a new and exciting life for himself.

CHAPTER 86

After shaking the sand from her sandals and her swimsuits, Madam quickly packed her things back into the suitcase that she had arrived with. She felt oddly relieved to be leaving, for although she was in love with the culture and the climate, she felt out of sorts being back in Puerto Vallarta. She had chosen for a time to cling to the memories that she had, the pleasant ones, memories of when her children were small, their days on the beach, the palm trees, the romance of the language, the fresh fish, surfing and the excitement of owning her own restaurant. She had always loved the live music and the sound of dishes and glassware clinking and chiming as the staff moved about hastily presenting her food wares to the patrons. She missed her life here but was prepared to move on. Sadly, leaving this country that she was so fond of, her passions for the culture, and her love for a man, behind.

Madam closed the door to the hotel room and walked the hallway towards the elevator which would take her to the lobby. With her sunglasses on to hide her swollen eyes she moved through a crowd of local people and approached the reception desk.

"Good Morning, I need to check out early please."

The clerk behind the desk seemed alarmed. "Is something not pleasing to you Madam? Can I do something to assist you?"

"No, it's nothing like that, I assure you. Regretfully there has been an emergency at home and I need to return. My departure has nothing to do with the hotel." Madam took her wallet from her handbag and placed her credit card on the desk in front of her.

"I see, my apologies Madam, Oh and Madam, there was a gentleman here this morning looking for you. He didn't want to wait and refused our offer to leave you a message or a note."

Madam wondered who it might have been and could think of no one that would be seeking her audience here. "Do you happen to know who it was? Did you get a name?"

"I'm sorry Madam, he wouldn't leave any information." The clerk continued with the check-out process, having Madam sign the credit card slip.

"Okay, I understand. Thank you so much, you have been so kind."

"Madam can we arrange a car for you to the airport? Or a taxi perhaps?"

"Yes, a taxi would be appreciated, thank you." Madam nodded and moved towards the vestibule, in front of her; a row of cars and people waiting to leave the hotel. She looked left and to the right. Scanning the faces of the tourists waiting to depart on sailing trips, the locals waiting to return home after a long evening of service within the hotel. She held her handbag, thinking of her mother, choosing not to allow herself to think of her father. A preferred state of composure was what she was attempting.

From behind her she heard her name being called. "Madam, *squize me*, Madam?"

She turned to see a smiling face, one that she hadn't seen for five years, but that she would never forget.

CHAPTER 87

Jorge's flight landed, without incident. He felt a sudden comfort being on land that he directed, that was under his control. He had felt like a fish out of water in Louisiana, foreign; as the inhabitants and tourists made each other feel. Each of the two groups observing and criticizing each other by instinct. Applying individual rules of expectation on the opposing group; ignorant of the others history or experience.

He was relieved to be home. He collected his bags, after embracing friends and comrades in the immigration office. He hailed a cab; directing the driver to the Police Station in the center of town.

The trip through town was like his flight had been, uneventful. He arrived at the station and entered the historical building through the front doors; the elaborate lobby impressive after being abroad for a few weeks.

Jorge unlocked the door to his office and entered throwing his suitcase on the floor next to the window. A pile of mail and messages filled his inbox. He thought about going through them and discarded the thought, knowing that everything that had been urgent would have been taken care of by the Sergeant overseeing his duties.

He picked up the phone and called the airline booking a flight to Vera Cruz for later in the afternoon. He then walked down the hallway towards the office of his detectives and entered the room which was filled with cigarette smoke and a handful of men's men. The unit greeted him warmly and reviewed the highlights of activity that occurred while he was absent. Following his debrief, one of his favorite detectives, a sergeant that had been with him for over a decade asked for a private moment.

The two men retreated to Chief Alvarez's office, Jorge taking a seat behind his desk the detective sitting on the window ledge next to his boss's suitcase. "Sergeant, I am only here for a few moments, regretfully my father has passed, and I am just here to switch out my cloths before taking off to Vera Cruz. My mother will be needing me. Lots to take care of."

"My condolences Chief, I didn't know. Is it okay if I share with the guys? They will want to know."

Jorge nodded. "Of course. I would appreciate it. What can I do for you?"

The detective placed his hand on his revolver, holstered on his left hip. "Chief, it's of a personal nature."

Jorge was surprised, having always kept a professional distance from the lives of his staff, hearing the details of their personal lives was unnatural to him. "What is it Sergeant? If there is something that I can do I am happy to help."

"Chief, it's not my personal life that I need to talk to you about, everything is good there, thank you though for your concern. It's actually yours that I would like to talk to you about. Or maybe I just need to share something that happened while you were away. Maybe that's a better way to put it."

"Now you have my attention, I'm not certain what part of my life could possibly be any of your business, so please indulge me." His expression was pensive, and stern. He waited for his employee to respond, anxious for a reply that might ease his curiosity.

"Well sir, you're probably right that it's none of my business. That's for sure. Last night I was here late, after my regular shift I mean. A lady came in looking for you. She left a note."

Jorge was intrigued, his mind still foggy from the effects of his father's passing, was uncertain where this particular conversation could be going. "Please, continue, who was this lady?"

"That's the thing Chief. I pretended like I didn't know who she was, when she came in. I didn't want to seem as though I knew her. But remember the lady with the kids? The ones that were kidnapped a few years back? We arrested her husband at the airport? Hard to forget her. She came in looking for you last night."

Jorge's heart stopped beating. "Are you sure Sergeant? You must have been mistaken."

The sergeant took a cigarette from the breast pocket of his white uniform. He lit it and shook his head. "No Chief, I'm sure it was her. Long dark curly hair; striking. It was her for sure."

"You said she left a note?" Jorge was having trouble remaining composed.

"She did, yeah. I have it in my desk, I will go get it now." He stood and moved towards the door. Jorge now on the edge of his seat, knowing that she was in town, he quickly filtered the thought of seeing her. He had just booked a trip to Vera Cruz, his mother waiting for his support. He had to move past her and stay focused on what was necessary, on what was important.

The sergeant returned with an envelope, neatly sealed and handed it to his superior, with his name neatly written on the front in her handwriting. "Did you read the contents of this Sergeant?"

"No Sir. I spoke with her but didn't read the note that she left for you. Wasn't my place, you know, none of my business."

Jorge took the envelope and placed it in the pocket of his chinos without opening it. "Thank you, Sergeant, I appreciate your discretion. No one knows about this but us then?"

"No sir, just us. I didn't say anything to anyone."

"Thank you, I will be leaving right away for Vera Cruz. I'm not certain how long I will be gone for. We will need to plan the funeral, I will help my mother with the arrangements and finalize my father's affairs, then I will come back. I will be in touch though. Call me if you need anything at all." The Chief of Police stood, picked up his suitcase from in front of the window, and left the building. He took a taxi to his condo, asked the driver to wait; repacked his bag with clothing appropriate for a funeral, and then headed to the airport to catch his flight. The envelope still in the back pocket of his pants.

CHAPTER 88

She sat with Her Grandfathers body, waiting with him quietly while Her Grandmother was busy on the phone. She knew that there were calls to make, and that people had to be notified. She was angry though that Her Grandmother had to do it all. She herself was hardly old enough, barely being just thirteen to do the calling, and Her brother was not responsible enough to do it. Her mother should be here. Her Mother should be the one helping, the one calling, the one doing the arranging. Her Mother should have been here.

She had told her. She knew, because the old woman had shared with Her that his passing was inevitable. She had shared that information and she had been ignored. She didn't like the idea of being disregarded or that Her ideas were thought to be imbecilic and childlike. She didn't see how anyone could assume that being warned of an oncoming event of such abysmal proportions was not pertinent or of grand enough nature to take seriously. She was appalled. Her inside voice was raging, telling Her stories of betrayal and delusion. She tried not to listen. She focused instead on the man that she sat with. The man that had been more of a father to Her than Her own dad had ever wanted to be. She held his hand, gently stroking the skin even though she knew that he was not able to feel Her gentle touch. She strained to listen to the telephone conversations that Her Grandmother was having. Repetitive, the same tale over, and over again. "It was sudden, no...no one expected it...it was very sudden yes.... I appreciate your support, thank you... I think we are fine, but yes, we will be sure to call if we need anything.... Yes of course there will be a service.... No, we haven't picked a day yet. We will wait for the boys to arrive in town before we make any decisions... yes of course he did love his sons you're so right.... I know and thank you so much, no...no flowers please.... That's right.... Yes, we will pick a charity. One of his favorites." Tears and sniffling.... "Thank you, God Bless you.... I appreciate it, bye now."

She felt sadness. Surging up and threatening to pour out of Her. She attempted to repress it. Managing Her emotions, she sat with him in this; his time of need. She didn't want Her Grandfather to be alone. Not now, not ever.

Her Grandmother had covered him with a pretty blanket. Not wanting him to feel cold. She thought it interesting how similar she was to Her Grandmother, while still being so very different. Both were worried, concerned for him. She knew that he was in a good place, that he had made his crossover effortlessly, and yet instinct told Her to continue to protect. And so, she engaged.

CHAPTER 89

Juan searched the globe, he looked in every place that he knew she had been, during life, and during her time of service. He revisited homes, he travelled to the beaches, and walked the cobblestone streets that she loved. She was nowhere to be found.

He stood still after the darkness of evening fell, seeking refuge in the stars and the mystery of the night sky. For a moment, he became lost in the immeasurable depth of the universe. The complexity of its creation, and the simplicity of its deliverance to man. He gave thanks as he questioned human understanding of their existence and praised the heavens for each new life that came unto the earth seeking awareness and enlightenment.

Juan repeated his prayer from years before. Begging the Lord to bring her back, longing for his dearest friend Mary Mack.

CHAPTER 90

Madam responded to the man calling her name. "Hello, I'm so sorry, I have to leave yet again. But I am so grateful that you found me." She placed her hand inside of her purse, still standing next to her suitcase, awaiting a taxi to take her to the airport.

"Madam, it's been such a long time. I thought I would never see you again. I thought that day that you left, that you were gone for good."

"As did I, I only came back for a short vacation, and now unfortunately I have to return. There's been an emergency at home."

He looked at her, wondering. "You are always leaving so quickly, never staying, always going. You're a bit like the wind."

Madam smiled at the thought, appreciative of the comment, not certain if it was intended as an insult, or presented as a compliment. "Yes, I suppose that I could be interpreted a bit like the wind. Sometimes a gentle breeze and other times a gusting hurricane."

He laughed at her interpretation. "Yes, not exactly as I was thinking, but an interesting perspective. I was thinking more as blowing on some days, and not others."

"I see." She responded. "I'm so glad that you found me. I have this for you." She handed him an envelope from her purse. The number 3447 written on the front in her own handwriting.

He reached forward, taking the envelope and opening it. He peeked inside and handed it back to her. "I can't Madam, I appreciate the gesture, but when you left so long ago I told you that I didn't have change for this hundred, and I don't today. I was wondering why you were looking for me."

Madam pushed the envelope back into driver 3447's hand. "Please I insist, on that day so long ago, you didn't take the hundred, but you let me go. You allowed me to escape this place and I found freedom. Please take it, and keep the change, for your trouble."

The cabbie took the envelope and shook Madam's hand, thankful that she was here, and appreciative of her generosity. He opened the door for Madam, who got into the taxi that was waiting to take her to the airport. He would stop on the way home and buy groceries, more than just the basics, today he would buy meat, milk, eggs and some fresh flowers for his wife.

CHAPTER 91

Jorge sat in the back of the taxi headed for the airport. The note from Madam burning a hole in his mind as they maneuvered through the streets of Puerto Vallarta. He took the envelope from his pocket, contemplating the idea of opening it. Then returned it to his pocket still sealed.

He recalled the words of his father, telling him to move on. That the message of Juan Maria de Salvatierra was not to be taken lightly. Then he thought of Madam's husband, and the concepts that he had eluded to. Who was she? Why were the two of them connected and what role did he have in all of it?

There were too many questions that needed answering, too many open doors, and not enough time to explore them all. As he headed to the airport he thought of nothing but her, however his thoughts were no longer of lust and raw emotion. They now consisted of concern and indecision. He would make his way home to Vera Cruz, to pay his respects as he should, mourn his father and support his mother. He would deal with the drama of Madam at a later date; or he might choose to not ever explore the idea of her ever again.

CHAPTER 90

She remained angry. A new and unfamiliar reaction
to an emotional state that she was not comfortable with, she
festered and with each passing moment she became more
enraged and frustrated with Her mother's actions. She
attempted but failed at supressing it, she prayed about the
anger, but only became more enraged with the verbalization
and articulation of the sentiment. She considered a time long
ago, when she had been angry with her Father, she had been
successful in obliterating the feeling through prayer and
meditation. She remembered the drive to Mexico like it had
happened yesterday. The coyote chase, the crossing of the
great river that divided the highway in two; the heat and
exhaustion. She had been strong enough at that time to
concur the anger, now she felt a slave to it. Bubbling around
in Her head, manifesting over, and over again. Confusing Her.

She knew that there was something here that she must learn, she longed for Mary Mack, for guidance, for solace. She was fully prepared to share Her feelings and to fully express the breadth of Her resentment.

She had not seen Mary Mack for over a week, she had no vessel to communicate with, no person to share with in Her wrath. She said a short prayer, pleading for the return of both Her mother and Her friend. She then waited calmly for answers and the return of both of them.

CHAPTER 92

Madam stood at the check in counter of Continental Airlines, providing for them the immigration documents requested and her passport. She looked at her watch and waited while the attendant weighed her bag and ran her passport number through their watch list on the computer.

The marble floors were clean and shone brightly under the fluorescent bulbs, above her the ceiling rose to elaborate heights. She noticed that one of the ceiling lights was about to burn out, blinking furiously in the distance. She watched the tourists passing her, dragging their luggage, darkly tanned and brightly clothed. She wondered why life was never easy for her. Why these people were able to live carefree, and yet she was plagued with trauma. It seemed never ending, and regardless of her belief that God provided and that through positive thinking and a touch of faith one could overcome any obstacle; she felt burdened. She had a hard time trusting in the idea that everything was going to work out.

She didn't know what she was going to do without her father, how she would navigate life in the absence of his wisdom. Without his carefree and loving manner, how would Sunday dinner be bearable? Birthdays wouldn't be the same without his wit, and Christmas might not be tolerable without his attention to detail, his careful selection of perfect gifts, and the thoughtful way in which he presented them. How might she forge ahead in her own life without his direction, without him assisting in decision making. She felt lost.

"Madam? Your passport requires a high-level security check. Madam?"

She looked sideways at him, pushing her hair behind her ear. "I'm sorry, what?"

"Your passport, Madam, I'm sorry but I am going to have to ask you to proceed to the gated area on the left. I'm sure it's nothing, but we are going to have to have a supervisor ask you a few questions." He was nervous. Small beads of sweat brewing on his brow. His upper lip quivering ever so slightly.

"What do you mean? There's nothing wrong with my passport." Anxiety suddenly burst within her.

"Like I said, I'm so very sorry Madam, but a supervisor will meet you down the hall, to the left. It's not that there is anything wrong, I just don't have the clearance to produce a boarding pass for you. You understand."

"No, no I don't understand. Not at all. This passport was good enough to get me into the country, are you suggesting that I can't leave?"

The attendant looked behind Madam to the line of travellers that were waiting to check in. He could see that they were becoming frustrated with the wait time. "Madam, I am not suggesting that there is anything wrong. I just really need you to move through the gated area to the left. I will check your bag and you will be done in just a moment. I promise you."

Madam took her passport and paperwork from him and moved to the left. "Fine. That's just fine. Thank you."

Jorge Alvarez moved through the airport and towards the check in counter. He carried his small bag, a structured suitcase with a hard shell. He had left his revolver at the station knowing that he would have no need for it on this trip home. He was now anxious to get there, and he was certain that his mother would be in desperate need of his support.

"Hello Chief." The attendant knew him well. As did every local.

"Hi there, how are you today?"

"Well, thank you sir. Where are you headed?"

Jorge set his passport on the countertop. "Vera Cruz."

"Okay, let's get you checked in, will you be checking your bag sir?'

"Yes, of course. Thank you."

"Sir, on that particular flight, it's direct to Vera Cruz from here, I can upgrade you to First. Are you okay with that?"

Jorge shook his head no. "No, that's fine thank you. That won't be necessary. I prefer economy class."

"No charge sir." The attendant winked at him. "My treat, for all of the good that you have done for the city, it's the least that we can do."

"Much obliged, thank you very much." Jorge was quite touched that this stranger appreciated his work, he took his boarding pass, his passport, and his cell phone and moved towards security. He passed the counter for Continental Airlines on the way, wondering why they had such a long line up of tourists waiting to check in.

CHAPTER 94

Rohan sat quietly on the plane, his first experience in the air was one of grandeur. Nervousness overwhelmed him at first, allowing his body to feel nauseous, allowing thoughts of doom to enter his mind, and dominate his meditative state.

He banished the ill feelings through prayer, silently with his seatbelt tightly fastened. Roh contemplated the construction and engineering of the airplane that moved himself and three hundred others from one side of the globe across a vast body of water, the international date line, and mountain ranges that touched the clouds. He questioned the safety; common sense suggesting that the journey was too far, the Atlantic Ocean too deep, and the plane not sound enough to make it across.

At first, he napped, succumbing to the stress of air travel, he then enjoyed a lovely plated meal, which he enjoyed immensely, noting that each passenger was offered a choice of beef or chicken. His chicken had been dry, the rice overcooked, and the vegetables sadly steamed beyond recognition. However, to Rohan it had been an offering, generously gifted, and equally relished. He washed down the chicken with a coca cola, another pleasure that he had never before participated in.

After meal trays had been removed, he watched a short movie and then eventually the flight crew began for their decent into Amsterdam. There he would clear customs and change planes, before continuing on his journey to Canada.

The Amsterdam airport proved to be as colorful and boisterous as Rohan had been told. He found the activities of so many to be humorous. He waited in line with a bright smile on his face, partially from the entertainment, and abundantly because on this journey he was embarking on a new life. A new country waited for him, a new people waited to hear him share the Word, take confessions and pray for the sick.

The sacrifice had at times limited his vision of the future. As a young boy, he had maintained a faithful heart, but in the quiet hours of the morning, before the rising of the sun, he often doubted his own abilities and sometimes those of the Lord. Now that his journey was unfolding in front of him; he felt awe in the greatness of it all. He was now able to see how the hand of God manipulated his movements, and decisions which had brought him to this place. Had his mother not been ill, and had she not been hospitalized, he would not have attended school at the monastery. Had he not been working by the side of the school janitor, he would not have had his support in the middle of the confrontation with Nigel regarding the Rolex watch. Had he not been strong and stood up for himself then, he would not have gone to University with Nigel and would not be friends with Nigel now. He appreciated the expression of faith in his life, and regarded his appointment in this new country, as an extension of the same.

Once he boarded the plane bound for Canada, Rohan settled into his seat, fastened his seat belt and prepared for the last leg of his initial journey. His decision to take the position within the Catholic Diocese in Canada was opening for him a door to a new world. He chose to pass through that door, and embark into unchartered waters, an Indian Priest, from a challenged past, with nothing but faith and perseverance to guide him.

CHAPTER 95

Madam waited patiently for the supervisor of the airline to finally appear. She checked her watch, she checked her cell phone for messages, and then checked her watch again. She tapped her passport on the desk in front of her and checked her watch one more time.

The woman entered after Madam had waited for fifteen minutes. Her uniform neat and tidy, her shoes practical for standing. Madam noted the tight bun she wore, and the bright red lipstick that made her olive skin seem sallow.

The supervisor sat carefully behind the desk, unbuttoning her blazer to ease sitting in the chair. "Buenas Tardes Madam. Thank you for visiting Puerto Vallarta. May I see your passport please?"

Madam gracefully handed her passport to the woman, gently touching her hand as she placed it in her grasp. She felt contempt, and anger radiating from the woman as she did; and so, Madam altered her sitting position so as to not present in an aggressive manner.

The supervisor looked at Madams passport carefully and her tourist visa, and then quickly stamped both of them. Using a red pen, she placed her signature on the visa, and then handed the documents back to Madam. "Thank you for your time, you can now return to the check in counter to retrieve an updated boarding pass."

Madam took her things but paused before leaving the small room. "Can you tell me what all of this was about? Why the delay in my checking in, and needing to wait for you?"

The supervisor wearing the red lip stick looked up at Madam from where she sat. "I'm sorry Madam, but I cannot. I simply do not have an explanation. Your documents are in order, there was no apparent reason for you to be delayed. Please accept my apologies on behalf of the airline."

Madam nodded and moved through the door. Juan stood behind the supervisor's desk and smiled quietly to himself, unseen to either Madam or the Continental Airlines supervisor. Relief rushed through his veins as blood had once done. He managed to keep Madam and Jorge from seeing one another. He was pleased.

Jorge boarded his flight with the first group of passengers, taking his seat in first class. He felt quite spoiled to have so much extra room. This was a pleasure that he had never indulged in, and one that he would never experience again.

The flight attendant brought him a flute of champagne and offered blankets, pillows and reading materials. He thanked her but refused all.

He watched the other passengers board, their carry-on luggage cumbersome and awkward. Fumbling and bumping down the aisle, mentally rushing to get to their seats.; physically impeded by the space surrounding them. In his hand, he held the envelope provided to him early that afternoon by his Sergeant. His own name clearly written across the front in her handwriting. Jorge feared opening it, his heart not capable of dealing with her today. Today was a day for his father. He placed the envelope carefully into the back pocket of his chinos once again. Lay his head back and closed his eyes, a much-needed rest taking over his body and drawing him to sleep.

Juan Maria de Salvatierra watched Madam board her flight twenty minutes after the Police Chief. He had successfully kept them from making an accidental contact and had deliberately with Mary Mack's assistance managed to keep them from reuniting at all. He was aware that Mary Mack did not agree with his position, and for today he was okay with that. His instructions had been to keep them apart, and he had done exactly as he was told. For Juan the necessity of a successful mission far outweighed any suggestions of emotional commitment or engagement. There was no place for love and absolutely no time for romance. His assignment took priority, his loyalty lie only with his maker; and Her.

CHAPTER 96

She waited patiently for Her mother to arrive by taxi. Sitting cross legged in front of the living room window, she counted passing cars and neighbors walking their dogs. She identified dog owners who were left handed, using their dominant hand to hold the leash, and dog owners who walked two dogs at the same time. She compared the number of silver vehicles versus the number of black, white, blue and red; acknowledging a silver majority. She wondered if Her mother would ever arrive.

After what had felt like an eternity to Her, she watched a taxi cab pull into the driveway. The grass on either side of the pavement was just beginning to turn a rich and lush green. From the backseat of the cab, Her mother emerged. Radiant as always, Her mother's smile stirred in Her a deep adoration. Her anger today boiled however, burning in Her stomach, directed at only Her mother, it erupted.

"You weren't here! I told you. I warned you and you didn't listen. I told you and you left anyway. How could you? How could you think only of yourself?" She stood from the spot in front of the window where she had been sitting; waiting, not wanting to linger for an answer, holding on to Her pain, wanting it to cultivate and grow, allowing it to manifest into a frenzy.

She turned Her back to Her mother, who stood in the doorway; holding her suitcase and her handbag. Her own broken heart hidden from sight, defeated from not seeing Jorge; the loss of her father standing firm on her shoulders, weighing her down. Rushing over her in waves, crushing her will to speak, not allowing her to retaliate, or defend herself. Madam felt her daughters' anguish and spoke tenderly.

"I'm so sorry Sweet-heart." Madam mumbled.

She turned Her back on Her mother, not looking at her when She spoke. "I hate you. I hate you! I hate that you weren't here, and I hate that you don't listen to me."

Madam's shoulders fell forward as she placed her suitcase on the floor. Not wanting to say the wrong thing, but desperately wanting to speak her mind, and clear the air with

Her. She took a deep breath and reached forward towards her daughter.

"I think you are very upset right now, and I understand. I don't think you meant what you said. I do not believe that you are capable of hate. I think you have misinterpreted anger for hatred, and I understand." Madam waited a moment for a response before continuing. "I am so sorry. I'm sorry that I wasn't here, and I am sorry if I did something that made you believe that I don't listen to you."

She turned towards Her mother, tears running freely down Her cheeks. "You cannot understand. You are never here. You are always at work. You are too busy to listen to me." She wiped Her nose using the back of Her hand. "You chase after things that you cannot catch, hoping for something that will never be; you have missed so much of what's happening right in front of you. And now he's gone. Grandpa is gone. And you weren't here. I was here, I was with him-not you."

Her mother reacted. "I was not chasing something. I was taking a few days for myself. I am so sorry."

"Why do you lie? Why do you bother telling me something that I know isn't true? I can see things. I know where you were, and I know what you were doing. You were chasing something that is forbidden. Don't you see that? You will be stuck until you let it go. Let it go! There is a plan for you, and it's so great, but you need to let go. Please. Please mother, let him go." She placed Her face on Her mother's abdomen, the two of them standing together, embraced and sobbing.

Silently She placed the moment into Her green box. For through Her own expression of Herself she had grown, she had pushed a boundary that had never before been tested, and she remained loved. She believed that she now understood Mary Mack fully. She was truly blessed.

CHAPTER 97

Jorge Alvarez sat on the porch on his parent's ranch, in the very spot in which his father had died two days before. The seat cushion of the chair was no longer warm from his Father's body, there was no smell of tequila in the air, no rumble of his hearty voice. The sun beat down on Jorge's face, drying the tears that were rolling down his cheeks. In his hand, he held the envelope left for him by Madam, her handwriting scrolled across the front, his name boldly identified. His fingers ran across the seal on the back side as he deliberated opening the message left just a few hours earlier at his place of work. He stuck his index finger into a small gap between the lapel and the backside of the envelope and slid it across, opening the envelope that concealed her message with a sudden rip.

He removed the paper from within, holding it tenderly in his hand. Eager to know what message had been left, but reluctant to heed the very same. He lifted the paper to his face, searching for her scent, inhaling deeply through his nose, in search of her fragrance. Memories of her lingered still in his mind, her hair falling forward on her face, the velvety feel of her skin on his own.

He opened the folds of paper to reveal words cleverly wound into a message that when he read it, drove him to wounded sobs.

My Dearest Jorge,

Alas we have missed again. Two starry eyed lovers, seeking but never finding each other in the dark. My love for you changes not today, nor tomorrow. I dreamt for so long of finding you, I imagined a time when our love would flourish, and fill my heart with joy. We cannot change circumstance, and geography just cannot be altered. I wish I could return to you, but I can't. Not again, not ever. No more can we change who we are than we can correct the wind. For it blows in so many directions, with varied speeds, and sudden gusts. Just when you think you might be there to connect with it, it's gone again.

*In my next life I promise, I will find you. I now know
what to look for... God Speed, forever loving you. XOXO
Madam*

Jorge moved inside the house with the intention of consoling his grieving mother. He entered the through the doorway, his large frame filling the opening in its entirety. His mother moved towards him, recognizing his pain. She saw her sons face filled with emotion; and embraced him. Together they wept, she for herself, and for her son; knowing that his heart was shattered, missing his father, but mourning the loss of his true love.

CHAPTER 98

The funeral was planned quickly. Her mother took the lead, ensuring that her Father's favourites were all present. His favourite friends, his favourite music and flowers, his favourite photos, his favourite suit and tie. She saw to the arrangements, helping her mother to contact everyone that her father knew, and soliciting help from trusted confidents. She made certain that his best shoes and belt were with his clothing items before the viewing and watched over the make-up artist that adjusted his coloring before he was put on display.

She despised the concept of viewing the body, of being seen in the absence of the human spirit. She had sat with Her grandfather when he passed, and She knew that he was no longer held captive within the body. The form that had once been him, was now just a corpse, just a skin bag of bones and organic material that would soon be cremated.

She watched Her mother executing tasks, she prayed for her, and consoled Her grandmother when She felt it was appropriate to do so. Her brother too was grieving and so She set out to spend time with him. He was growing tall, his blond hair darkening as he grew older, his shoulders broadening, she noted that he was beginning to turn into a man. His voice was an octave lower, his thoughts often on the pretty girl who lived around the corner.

"Hey, what are you doing?" She asked him.

"Just looking at some of Grandpa's note books. These things are pretty cool, they start when he was about I dunno, my age maybe. Fourteen or fifteen; like diaries, but lots of random thoughts and information. Some pretty good stuff in here. Look." He slid a notebook towards Her, open to a page where in Her grandfather's handwriting was written the following.

(with reference to1.COR 13) THE MEANING OF SUCH SHOULD BE UNDERSTOOD TO HAVE NO BOUNDARIES. NO LIMITATIONS OR CONDITIONS. IT SHOULD APPLY TO ALL AND BE INCLUSIVE OF EVERYONE. THE PLAN OF WHICH WILL RESULT IN ETERNAL HAPPINESS AND PEACE FOR MANKIND.

-LOVE IS PATIENT, LOVE IS KIND. IT DOES NOT ENVY, IT DOES NOT BOAST, IT IS NOT PROUD. IT IS NOT RUDE, IT IS NOT SELF SEEKING, IT IS NOT EASILY ANGERED, IT KEEPS NO RECORD OF WRONGS. LOVE DOES NOT DELIGHT IN EVIL BUT REJOICES WITH THE TRUTH. IT ALWAYS PROTECTS, ALWAYS TRUSTS ALWAYS PERSEVERES. LOVE NEVER FAILS. - (1.COR 13)

She looked at Her brother. "Do you understand the meaning of this passage, and of the note written by grandpa?"

His gaze remained focused on the notebook when he responded. "I do. Yes, to both of your questions. The biblical reference is self-explanatory, simple really, but holds a profound message. Grandpa's note above it, refers to comprehension of the word, and application of it, in its entirety. If we take note of the word and put it to action, the world would or could be a better place. Most people I think though, never see these words, or never listen to understand their meaning. Either way, the message is that good is going to win. God is love. Right?"

She nodded. "Love concurs. If we use love in our daily lives, then yes; if everyone did the world would be filled with love. Love breeds love. Eventually hatred and the darkness that oppresses humanity would subside."

Her brother observed Her for a moment. Noting the soft fall of Her auburn hair, the curls falling down Her back, Her eyebrows thick, elegantly framing Her dark brown eyes. "Have you ever wondered why your hair is red? Mine is blond, mothers is dark, we are all so different."

"I never thought about it."

"Our father's hair is also dark. So, from a genetic perspective, we are mutants. Your red hair is a recessive gene. My eyes are blue, also recessive. Mothers eyes are dark, her hair is dark. Where did my blonde hair come from? Recessive. Why would the recessive genes be prominent in both of us? And to have red hair and brown eyes? How does that happen? Why does that happen? Don't you wonder? Do you think about why you were sick? And then you weren't. Like it was erased. As though someone turned the channel on the television, and you got a new program. Why are we here? Can you answer that? I wonder a lot; about a lot of different things... I hear things. Strange things that I cannot explain."

She watched him as he spoke, his thoughts eloquently presented in the form of questions. Exposure of himself allowing for vulnerability, his questions relative, but not answerable. "What kind of things do you hear?"

"I hear voices, and I smell things. When there is no one in the room with me, sometimes I smell stinky feet, or the smell of alcohol, I can hear mumbling, but I can never really make out what is being said. Almost like I am underwater listening to someone talking."

She raised Her eyebrows. "Smells? Interesting, anything good like cinnamon buns or cookies baking?"

"Yeah, no, sometimes perfume, or cigarettes... whatever. Mrs. Potts says it's just my imagination." He said.

"You told your teacher? Why would you tell Mrs. Potts?" She was taken aback by the sharing of facts with strangers.

"Because it sort of bothers me, and I needed to talk to someone. I can't figure everything out on my own like you. I can study stuff, and I can learn it. But you, you can figure it out with reason alone. This is foreign to me. I have to have the information placed in front of me. Laid out, then I can absorb it. You do it more by feeling. I think."

"Instinct actually. I learn by instinct. As though I have learned it before. There are things that just come to me. Like languages for instance. I just know them." She thought through what he was saying, his questions and his observations. She pondered the concept of achievements through his manner of adaptation; persistence and diligent application of self. He focused on the necessary tools, found them and worked through obstacles. She on the other hand, followed Her own intuition, believing that she had the tools, and already knew how to apply them.

Her conclusion was that they were not similar. The two of them, one blond, one with auburn hair, one with blue eyes, one with brown, were as different intellectually as they were physically. Their manners of receiving and processing information were completely different. Opposites. "Tell me more about the things that you hear."

"I can't really tell you more. I don't understand it. I have to do some research so that I can figure out what it is. Then we can talk." He turned back to the journals written by their grandfather. "Right now, I want to read through more of these. I feel closer to him now, I better understand him. He was really smart, but not just smart like with knowledge, he was smart about humanity, about the human spirit. I need to understand the things that he was sharing here. So that I can understand myself. I feel most of the time like an oddball. Like I'm the strange one, the one that doesn't fit with the others."

"I love that you are investigating yourself. Like trying to understand who you are. I often question many things, why I am here, what my purpose is, how I fit in. I respect your journey." She smiled at him, taking in the moment, relishing in their relationship.

Her brother was relieved that his fears, and uncertainties were so well received by Her. "Thank you. I appreciate that."

"Just don't mess it up. If you need to search for yourself within the writings, and the literature, that's cool, do it, but I can see you just fine. I can see who you are; even when you can't. You are not lost, you just don't have all of the information that you believe you need. For me, that comes from faith. Perhaps while you are looking, you might find a higher power. A greater understanding of why doesn't necessarily come from within yourself, but from God." She ran her hands through Her rich thick hair, pulling it back from Her face.

"I don't know if I believe in God. How can a God that is supposed to be all loving make you sick, and then take our grandfather before his time? How can God allow children to starve, war to continue and illness to dominate the poor? How can that be? I'm just not sure. I am going to read Grandpa's journals, I hope that from his understandings I can find some of the answers that I need. I hope that the words within these notes and thoughts of his can help me to find the same hope that he had, for love and for humanity. If that means in the end that I believe in God, then that's fine with me. But it also might mean that I do not." Her brother sat back and looked at his younger sister with a soft and genuine smile. His heart was full of love for Her. Deep within himself he knew that he was here for a reason, for a greater purpose; but he wasn't able to determine what that purpose was. He knew that it involved Her, he knew that he loved Her immensely, and he knew that he was to protect Her. But to be able to say that he knew his purpose was going to take some time.

CHAPTER 99

It rained on the morning of the funeral, as if washing away the past. Everyone wore black. She thought it interesting that when a loved one died everyone chose to wear black. An absence of color, signifying the absence now of the person, the loved one that was now gone. Representing fear of the unknown, and great power. All things that were prevalent during a time of mourning. She thought it interesting and rather appropriate.

Her mother was sad, she could see that. Her grandmother was strong. She showed limited emotion when surrounded by people. She played the game. She was regal, conditioned to show restraint. She saved her emotions for private moments, reflection of self; not outward expression. Her mother was much the same, but her pain was evident on her face, and in the way that she carried herself.

She took the entire day's events and placed them safely in Her Purple Box, purple for faith events. She knew that Her grandfather was okay where he was, he was finally there. The place that everyone wondered about and no one wanted to talk about. She didn't feel like She needed a plan, not like Her brother did, she didn't need to understand everything in the world, she didn't need to have a handle on higher powers and the force that drives humanity. She was okay with just trusting that the Universe was on Her side. She opted to breath, live each day as it came, and see what happened. She chose trust. Today She chose purple, a purple box for faith, and She was trusting that it was the right choice.

CHAPTER 100

Rohan arrived in Canada, greeted by a member of the Diocese that he would be presiding in. He cleared customs and immigration, and then left the baggage area to find a smiling face holding ten by twelve-inch card board signage bearing his name. "Fr. Rohan Gupta."

Nerves rumbled in his gut, anxiety brought on by excitement, anticipation and uncertainty. He moved towards the friendly greeter and held out his hand. "Hello, I am Fr. Rohan, Rohan Gupta."

His handshake was accepted. "Fr. Gupta, hello, such an honour to meet you sir. Welcome! Welcome to Canada!"

"Thank you! I appreciate your warm reception."

His small suitcase was taken from him. "You must be exhausted. Such a long trip let me help you with your bag, we are going to exit right over there. By the 'C' door. I parked my car in the loading zone, so it's good that you came through quickly."

"Thank you, for coming. I will follow you then."

The tall and lanky young man moved towards the terminal exit, with Rohan right behind him. "My names Paul, by the way. You will stay with me tonight, and then tomorrow we will get you settled into your own space. The church will be providing accommodations for you. I hope that it's okay. That you are staying with me tonight I mean."

Rohan was accosted by the chill in the air. Never before had he felt such a brutally cold breeze, one that snapped through his skin to the core of his bones. He looked quickly from left to right, seeing a maze of shiny new cars and small trucks moving in front of the building that they were leaving. "So many cars."

"Oh, not really Father, you have arrived at a quiet time. Which was lucky for me; just over here." Paul pointed to where he had left the car.

"Is this your car here?" Rohan commented on the shiny blue Nissan parked in the waiting zone.

"Yes, it is, please excuse the mess inside. Student. I have a ton of books there in the back, and papers piled on the seat that I have written or that I am working on." Paul placed

Rohan's small suitcase in the trunk before moving around to the driver side of the vehicle.

Rohan smiled at his new companion. "Lovely, you must be from a very wealthy family. Your parents, they must have an abundance."

Paul looked at him from the driver seat, unsure of what he meant exactly. "No, not at all. I come from hardworking people. My dad is a cop and my mother is a teacher. Just usual, normal people. Nothing wealthy about us. Why would you think that?"

"Oh, I am sorry to have offended you. In India, where I come from, cars are a luxury, only the very wealthy have new cars. Some have cars for working, small pick-up trucks and things. But never usual normal people like you say."

"Father, cars are a necessity. You can't move around without one. Everyone has a vehicle of some kind. And cars are very affordable. You will be given a car by the church, part of your package I guess."

"I will be given a car? Good Heavens whatever for? I don't drive! I never have. I only take the bus, or I walk. Trains too, I like trains, but never driving myself." Rohan was surprised by the noted luxury addition to his salary package.

Paul chuckled. "Well Father, you're going to need to learn."

Paul navigated his way to the freeway and then the two men travelled at a very high speed on a roadway the likes of which Rohan had never seen before. He held on tightly to the door handle with his right hand, terrified of an impending crash. He found himself pushing all of his weight through his legs into the seatback of the passenger seat, his feet pressing firmly onto the floorboards. With his left hand he touched his clerical collar, securely fastened to the collar of his plain black clergy shirt; buttons neatly hidden from sight. He silently prayed for his own safety, and for a quick and painless arrival at their destination.

CHAPTER 101

The summer came and brought with it, warmer temperatures, sunshine and blue skies. The trees were full of leaves and those that blossomed every spring had dropped their blooms. The grass in areas where it grew was a deep rich green, cool on the feet in shady areas. It was alive, it was inviting, and giving to the soul.

Her brother sat alone under the Choke Cherry tree, willing it to turn from green to the lush purple that it is traditionally notorious for. He peered through the leaves and branches, to the blue sky above, his mind wandering randomly through his memories, attempting to focus on his Grandfather.

He cherished the moments that he had had with his Grandfather, especially the last ones that she had included him in. He was grateful to Her, to have taken him with Her that day, into the light, to a place where he was able to see not only his Grandfather, but also many others that had come and gone before. He hadn't shared his experience with anyone, no one had asked him what he had seen, or how he perceived the transcendence to the other side.

He questioned whether she too had seen the group of people sent to receive their Grandfather, he assumed that she must have. He had seen so many, waiting on the other side of the light with outreached hands. He was confident now having seen it, that there was not only a heaven, but that those who crossed over were always prepared to receive the newly departed. He wasn't certain though about the concept of one individual ruling or controlling the afterlife. He couldn't be sure about God and felt certain that he needed additional information before he could develop an opinion that would hold any weight. His own mind was unclear, there were too many grey areas, too many unanswered questions. He wasn't clear on where to look for the information that he sought, but he did know that he would search until he found the answers that he needed.

As Her brother, he learned a lot just from watching Her, he saw the world differently than she did, and chased things that were of no interest to Her. He enjoyed Her playful awareness of the world, Her unique and hungry eagerness to heal and to help those in need. He appreciated Her ability to rely on faith and to whole heartedly believe in something that no one could see. They were formed from the same skin, and yet moulded to be so different. He marvelled in change, and in picking things apart. Analyzing and seeking clarity, seeking reason. He did not possess Her instinct to blindly believe. He sought scientific support, proof; he wanted to know the mechanics of everything. He yearned for answers, knowing that things were rarely as they seemed, that naturally people see things not as they are; but as they are themselves. He believed in reason. He wished for insight into the Universe and its wonder. He hoped for clarity. *She knew it was there.*

Her too...